Arthur Sumner Walpole,   Euripides, John Bond

The Hecuba of Euripides

a revised text with notes and an introduction

Arthur Sumner Walpole, Euripides, John Bond

The Hecuba of Euripides
a revised text with notes and an introduction

ISBN/EAN: 9783337378202

Printed in Europe, USA, Canada, Australia, Japan

Cover: Foto ©Andreas Hilbeck / pixelio.de

More available books at **www.hansebooks.com**

Elementary Classics.

THE HECUBA

OF

EURIPIDES.

*A REVISED TEXT WITH NOTES AND AN
INTRODUCTION*

BY THE

REV. JOHN BOND, M.A.

CHAPLAIN AND CLASSICAL INSTRUCTOR ROYAL MILITARY ACADEMY, WOOLWICH ;
FORMERLY SCHOLAR OF ST JOHN'S COLLEGE, OXFORD ;

AND

ARTHUR SUMNER WALPOLE, M.A.

FORMERLY SCHOLAR OF WORCESTER COLLEGE, OXFORD.'

London

MACMILLAN AND CO.

1882

PREFACE.

THE present edition of the *Hecuba* is mainly intended to explain and illustrate the play itself. But
it being impossible to treat a Greek play as a separate
and isolated whole we have tried to make sure that
a boy after carefully and intelligently studying our
commentary shall not merely be able to pass a close
examination in the *Hecuba* itself, but shall know
more both of Euripides and of Greek scholarship in
general.

Our obligations to previous editors are very great:
but we have carefully avoided the mistake of writing
a mere compilation, which must needs be crude and
therefore unsatisfactory. The editors to whom our
acknowledgments are more especially due are Porson,
Pflugk, Hermann, Dindorf, Kirchhoff, Nauck, Paley,
Wecklein and Weil.

Our text is for the most part conservative, following—(as all modern editors must)—the lead of Kirch-

hoff, whose edition of 1855 placed the text of Euripides on a new footing. With him we have given great weight to the best class of MSS., viz. the *Marcian* (xii. cent.), the *Vatican* (xiii. ?), and the two *Parisian*, 2712, 2713; denoted by Prinz A, B, E, *a* respectively. The 'best MS.' occasionally mentioned in the commentary is the first of these.

All quotations have been given in full, and the only book to which mere references have been made is Prof. Goodwin's excellent *School Greek Grammar.* We gratefully acknowledge valuable help and advice from the well-known scholars Prof. Kennedy, Mr E. S. Shuckburgh and Mr A. W. Verrall.

INTRODUCTION.

EURIPIDES was born B.C. 480, perhaps on the very day when in '*the** battle' at 'sea-born Salamis' Athens under Themistokles destroyed the great Persian force which Xerxes had brought against Hellas, and won the fight of civilisation and progress over stagnation and barbarism. His lot was therefore cast in the most brilliant epoch of Athenian history, and while he was growing up to manhood the life of the whole of Hellas ran high, all was movement and vigour tempered by Athenian taste into an artistic beauty dignified by power. The literary form which this outburst of energy took was, as in Elizabethan England, the drama. Aeschylus born B.C. 525 and Sophokles born B.C. 495 had perfected the form of tragedy, the one ruggedly grand, the latter ideally perfect. It was reserved for their great successor Euripides to make tragedy not heroic but human, to paint men not as they ought to be but as they are when toiling, rejoicing, sorrowing in the high-ways and the byeways of everyday life. We may everywhere see

' Our Euripides the human
With his droppings of warm tears
And his touches of things common
Till they rose to touch the spheres '.

* Xen. *Anab.* I. 2. 9.

'His object was to excite interest, not by distant grandeur like Aeschylus, nor by ideals however touching and poetic like Sophokles, but by bringing real men and women on the stage, with real human passions and feelings as his countrymen saw them every day in Athens. The strong side of this realism is clearly 'the touch of nature', the weak side is the danger of its losing all effect and becoming commonplace and undignified'.

The HECUBA tells the story of the Trojan queen's sorrows,—the hateful exchange of slavery for royal estate, the foul murder of her son, the sacrifice of her daughter,—and the bloody revenge wreaked by her upon the slayer of her boy. It abounds with the good and bad points of the poet. It is, as Aristotle said, the 'most tragic' of dramas, and is full of pathetic power. But the set harangues on the possibility of teaching virtue and on the value of rhetoric (traces of the poet's intimate relations with Sokrates, Anaxagoras and other leading spirits of his day,) sound cold and in bad taste, coming as they do from the mouth of a mother steeped in bitter woe. Again, the loose joining of the two parts of which the play is composed indicates a weak point in the poet. The death of Polyxena and the cruel revenge upon Polymestor are really two separate pieces which Euripides has not cared to weld into one very fast whole. For whereas Sophokles contrived that every scene should lead up to the catastrophe, Euripides relied upon the telling nature of particular situations.

It is somewhat strange that, while Euripides gained the first prize but five times in the course of his long dramatic career, so many as 18 of his plays have come down to us as against seven of Sophokles and Aeschylus respectively. His tender pathos and modern spirit will account for his popularity in modern times; for his want of success in his own days, 'why crown whom Zeus has crowned in soul before?'

In criticising such prologues as that spoken by the shade of Polydorus, we must remember that every Athenian in the theatre knew perfectly well already the whole tale of 'the mobled queen.' But he would watch with breathless interest to see how the poet would work out and develop the familiar story, and the prize would be adjudged accordingly. The audience was probably as highly educated as our own Commons; 'for the house is clever', said Aristophanes, one of the cleverest of them all. Macaulay truly says, 'An Athenian citizen might possess very few volumes; and the largest library to which he had access might be much less valuable than Johnson's bookcase in Bolt Court. But the Athenian might pass every morning in conversation with Socrates, and might hear Pericles speak four or five times in a month. He saw the plays of Sophocles and Aristophanes: he walked amidst the friezes of Phidias and the paintings of Zeuxis: he knew by heart the choruses of Aeschylus'.

The date of the *Hecuba* is fixed with fair precision to B. C. 425 or thereabouts. For Aristophanes in the *Clouds**, which came out B. C. 423, parodies v. 172; compare also the notes on 462, 650. Its moral is the antithesis of barbarism and savagery to Hellenic culture and the reign of law, together with a practical illustration of the favourite Greek saying δράσαντι παθεῖν. The scene is laid in the Thracian Chersonese, over against Troy, where the anger of Achilles has held back the favourable wind from the Greek fleet. His Shade has just appeared above his tomb, demand-

* 1165.

ing as sacrifice the fairest of the Trojan maidens. A Greek council of war votes that Hecuba's daughter Polyxena shall die. Here the action of the play opens.

Structure of the Play.

I. Prologue, 1—99 = that part of a tragedy which precedes the first entrance of the chorus.

II. Parodus, 100—154 = the song of the chorus as they march into the orchestra and take their place.

III. *First* Episode, 155—443.

IV. *First* Stasimon, 444—483. A *Stasimon* is a song sung by the chorus from their station.

V. *Second* Episode, 484—628.

VI. *Second* Stasimon, 629—657.

VII. *Third* Episode, 658—904.

VIII. *Third* Stasimon, 905—952.

IX. Exodus, 953—end.

Episodes are the dialogues which come between two choral odes, and it will be seen that they roughly divide the whole play into acts. The Doric poet Alkman gave an artistic form to the choral lyric by arranging that the chorus, while singing stasima, should execute alternately a movement to the right (STROPHE turning) and a movement to the left (ANTISTROPHE); and he composed the songs which the chorus was to sing in couples of stanzas called STROPHE and ANTISTROPHE, answering to these balanced movements. Tisias of Sicily (surnamed Stesichorus, 'marshal of choruses',) perfected the form of the choral lyric by adding to STROPHE and ANTISTROPHE a third part, the

EPODOS, sung by the chorus while it remained station-
ary after the movements to right and left.

It is advisable to add a few words in explanation of
the *scholia* which are sometimes cited in the commentary. The scholia of Euripides consist of a putting
together of two continuous commentaries, the fuller one
the work of Dionysius, the other by an anonymous
writer, both drawing from Alexander, who again
drew largely from Didymus: he for the most part re-
produced the opinions of earlier commentators. The
genealogy therefore is (1) Didymus, (2) Alexander,
(3) (*a*) Dionysius, (*b*) Anon., (4) the *Scholia* themselves.

ΕΚΑΒΗ.

ΤΑ ΤΟΥ ΔΡΑΜΑΤΟΣ ΠΡΟΣΩΠΑ.

ΠΟΛΥΔΩΡΟΥ ΕΙΔΩΛΟΝ.

ΕΚΑΒΗ.

ΧΟΡΟΣ ΑΙΧΜΑΛΩΤΙΔΩΝ ΓΥΝΑΙΚΩΝ.

ΠΟΛΥΞΕΝΗ.

ΟΔΥΣΣΕΥΣ.

ΤΑΛΘΥΒΙΟΣ.

ΘΕΡΑΠΑΙΝΑ.

ΑΓΑΜΕΜΝΩΝ.

ΠΟΛΥΜΗΣΤΩΡ ΚΑΙ ΟΙ ΠΑΙΔΕΣ ΑΥΤΟΥ.

The scene is laid throughout in the Grecian encampment on the shores of the Thracian Chersonese.

ΕΚΑΒΗ.

ΠΟΛΥΔΩΡΟΥ ΕΙΔΩΛΟΝ.

Ἥκω, νεκρῶν κευθμῶνα καὶ σκότου πύλας
λιπών, ἵν' Ἅιδης χωρὶς ᾤκισται θεῶν,
Πολύδωρος, Ἑκάβης παῖς γεγὼς τῆς Κισσέως,
Πριάμου τε πατρὸς, ὅς μ', ἐπεὶ Φρυγῶν πόλιν
κίνδυνος ἔσχε δορὶ πεσεῖν Ἑλληνικῷ,   5
δείσας ὑπεξέπεμψε Τρωικῆς χθονὸς
Πολυμήστορος πρὸς δῶμα, Θρηκίου ξένου,
ὃς τήνδ' ἀρίστην Χερσονησίαν πλάκα
σπείρει, φίλιππον λαὸν εὐθύνων δορί.
πολὺν δὲ σὺν ἐμοὶ χρυσὸν ἐκπέμπει λάθρα   10
πατὴρ, ἵν', εἴ ποτ' Ἰλίου τείχη πέσοι,
τοῖς ζῶσιν εἴη παισὶ μὴ σπάνις βίου.
νεώτατος δ' ἦν Πριαμιδῶν· ὃ καί με γῆς
ὑπεξέπεμψεν· οὔτε γὰρ φέρειν ὅπλα
οὔτ' ἔγχος οἷός τ' ἦν νέῳ βραχίονι.   15
ἕως μὲν οὖν γῆς ὄρθ' ἔκειθ' ὁρίσματα,
πύργοι τ' ἄθραυστοι Τρωικῆς ἦσαν χθονὸς,
Ἕκτωρ τ' ἀδελφὸς οὑμὸς ηὐτύχει δορὶ,
καλῶς παρ' ἀνδρὶ Θρηκὶ, πατρῴῳ ξένῳ,
τροφαῖσιν, ὥς τις πτόρθος, ηὐξόμην τάλας.   20

ἐπεὶ δὲ Τροία θ' Ἕκτορός τ' ἀπόλλυται
ψυχή, πατρῷα θ' ἑστία κατεσκάφη,
αὐτὸς δὲ βωμῷ πρὸς θεοδμήτῳ πίτνει,
σφαγεὶς Ἀχιλλέως παιδὸς ἐκ μιαιφόνου,
κτείνει με χρυσοῦ τὸν ταλαίπωρον χάριν   25
ξένος πατρῷος, καὶ κτανὼν ἐς οἶδμ' ἁλὸς
μεθῆχ', ἵν' αὐτὸς χρυσὸν ἐν δόμοις ἔχῃ.
κεῖμαι δ' ἐπ' ἀκτῆς, ἄλλοτ' ἐν πόντου σάλῳ,
πολλοῖς διαύλοις κυμάτων φορούμενος,
ἄκλαυστος, ἄταφος· νῦν δ' ὑπὲρ μητρὸς φίλης   30
Ἑκάβης ἀίσσω, σῶμ' ἐρημώσας ἐμὸν,
τριταῖον ἤδη φέγγος αἰωρούμενος,
ὅσονπερ ἐν γῇ τῇδε Χερσονησίᾳ
μήτηρ ἐμὴ δύστηνος ἐκ Τροίας πάρα.
πάντες δ' Ἀχαιοὶ ναῦς ἔχοντες ἥσυχοι   35
θάσσουσ' ἐπ' ἀκταῖς τῆσδε Θρηκίας χθονός·
ὁ Πηλέως γὰρ παῖς ὑπὲρ τύμβου φανεὶς
κατέσχ' Ἀχιλλεὺς πᾶν στράτευμ' Ἑλληνικόν,
πρὸς οἶκον εὐθύνοντας ἐναλίαν πλάτην·
αἰτεῖ δ' ἀδελφὴν τὴν ἐμὴν Πολυξένην   40
τύμβῳ φίλον πρόσφαγμα καὶ γέρας λαβεῖν.
καὶ τεύξεται τοῦδ', οὐδ' ἀδώρητος φίλων
ἔσται πρὸς ἀνδρῶν· ἡ πεπρωμένη δ' ἄγει
θανεῖν ἀδελφὴν τῷδ' ἐμὴν ἐν ἤματι.
δυοῖν δὲ παίδοιν δύο νεκρὼ κατόψεται   45
μήτηρ, ἐμοῦ τε τῆς τε δυστήνου κόρης.
φανήσομαι γάρ, ὡς τάφου τλήμων τύχω,
δούλης ποδῶν πάροιθεν ἐν κλυδωνίῳ.
τοὺς γὰρ κάτω σθένοντας ἐξῃτησάμην

τύμβου κυρῆσαι, κἀς χέρας μητρὸς πεσεῖν. 50
τοὐμὸν μὲν οὖν ὅσονπερ ἤθελον τυχεῖν
ἔσται· γεραιᾷ δ᾽ ἐκποδὼν χωρήσομαι
Ἑκάβῃ· περᾷ γὰρ ἥδ᾽ ὑπὸ σκηνῆς πόδα
Ἀγαμέμνονος, φάντασμα δειμαίνουσ᾽ ἐμόι.
φεῦ·
ὦ μῆτερ, ἥτις ἐκ τυραννικῶν δόμων 55
δούλειον ἦμαρ εἶδες, ὡς πράσσεις κακῶς,
ὅσονπερ εὖ ποτ᾽. ἀντισηκώσας δέ σε
φθείρει θεῶν τις τῆς πάροιθ᾽ εὐπραξίας.

ΕΚΑΒΗ.

ἄγετ᾽, ὦ παῖδες, τὴν γραῦν πρὸ δόμων,
ἄγετ᾽, ὀρθοῦσαι τὴν ὁμόδουλον, 60
Τρῳάδες, ὑμῖν, πρόσθε δ᾽ ἄνασσαν.
λάβετε, φέρετε, πέμπετ᾽, ἀείρετέ μου
γεραιᾶς χειρὸς προσλαζύμεναι·
κἀγὼ σκολιῷ σκίπωνι χερὸς 65
διερειδομένα, σπεύσω βραδύπουν
ἤλυσιν ἄρθρων προτιθεῖσα.
ὦ στεροπὰ Διὸς, ὦ σκοτία νὺξ,
τί ποτ᾽ αἴρομαι ἔννυχος οὕτω
δείμασι, φάσμασιν; ὦ ποτνια χθὼν, 70
μελανοπτερύγων μᾶτερ ὀνείρων,
ἀποπέμπομαι ἔννυχον ὄψιν,
ἂν περὶ παιδὸς ἐμοῦ τοῦ σωζομένου κατὰ Θρήκην
ἀμφὶ Πολυξείνης τε φίλης θυγατρὸς δι᾽ ὀνείρων 75
φοβερὰν [ὄψιν ἔμαθον,] ἐδάην.
ὦ χθόνιοι θεοὶ, σώσατε παῖδ᾽ ἐμὸν,

ὃς μόνος οἴκων ἄγκυρ' ἄτ' ἐμῶν,   80
τὴν χιονώδη Θρῄκην κατέχει,
ξείνου πατρίου φυλακαῖσιν.
ἔσται τι νέον,
ἥξει τι μέλος γοερὸν γοεραῖς.
οὔποτ' ἐμὰ φρὴν ὧδ' ἀλίαστος   85
φρίσσει, ταρβεῖ.
ποῦ ποτε θείαν Ἑλένου ψυχὰν
ἢ Κασάνδρας ἐσίδω, Τρῳάδες,
ὣς μοι κρίνωσιν ὀνείρους;
εἶδον γὰρ βαλιὰν ἔλαφον λύκου αἵμονι χαλᾷ   90
σφαζομέναν, ἀπ' ἐμῶν γονάτων σπασθεῖσαν ἀνοίκ-
     τως.
καὶ τόδε δεῖμά μοι·
ἦλθ' ὑπὲρ ἄκρας τύμβου κορυφᾶς
φάντασμ' Ἀχιλέως·   95
ᾔτει δὲ γέρας τῶν πολυμόχθων
τινὰ Τρωιάδων.
ἀπ' ἐμᾶς οὖν, ἀπ' ἐμᾶς τόδε παιδὸς
πέμψατε, δαίμονες, ἱκετεύω.
                    ΧΟΡΟΣ.
Ἑκάβη, σπουδῇ πρός σ' ἐλιάσθην,   100
τὰς δεσποσύνους σκηνὰς προλιποῦσ',
ἵν' ἐκληρώθην καὶ προσετάχθην
δούλη, πόλεως ἀπελαυνομένη
τῆς Ἰλιάδος, λόγχης αἰχμῇ
δοριθήρατος πρὸς Ἀχαιῶν,   105
οὐδὲν παθέων ἀποκουφίζουσ',
ἀλλ' ἀγγελίας βάρος ἀραμένη

μέγα, σοί τε, γύναι, κῆρυξ ἀχέων.
ἐν γὰρ Ἀχαιῶν πλήρει ξυνόδῳ
λέγεται δόξαι σὴν παῖδ' Ἀχιλεῖ   110
σφάγιον θέσθαι· τύμβου δ' ἐπιβὰς
οἶσθ' ὅτε χρυσέοις ἐφάνη σὺν ὅπλοις,
τὰς ποντοπόρους δ' ἔσχε σχεδίας,
λαίφη προτόνοις ἐπερειδομένας,
τάδε θωύσσων,   115
ποῖ δὴ, Δαναοί, τὸν ἐμὸν τύμβον
στέλλεσθ' ἀγέραστον ἀφέντες ;
πολλῆς δ' ἔριδος ξυνέπαισε κλύδων,
δόξα δ' ἐχώρει δίχ' ἀν' Ἑλλήνων
στρατὸν αἰχμητὴν, τοῖς μὲν διδόναι   120
τύμβῳ σφάγιον, τοῖς δ' οὐχὶ δοκοῦν.
ἦν δὲ τὸ μὲν σὸν σπεύδων ἀγαθὸν
τῆς μαντιπόλου βάκχης ἀνέχων
λέκτρ' Ἀγαμέμνων·
τὼ Θησείδα δ', ὄζω Ἀθηνῶν,   125
δισσῶν μύθων ῥήτορες ἦσαν·
γνώμῃ δὲ μιᾷ ξυνεχωρείτην,
τὸν Ἀχίλλειον τύμβον στεφανοῦν
αἵματι χλωρῷ, τὰ δὲ Κασάνδρας
λέκτρ' οὐκ ἐφάτην τῆς Ἀχιλείας   130
πρόσθεν θήσειν ποτὲ λόγχης.
σπουδαὶ δὲ λόγων κατατεινομένων
ἦσαν ἴσαι πως, πρὶν ὁ ποικιλόφρων
κόπις, ἡδυλόγος, δημοχαριστὴς
Λαερτιάδης πείθει στρατιὰν   135
μὴ τὸν ἄριστον Δαναῶν πάντων

E. II.   2

δούλων σφαγίων οὕνεκ' ἀπωθεῖν,
μηδέ τιν' εἰπεῖν παρὰ Περσεφόνῃ
στάντα φθιμένων
ὡς ἀχάριστοι Δαναοὶ Δαναοῖς   140
τοῖς οἰχομένοις ὑπὲρ Ἑλλήνων
Τροίας πεδίων ἀπέβησαν.
ἥξει δ' Ὀδυσεὺς ὅσον οὐκ ἤδη,
πῶλον ἀφέλξων σῶν ἀπὸ μαστῶν,
ἔκ τε γεραιᾶς χερὸς ὁρμήσων.   145
ἀλλ' ἴθι ναούς, ἴθι πρὸς βωμούς,
ἵζ' Ἀγαμέμνονος ἱκέτις γονάτων·
κήρυσσε θεοὺς τούς τ' οὐρανίδας
τούς θ' ὑπὸ γαῖαν.
ἢ γάρ σε λιταὶ διακωλύσουσ'   150
ὀρφανὸν εἶναι παιδὸς μελέας,
ἢ δεῖ σ' ἐπιδεῖν τύμβου προπετῆ
φοινισσομένην αἵματι παρθένον
ἐκ χρυσοφόρου
δειρῆς νασμῷ μελαναυγεῖ.

ΕΚ.   οἲ 'γὼ μελέα, τί ποτ' ἀπύσω;   155
ποίαν ἀχώ; ποῖον ὀδυρμόν;
δειλαία δειλαίου γήρως,
δουλείας τᾶς οὐ τλατᾶς,
τᾶς οὐ φερτᾶς· ὤμοι μοι.
τίς ἀμύνει μοι; ποία γέννα,   160
ποία δὲ πόλις;
φροῦδος πρέσβυς, φροῦδοι παῖδες.
ποίαν, ἢ ταύταν ἢ κείναν,
στείχω; ποῖ δ' ἥσω; ποῦ τις

θεῶν ἢ δαίμων ἐπαρωγός ;   165
ὦ κάκ' ἐνεγκοῦσαι Τρῳάδες, ὦ
κάκ' ἐνεγκοῦσαι
πήματ', ἀπωλέσατ', ὠλέσατ'· οὐκέτι μοι βίος
ἀγαστὸς ἐν φάει.
ὦ τλάμων, ἄγησαί μοι, ποὺς,   17ɔ
ἄγησαι τᾷ γηραιᾷ
πρὸς τάνδ' αὐλάν· ὦ τέκνον, ὦ παῖ
δυστανοτάτας ματέρος, ἔξελθ'
ἔξελθ' οἴκων· ἄῐε ματέρος
αὐδὰν, ὦ τέκνον, ὡς εἰδῇς   175
οἵαν οἵαν ἀΐω φάμαν
περὶ σᾶς ψυχᾶς.

ΠΟΛΥΞΕΝΗ.
ἰὼ,
μᾶτερ μᾶτερ, τί βοᾷς ; τί νέον
καρύξασ' οἴκων μ', ὥστ' ὄρνιν,
θάμβει τῷδ' ἐξέπταξας ;   18ɔ
ΕΚ. ἰώ μοι, τέκνον.
ΠΟΛΥΞ. τί με δυσφημεῖς ; φροίμια μοι κακά.
ΕΚ. αἰαῖ, σᾶς ψυχᾶς.
ΠΟΛΥΞ. ἐξαύδα, μὴ κρύψῃς δαρόν.
δειμαίνω δειμαίνω, μᾶτερ,   185
τί ποτ' ἀναστένεις.
ΕΚ. τέκνον ὦ, τέκνον μελέας ματρός.
ΠΟΛΥΞ. τί τόδ' ἀγγέλλεις ;
ΕΚ. σφάξαι σ' Ἀργείων κοινὰ
ξυντείνει πρὸς τύμβον γνώμα   190

2—2

Πηλείᾳ γέννᾳ.

ΠΟΛΥΞ. οἴμοι, μᾶτερ, πῶς φθέγγει
ἀμέγαρτα κακῶν; μάνυσόν μοι
μάνυσον, μᾶτερ.

ΕΚ. αὐδῶ, παῖ, δυσφήμους φάμας·   195
ἀγγέλλουσ᾽ Ἀργείων δόξαι
ψήφῳ τᾶς σᾶς περί μοι ψυχᾶς.

ΠΟΛΥΞ. ὦ δεινὰ παθοῦσ᾽, ὦ παντλάμων,
ὦ δυστάνου μᾶτερ βιοτᾶς,
οἵαν οἵαν αὖ σοι λώβαν   200
ἐχθίσταν ἀρρήταν τ᾽
ὦρσέν τις δαίμων.
οὐκέτι σοι παῖς ἅδ᾽ οὐκέτι δὴ
γήρᾳ δειλαία δειλαίῳ
ξυνδουλεύσω.
σκύμνον γάρ μ᾽ ὥστ᾽ οὐριθρέπταν
μόσχον δειλαία δειλαίαν   205
εἰσόψει χειρὸς ἀναρπαστὰν
σᾶς ἄπο, λαιμότομόν θ᾽ Ἅιδᾳ
γᾶς ὑποπεμπομέναν σκότον, ἔνθα νεκρῶν μέτα
τάλαινα κείσομαι.   210
σὲ μὲν, ὦ μᾶτερ δύστανε βίον,
κλαίω πανδύρτοις θρήνοις·
τὸν ἐμὸν δὲ βίον, λώβαν λύμαν τ᾽,
οὐ μετακλαίομαι, ἀλλὰ θανεῖν μοι
ξυντυχία κρείσσων ἐκύρησεν.   215

ΧΟ. καὶ μὴν Ὀδυσσεὺς ἔρχεται σπουδῇ ποδὸς,
Ἑκάβη, νέον τι πρὸς σὲ σημαίνων ἔπος.

ΟΔΥΣΣΕΥΣ.

γύναι, δοκῶ μέν σ' εἰδέναι γνώμην στρατοῦ
ψῆφόν τε τὴν κρανθεῖσαν, ἀλλ' ὅμως φράσω.
ἔδοξ' Ἀχαιοῖς παῖδα σὴν Πολυξένην   220
σφάξαι πρὸς ὀρθὸν χῶμ' Ἀχιλλείου τάφου.
ἡμᾶς δὲ πομποὺς καὶ κομιστῆρας κόρης
τάσσουσιν εἶναι· θύματος δ' ἐπιστάτης
ἱερεύς τ' ἔπεσται τοῦδε παῖς Ἀχιλλέως.
οἶσθ' οὖν ὃ δρᾶσον; μήτ' ἀποσπασθῇς βίᾳ   225
μήτ' ἐς χερῶν ἅμιλλαν ἐξέλθῃς ἐμοί·
γίγνωσκε δ' ἀλκὴν καὶ παρουσίαν κακῶν
τῶν σῶν. σοφόν τοι κἀν κακοῖς ἃ δεῖ φρονεῖν.

EK. αἰαῖ· παρέστηχ', ὡς ἔοικ', ἀγὼν μέγας,
πλήρης στεναγμῶν οὐδὲ δακρύων κενός.   230
κἄγωγ' ἄρ' οὐκ ἔθνησκον οὗ μ' ἐχρῆν θανεῖν,
οὐδ' ὤλεσέν με Ζεύς, τρέφει δ', ὅπως ὁρῶ
κακῶν κάκ' ἄλλα μείζον' ἢ τάλαιν' ἐγώ.
εἰ δ' ἔστι τοῖς δούλοισι τοὺς ἐλευθέρους
μὴ λυπρὰ μηδὲ καρδίας δηκτήρια   235
ἐξιστορῆσαι, σοὶ μὲν εἰρῆσθαι χρεών,
ἡμᾶς δ' ἀκοῦσαι τοὺς ἐρωτῶντας τάδε.

ΟΔ. ἔξεστ', ἐρώτα· τοῦ χρόνου γὰρ οὐ φθονῶ.

EK. οἶσθ' ἡνίκ' ἦλθες Ἰλίου κατάσκοπος,
δυσχλαινίᾳ τ' ἄμορφος, ὀμμάτων τ' ἄπο   240
φόνου σταλαγμοὶ σὴν κατέσταζον γένυν;

ΟΔ. οἶδ'· οὐ γὰρ ἄκρας καρδίας ἔψαυσέ μου.

EK. ἔγνω δέ σ' Ἑλένη, καὶ μόνῃ κατεῖπ' ἐμοί;

ΟΔ. μεμνήμεθ ἐς κίνδυνον ἐλθόντες μέγαν.

EK. ἧψω δὲ γονάτων τῶν ἐμῶν ταπεινὸς ὤν;   245

ΟΔ. ὥστ᾽ ἐνθανεῖν γε σοῖς πέπλοισι χεῖρ᾽ ἐμήν

ΕΚ. τί δῆτ᾽ ἔλεξας, δοῦλος ὢν ἐμὸς τότε;

ΟΔ. πολλῶν λόγων εὕρημαθ᾽, ὥστε μὴ θανεῖν.

ΕΚ. ἔσωσα δῆτά σ᾽, ἐξέπεμψά τε χθονός;

ΟΔ. ὥστ᾽ εἰσορᾶν γε φέγγος ἡλίου τόδε.   250

ΕΚ. οὔκουν κακύνει τοῖσδε τοῖς βουλεύμασιν,
    ὃς ἐξ ἐμοῦ μὲν ἔπαθες οἷα φὴς παθεῖν,
    δρᾷς δ᾽ οὐδὲν ἡμᾶς εὖ, κακῶς δ᾽ ὅσον δύνῃ;
    ἀχάριστον ὑμῶν σπέρμ᾽, ὅσοι δημηγόρους
    ζηλοῦτε τιμάς· μηδὲ γιγνώσκοισθέ μοι,   255
    οἳ τοὺς φίλους βλάπτοντες οὐ φροντίζετε,
    ἢν τοῖσι πολλοῖς πρὸς χάριν λέγητέ τι.
    ἀτὰρ τί δὴ σόφισμα τοῦθ᾽ ἡγούμενοι
    ἐς τήνδε παῖδα ψῆφον ὥρισαν φόνου;
    πότερα τὸ χρῆν σφ᾽ ἐπήγαγ᾽ ἀνθρωποσφαγεῖν   260
    πρὸς τύμβον, ἔνθα βουθυτεῖν μᾶλλον πρέπει;
    ἢ τοὺς κτανόντας ἀνταποκτεῖναι θέλων
    ἐς τήνδ᾽ Ἀχιλλεὺς ἐνδίκως τείνει φόνον;
    ἀλλ᾽ οὐδὲν αὐτὸν ἥδε γ᾽ εἴργασται κακόν.
    Ἑλένην νιν. αἰτεῖν χρῆν τάφῳ προσφάγματα·   265
    κείνη γὰρ ὤλεσέν νιν ἐς Τροίαν τ᾽ ἄγει.
    εἰ δ᾽ αἰχμάλωτον χρή τιν᾽ ἔκκριτον θανεῖν
    κάλλει θ᾽ ὑπερφέρουσαν, οὐχ ἡμῶν τόδε·
    ἡ Τυνδαρὶς γὰρ εἶδος ἐκπρεπεστάτη,
    ἀδικοῦσά θ᾽ ἡμῶν οὐδὲν ἧσσον ηὑρέθη.   270
    τῷ μὲν δικαίῳ τόνδ᾽ ἁμιλλῶμαι λόγον·
    ἃ δ᾽ ἀντιδοῦναι δεῖ σ᾽, ἀπαιτούσης ἐμοῦ,
    ἄκουσον. ἥψω τῆς ἐμῆς, ὡς φὴς, χερὸς
    καὶ τῆσδε γραίας προσπίτνων παρηΐδος·

ἀνθάπτομαί σου τῶνδε τῶν αὐτῶν ἐγώ, 275
χάριν τ᾽ ἀπαιτῶ τὴν τόθ᾽, ἱκετεύω τέ σε,
μή μου τὸ τέκνον ἐκ χερῶν ἀποσπάσῃς,
μηδὲ κτάνητε. τῶν τεθνηκότων ἅλις·
ταύτῃ γέγηθα κἀπιλήθομαι κακῶν·
ἥ δ᾽ ἀντὶ πολλῶν ἐστί μοι παραψυχή, 280
πόλις, τιθήνη, βάκτρον, ἡγεμὼν ὁδοῦ.
οὐ τοὺς κρατοῦντας χρὴ κρατεῖν ἃ μὴ χρεών,
οὐδ᾽ εὐτυχοῦντας εὖ δοκεῖν πράξειν ἀεί.
κἀγὼ γὰρ ἦν ποτ᾽, ἀλλὰ νῦν οὐκ εἴμ᾽ ἔτι,
τὸν πάντα δ᾽ ὄλβον ἦμαρ ἕν μ᾽ ἀφείλετο. 285
ἀλλ᾽, ὦ φίλον γένειον, αἰδέσθητί με,
οἴκτειρον· ἐλθὼν δ᾽ εἰς Ἀχαϊκὸν στρατὸν
παρηγόρησον, ὡς ἀποκτείνειν φθόνος
γυναῖκας, ἃς τὸ πρῶτον οὐκ ἐκτείνατε
βωμῶν ἀποσπάσαντες, ἀλλ᾽ ᾠκτείρατε. 290
νόμος δ᾽ ἐν ὑμῖν τοῖς τ᾽ ἐλευθέροις ἴσος
καὶ τοῖσι δούλοις αἵματος κεῖται πέρι.
τὸ δ᾽ ἀξίωμα, κἂν κακῶς λέγῃ, τὸ σὸν
πείσει· λόγος γὰρ ἔκ τ᾽ ἀδοξούντων ἰὼν
κἀκ τῶν δοκούντων αὐτὸς οὐ ταὐτὸν σθένει. 295
ΧΟ. οὐκ ἔστιν οὕτω στερρὸς ἀνθρώπου φύσις,
ἥτις γόων σῶν καὶ μακρῶν ὀδυρμάτων
κλύουσα θρήνους οὐκ ἂν ἐκβάλοι δάκρυ.
ΟΔ. Ἑκάβη, διδάσκου, μηδὲ τῷ θυμουμένῳ
τὸν εὖ λέγοντα δυσμενῆ ποιοῦ φρενί. 300
ἐγὼ τὸ μὲν σὸν σῶμ᾽, ὑφ᾽ οὗπερ ηὐτύχουν,
σώζειν ἕτοιμός εἰμι, κοὐκ ἄλλως λέγω·
ἃ δ᾽ εἶπον εἰς ἅπαντας, οὐκ ἀρνήσομαι,

Τροίας ἁλούσης ἀνδρὶ τῷ πρώτῳ στρατοῦ
σὴν παῖδα δοῦναι σφάγιον ἐξαιτουμένῳ.　　305
ἐν τῷδε γὰρ κάμνουσιν αἱ πολλαὶ πόλεις,
ὅταν τις ἐσθλὸς καὶ πρόθυμος ὢν ἀνὴρ
μηδὲν φέρηται τῶν κακιόνων πλέον.
ἡμῖν δ᾽ Ἀχιλλεὺς ἄξιος τιμῆς, γύναι,
θανὼν ὑπὲρ γῆς Ἑλλάδος κάλλιστ᾽ ἀνήρ.　　310
οὔκουν τόδ᾽ αἰσχρὸν, εἰ βλέποντι μὲν φίλῳ
χρώμεσθ᾽, ἐπεὶ δ᾽ ὄλωλε, μὴ χρώμεσθ᾽ ἔτι;
εἶεν· τί δῆτ᾽ ἐρεῖ τις, ἤν τις αὖ φανῇ
στρατοῦ τ᾽ ἄθροισις πολεμίων τ᾽ ἀγωνία;
πότερα μαχούμεθ᾽, ἢ φιλοψυχήσομεν,　　315
τὸν κατθανόνθ᾽ ὁρῶντες οὐ τιμώμενον;
καὶ μὴν ἔμοιγε ζῶντι μὲν, καθ᾽ ἡμέραν
κεἰ σμίκρ᾽ ἔχοιμι, πάντ᾽ ἂν ἀρκούντως ἔχοι·
τύμβον δὲ βουλοίμην ἂν ἀξιούμενον
τὸν ἐμὸν ὁρᾶσθαι· διὰ μακροῦ γὰρ ἡ χάρις.　320
εἰ δ᾽ οἰκτρὰ πάσχειν φῇς, τάδ᾽ ἀντάκουέ μου·
εἰσὶν παρ᾽ ἡμῖν οὐδὲν ἧσσον ἄθλιαι
γραῖαι γυναῖκες ἠδὲ πρεσβῦται σέθεν,
νύμφαι τ᾽ ἀρίστων νυμφίων τητώμεναι,
ὧν ἥδε κεύθει σώματ᾽ Ἰδαία κόνις.　　325
τόλμα τάδ᾽· ἡμεῖς δ᾽, εἰ κακῶς νομίζομεν
τιμᾶν τὸν ἐσθλὸν, ἀμαθίαν ὀφλήσομεν·
οἱ βάρβαροι δὲ μήτε τοὺς φίλους φίλους
ἡγεῖσθε μήτε τοὺς καλῶς τεθνηκότας
θαυμάζεθ᾽, ὡς ἂν ἡ μὲν Ἑλλὰς εὐτυχῇ,　330
ὑμεῖς δ᾽ ἔχηθ᾽ ὅμοια τοῖς βουλεύμασιν.
ΧΟ. αἰαῖ· τὸ δοῦλον ὡς κακὸν πέφυκ᾽ ἀεὶ,

τολμᾷ θ' ἃ μὴ χρῇ, τῇ βίᾳ κρατούμενον.

ΕΚ. ὦ θύγατερ, οὑμοὶ μὲν λόγοι πρὸς αἰθέρα
φροῦδοι μάτην ῥιφθέντες ἀμφὶ σοῦ φόνου·   335
σὺ δ' εἴ τι μείζω δύναμιν ἢ μήτηρ ἔχεις,
σπούδαζε, πάσας ὥστ' ἀηδόνος στόμα
φθογγὰς ἱεῖσα, μὴ στερηθῆναι βίου.
πρόσπιπτε δ' οἰκτρῶς τοῦδ' Ὀδυσσέως γόνυ,
καὶ πεῖθ'. ἔχεις δὲ πρόφασιν· ἔστι γὰρ τέκνα   340
καὶ τῷδε, τὴν σὴν ὥστ' ἐποικτεῖραι τύχην.

ΠΟΛΥΞ. ὁρῶ σ', Ὀδυσσεῦ, δεξιὰν ὑφ' εἵματος
κρύπτοντα χεῖρα, καὶ πρόσωπον ἔμπαλιν
στρέφοντα, μή σου προσθίγω γενειάδος.
θάρσει· πέφευγας τὸν ἐμὸν ἱκέσιον Δία·   345
ὡς ἕψομαί γε, τοῦ τ' ἀναγκαίου χάριν
θανεῖν τε χρῄζουσ'· εἰ δὲ μὴ βουλήσομαι,
κακὴ φανοῦμαι καὶ φιλόψυχος γυνή.
τί γάρ με δεῖ ζῆν; ᾗ πατὴρ μὲν ἦν ἄναξ
Φρυγῶν ἁπάντων· τοῦτό μοι πρῶτον βίου·   350
ἔπειτ' ἐθρέφθην ἐλπίδων καλῶν ὕπο,
βασιλεῦσι νύμφη, ζῆλον οὐ σμικρὸν γάμων
ἔχουσ', ὅτου δῶμ' ἑστίαν τ' ἀφίξομαι·
·δέσποινα δ' ἡ δύστηνος Ἰδαίαισιν ἦν
γυναιξὶ, παρθένοις τ' ἀπόβλεπτος μέτα,   355
ἴση θεοῖσι, πλὴν τὸ κατθανεῖν μόνον·
νῦν δ' εἰμὶ δούλη. πρῶτα μέν με τοὔνομα
θανεῖν ἐρᾶν τίθησιν, οὐκ εἰωθὸς ὄν·
ἔπειτ' ἴσως ἂν δεσποτῶν ὠμῶν φρένας
τύχοιμ' ἄν, ὅστις ἀργύρου μ' ὠνήσεται,   360
τὴν Ἕκτορός τε χἀτέρων πολλῶν κάσιν,

προσθεὶς δ' ἀνάγκην σιτοποιὸν ἐν δόμοις,
σαίρειν τε δῶμα κερκίσιν τ' ἐφεστάναι
λυπρὰν ἄγουσαν ἡμέραν μ' ἀναγκάσει·
λέχη δὲ τἀμὰ δοῦλος ὠνητός ποθεν   365
χρανεῖ, τυράννων πρόσθεν ἠξιωμένα.
οὐ δῆτ'· ἀφίημ' ὀμμάτων ἐλεύθερον
φέγγος τόδ', Ἅιδῃ προστιθεῖσ' ἐμὸν δέμας.
ἄγ' οὖν μ', Ὀδυσσεῦ, καὶ διέργασαί μ' ἄγων·
οὔτ' ἐλπίδος γὰρ οὔτε του δόξης ὁρῶ   370
θάρσος παρ' ἡμῖν ὥς ποτ' εὖ πρᾶξαί με χρή.
μῆτερ, σὺ δ' ἡμῖν μηδὲν ἐμποδὼν γένῃ
λέγουσα μητὲ δρῶσα· συμβούλου δέ μοι
θανεῖν, πρὶν αἰσχρῶν μὴ κατ' ἀξίαν τυχεῖν.
ὅστις γὰρ οὐκ εἴωθε γεύεσθαι κακῶν,   375
φέρει μὲν, ἀλγεῖ δ' αὐχέν' ἐντιθεὶς ζυγῷ·
θανὼν δ' ἂν εἴη μᾶλλον εὐτυχέστερος
ἢ ζῶν· τὸ γὰρ ζῆν μὴ καλῶς μέγας πόνος.
ΧΟ. δεινὸς χαρακτὴρ κἀπίσημος ἐν βροτοῖς
ἐσθλῶν γενέσθαι, κἀπὶ μεῖζον ἔρχεται   380
τῆς εὐγενείας ὄνομα τοῖσιν ἀξίοις.
ΕΚ. καλῶς μὲν εἶπας, θύγατερ· ἀλλὰ τῷ καλῷ
λύπη πρόσεστιν. εἰ δὲ δεῖ τῷ Πηλέως
χάριν γενέσθαι παιδί, καὶ ψόγον φυγεῖν
ὑμᾶς, Ὀδυσσεῦ, τήνδε μὲν μὴ κτείνετε,   385
ἡμᾶς δ' ἄγοντες πρὸς πυρὰν Ἀχιλλέως
κεντεῖτε, μὴ φείδεσθ'· ἐγὼ 'τεκον Πάριν
ὃς παῖδα Θέτιδος ὤλεσεν τόξοις βαλών.
ΟΔ. οὐ σ', ὦ γεραιά, κατθανεῖν Ἀχιλλέως
φάντασμ' Ἀχαιοὺς, ἀλλὰ τήνδ', ᾐτήσατο.   390

ΕΚ. ὑμεῖς δέ μ' ἀλλὰ θυγατρὶ συμφονεύσατε,
    καὶ δὶς τόσον πῶμ' αἵματος γενήσεται
    γαίᾳ νεκρῷ τε τῷ τάδ' ἐξαιτουμένῳ.
ΟΔ. ἅλις κόρης εἷς θάνατος· οὐ προσοιστέος
    ἄλλος πρὸς ἄλλῳ· μηδὲ τόνδ' ὠφείλομεν.   395
ΕΚ. πολλή γ' ἀνάγκη θυγατρὶ συνθανεῖν ἐμέ.
ΟΔ. πῶς; οὐ γὰρ οἶδα δεσπότας κεκτημένος.
ΕΚ. ὁποῖα κισσὸς δρυὸς ὅπως τῆσδ' ἕξομαι.
ΟΔ. οὔκ, ἤν γε πείθῃ τοῖσι σοῦ σοφωτέροις.
ΕΚ. ὡς τῆσδ' ἑκοῦσα παιδὸς οὐ μεθήσομαι.   400
ΟΔ. ἀλλ' οὐδ' ἐγὼ μὴν τήνδ' ἄπειμ' αὐτοῦ λιπών.
ΠΟΛΥΞ. μῆτερ, πιθοῦ μοι· καὶ σύ, παῖ Λαερτίου,
    χάλα τοκεῦσιν εἰκότως θυμουμένοις,
    σύ τ', ὦ τάλαινα, τοῖς κρατοῦσι μὴ μάχου.
    βούλει πεσεῖν πρὸς οὖδας, ἑλκῶσαί τε σὸν   405
    γέροντα χρῶτα πρὸς βίαν ὠθουμένη,
    ἀσχημονῆσαί τ' ἐκ νέου βραχίονος
    σπασθεῖσ'; ἃ πείσει· μὴ σύ γ'· οὐ γὰρ ἄξιον.
    ἀλλ', ὦ φίλη μοι μῆτερ, ἡδίστην χέρα
    δὸς καὶ παρειὰν προσβαλεῖν παρηίδι·   410
    ὡς οὔποτ' αὖθις, ἀλλὰ νῦν πανύστατον
    ἀκτῖνα κύκλον θ' ἡλίου προσόψομαι.
    τέλος δέχει δὴ τῶν ἐμῶν προσφθεγμάτων.
    ὦ μῆτερ, ὦ τεκοῦσ', ἄπειμι δὴ κάτω.
ΕΚ. ὦ θύγατερ, ἡμεῖς δ' ἐν φάει δουλεύσομεν.   415
ΠΟΛΥΞ. ἄνυμφος, ἀνυμέναιος, ὧν μ' ἐχρῆν τυχεῖν.
ΕΚ. οἰκτρὰ σύ, τέκνον, ἀθλία δ' ἐγὼ γυνή.
ΠΟΛΥΞ. ἐκεῖ δ' ἐν Ἅιδου κείσομαι χωρὶς σέθεν.
ΕΚ. οἴμοι τί δράσω; ποῖ τελευτήσω βίον;

ΠΟΛΥΞ. δούλη θανοῦμαι, πατρὸς οὖσ᾽ ἐλευθέρου.   420

ΕΚ. ἡμεῖς δὲ πεντήκοντά γ᾽ ἄμμοροι τέκνων.

ΠΟΛΥΞ. τί σοι πρὸς Ἕκτορ᾽ ἢ γέροντ᾽ εἴπω πόσιν;

ΕΚ. ἄγγελλε πασῶν ἀθλιωτάτην ἐμέ.

ΠΟΛΥΞ. ὦ στέρνα, μαστοί θ᾽, οἵ μ᾽ ἐθρέψαθ᾽ ἡδέως.

ΕΚ. ὦ τῆς ἀώρου θύγατερ ἀθλία τύχης.   425

ΠΟΛΥΞ. χαῖρ᾽, ὦ τεκοῦσα, χαῖρε Κασάνδρα τέ μοι.

ΕΚ. χαίρουσιν ἄλλοι, μητρὶ δ᾽ οὐκ ἔστιν τόδε.

ΠΟΛΥΞ. ὅ τ᾽ ἐν φιλίπποις Θρῃξὶ Πολύδωρος κάσις.

ΕΚ. εἰ ζῇ γ᾽· ἀπιστῶ δ᾽ ὧδε πάντα δυστυχῶ.

ΠΟΛΥΞ. ζῇ καὶ θανούσης ὄμμα συγκλήσει τὸ σόν.   430

ΕΚ. τέθνηκ᾽ ἔγωγε πρὶν θανεῖν κακῶν ὕπο.

ΠΟΛΥΞ. κόμιζ᾽, Ὀδυσσεῦ, μ᾽ ἀμφιθεὶς κάρα πέπλοις·
ὡς πρὶν σφαγῆναί γ᾽ ἐκτέτηκα καρδίαν
θρήνοισι μητρός, τήνδε τ᾽ ἐκτήκω γόοις.
ὦ φῶς· προσειπεῖν γὰρ σὸν ὄνομ᾽ ἔξεστί μοι, 435
μέτεστι δ᾽ οὐδὲν πλὴν ὅσον χρόνον ξίφους
βαίνω μεταξὺ καὶ πυρᾶς Ἀχιλλέως.

ΕΚ. οἲ ᾽γώ· προλείπω· λύεται δέ μου μέλη.
ὦ θύγατερ, ἅψαι μητρός, ἔκτεινον χέρα,
δός· μὴ λίπῃς μ᾽ ἄπαιδ᾽. ἀπωλόμην, φίλαι.   440
[ὡς τὴν Λάκαιναν ξύγγονον Διοσκόροιν
Ἑλένην ἴδοιμι· διὰ καλῶν γὰρ ὀμμάτων
αἴσχιστα Τροίαν εἷλε τὴν εὐδαίμονα.]

ΧΟ. αὔρα, ποντιὰς αὔρα,   στρ. α΄.
ἅτε ποντοπόρους κομίζεις   445
θοὰς ἀκάτους ἐπ᾽ οἶδμα λίμνας,
ποῖ με τὰν μελέαν πορεύσεις;
τῷ δουλόσυνος πρὸς οἶκον

κτηθεῖσ' ἀφίξομαι;
ἢ Δωρίδος ὅρμον αἴας, 450
ἢ Φθιάδος, ἔνθα τὸν
καλλίστων ὑδάτων πατέρα
φασὶν Ἀπιδανὸν γύας λιπαίνειν;
ἢ νάσων, ἁλιήρει ἀντ. ά. 455
κώπᾳ πεμπομέναν τάλαιναν,
οἰκτρὰν βιοτὰν ἔχουσαν οἴκοις,
ἔνθα πρωτόγονός τε φοῖνιξ
δάφνα θ' ἱεροὺς ἀνέσχε
πτόρθους Λατοῖ φίλᾳ 460
ὠδῖνος ἄγαλμα δίας;
σὺν Δηλιάσιν τε κού-
ραισιν Ἀρτέμιδός τε θεᾶς
χρυσέαν ἄμπυκα τόξα τ' εὐλογήσω; 465
ἢ Παλλάδος ἐν πόλει στρ. β'.
τᾶς καλλιδίφρου θεᾶς
ναίουσ' ἐν κροκέῳ πέπλῳ
ζεύξομαι ἆρα πώ-
λους, ἐν δαιδαλέαισι ποι- 470
κίλλουσ' ἀνθοκρόκοισι πήναις;
ἢ Τιτάνων γενεὰν,
τὰν Ζεὺς ἀμφιπύρῳ
κοιμίζει φλογμῷ Κρονίδας;
ὤμοι τεκέων ἐμῶν, ἀντ. β'. 475
ὤμοι πατέρων, χθονός θ'
ἃ καπνῷ κατερείπεται
τυφομένα, δορί-
κτητος Ἀργείων· ἐγὼ δ'

ἐν ξείνᾳ χθονὶ δὴ κέκλημαι   480
δούλα, λιποῦσ᾽ Ἀσίαν
Εὐρώπας θεράπναν,
ἀλλάξασ᾽ Ἅιδα θαλάμους.

ΤΑΛΘΥΒΙΟΣ.

ποῦ τὴν ἄνασσαν δήποτ᾽ οὖσαν Ἰλίου
Ἑκάβην ἂν ἐξεύροιμι, Τρῳάδες κόραι ;   485
ΧΟ. αὕτη πέλας σου, νῶτ᾽ ἔχουσ᾽ ἐπὶ χθονὶ,
Ταλθύβιε, κεῖται, συγκεκλημένη πέπλοις.
ΤΑ. ὦ Ζεῦ, τί λέξω ; πότερά σ᾽ ἀνθρώπους ὁρᾶν ;
ἢ δόξαν ἄλλως τήνδε κεκτῆσθαι μάτην
[ψευδῆ, δοκοῦντας δαιμόνων εἶναι γένος,]   490
τύχην δὲ πάντα τὰν βροτοῖς ἐπισκοπεῖν ;
οὐχ ἥδ᾽ ἄνασσα τῶν πολυχρύσων Φρυγῶν ;
οὐχ ἥδε Πριάμου τοῦ μέγ᾽ ὀλβίου δάμαρ ;
καὶ νῦν πόλις μὲν πᾶσ᾽ ἀνέστηκεν δορὶ,
αὐτὴ δὲ δούλη, γραῦς, ἄπαις, ἐπὶ χθονὶ   495
κεῖται, κόνει φύρουσα δύστηνον κάρα.
φεῦ φεῦ. γέρων μέν εἰμ᾽· ὅμως δέ μοι θανεῖν
εἴη, πρὶν αἰσχρᾷ περιπεσεῖν τύχῃ τινί.
ἀνίστασ᾽, ὦ δύστηνε, καὶ μετάρσιον
πλευρὰν ἔπαιρε καὶ τὸ πάλλευκον κάρα.   500
ΕΚ. ἔα· τίς οὗτος σῶμα τοὐμὸν οὐκ ἐᾷς
κεῖσθαι ; τί κινεῖς μ᾽, ὅστις εἶ, λυπουμένην ;
ΤΑ. Ταλθύβιος ἥκω, Δαναϊδῶν ὑπηρέτης,
Ἀγαμέμνονος πέμψαντος, ὦ γύναι, μέτα.
ΕΚ. ὦ φίλτατ᾽, ἆρα κἄμ᾽ ἐπισφάξαι τάφῳ   505
δοκοῦν Ἀχαιοῖς ἦλθες ; ὡς φίλ᾽ ἂν λέγοις.

σπεύδωμεν, ἐγκονῶμεν, ἡγοῦ μοι, γέρον.

ΤΑ. σὴν παῖδα κατθανοῦσαν ὡς θάψῃς, γύναι,
ἥκω μεταστείχων σε· πέμπουσιν δέ με
δισσοί τ᾽ Ἀτρεῖδαι καὶ λεὼς Ἀχαιϊκός. 510

ΕΚ. οἴμοι, τί λέξεις; οὐκ ἄρ᾽ ὡς θανουμένους
μετῆλθες ἡμᾶς, ἀλλὰ σημανῶν κακά;
ὄλωλας, ὦ παῖ, μητρὸς ἁρπασθεῖσ᾽ ἄπο·
ἡμεῖς δ᾽ ἄτεκνοι τοὐπὶ σ᾽· ὦ τάλαιν᾽ ἐγώ.
πῶς καί νιν ἐξεπράξατ᾽; ἆρ᾽ αἰδούμενοι; 515
ἢ πρὸς τὸ δεινὸν ἤλθεθ᾽, ὡς ἐχθρὰν, γέρον,
κτείνοντες; εἰπέ, καίπερ οὐ λέξων φίλα.

ΤΑ. διπλᾶ με χρῄζεις δάκρυα κερδᾶναι, γύναι,
σῆς παιδὸς οἴκτῳ· νῦν τε γὰρ λέγων κακὰ
τέγξω τόδ᾽ ὄμμα, πρὸς τάφῳ θ᾽, ὅτ᾽ ὤλλυτο. 520
παρῆν μὲν ὄχλος πᾶς Ἀχαιϊκοῦ στρατοῦ
πλήρης πρὸ τύμβου σῆς κόρης ἐπὶ σφαγάς·
λαβὼν δ᾽ Ἀχιλλέως παῖς Πολυξένην χερὸς
ἔστησ᾽ ἐπ᾽ ἄκρου χώματος, πέλας δ᾽ ἐγώ·
λεκτοί τ᾽ Ἀχαιῶν ἔκκριτοι νεανίαι, 525
σκίρτημα μόσχου σῆς καθέξοντες χεροῖν,
ἕσποντο· πλῆρες δ᾽ ἐν χεροῖν λαβὼν δέπας
πάγχρυσον, αἴρει χειρὶ παῖς Ἀχιλλέως
χοὰς θανόντι πατρί· σημαίνει δέ μοι
σιγὴν Ἀχαιῶν παντὶ κηρῦξαι στρατῷ. 530
κἀγὼ παραστὰς εἶπον ἐν μέσοις τάδε·
'σιγᾶτ᾽, Ἀχαιοί, σῖγα πᾶς ἔστω λεώς·
σίγα, σιώπα·' νήνεμον δ᾽ ἔστησ᾽ ὄχλον.
ὁ δ᾽ εἶπεν, 'ὦ παῖ Πηλέως, πατὴρ δ᾽ ἐμὸς,
δέξαι χοάς μοι τάσδε κηλητηρίους, 535

νεκρῶν ἀγωγούς· ἐλθὲ δ', ὡς πίῃς μέλαν
κόρης ἀκραιφνὲς αἶμ', ὅ σοι δωρούμεθα
στρατός τε κἀγώ· πρευμενὴς δ' ἡμῖν γενοῦ,
λῦσαί τε πρύμνας καὶ χαλινωτήρια
νεῶν δὸς ἡμῖν, πρευμενοῦς τ' ἀπ' Ἰλίου   54ᴣ
νόστου τυχόντας πάντας ἐς πάτραν μολεῖν.'
τοσαῦτ' ἔλεξε, πᾶς δ' ἐπηύξατο στρατός.
εἶτ' ἀμφίχρυσον φάσγανον κώπης λαβὼν
ἐξεῖλκε κολεοῦ, λογάσι δ' Ἀργείων στρατοῦ
νεανίαις ἔνευσε παρθένον λαβεῖν.   545
ἡ δ', ὡς ἐφράσθη, τόνδ' ἐσήμηνεν λόγον·
ὦ τὴν ἐμὴν πέρσαντες Ἀργεῖοι πόλιν,
ἑκοῦσα θνῄσκω· μή τις ἅψηται χροὸς
τοὐμοῦ· παρέξω γὰρ δέρην εὐκαρδίως.
ἐλευθέραν δέ μ', ὡς ἐλευθέρα θάνω,   550
πρὸς θεῶν μεθέντες κτείνατ'· ἐν νεκροῖσι γὰρ
δούλη κεκλῆσθαι βασιλὶς οὖσ' αἰσχύνομαι.
λαοὶ δ' ἐπερρόθησαν, Ἀγαμέμνων τ' ἄναξ
εἶπεν μεθεῖναι παρθένον νεανίαις.
[οἱ δ', ὡς τάχιστ' ἤκουσαν ὑστάτην ὄπα,   555
μεθῆκαν, οὗπερ καὶ μέγιστον ἦν κράτος.]
κἀπεὶ τόδ' εἰσήκουσε δεσποτῶν ἔπος,
λαβοῦσα πέπλους ἐξ ἄκρας ἐπωμίδος
ἔρρηξε λαγόνος ἐς μέσον παρ' ὀμφαλὸν,
μαστούς τ' ἔδειξε στέρνα θ', ὡς ἀγάλματος,   560
κάλλιστα· καὶ καθεῖσα πρὸς γαῖαν γόνυ
ἔλεξε πάντων τλημονέστατον λόγον·
ἰδοὺ τόδ', εἰ μὲν στέρνον, ὦ νεανία,
παίειν προθυμεῖ, παῖσον, εἰ δ' ὑπ' αὐχένα

χρήζεις, πάρεστι λαιμὸς εὐτρεπὴς ὅδε.   565
ὁ δ᾽ οὐ θέλων τε καὶ θέλων, οἴκτῳ κόρης,
τέμνει σιδήρῳ πνεύματος διαρροάς·
κρουνοὶ δ᾽ ἐχώρουν· ἡ δὲ καὶ θνήσκουσ᾽ ὅμως
πολλὴν πρόνοιαν εἶχεν εὐσχήμως πεσεῖν,
[κρύπτουσ᾽ ἃ κρύπτειν ὄμματ᾽ ἀρσένων χρεών.] 570
ἐπεὶ δ᾽ ἀφῆκε πνεῦμα θανασίμῳ σφαγῇ,
οὐδεὶς τὸν αὐτὸν εἶχεν Ἀργείων πόνον,
ἀλλ᾽ οἱ μὲν αὐτῶν τὴν θανοῦσαν ἐκ χερῶν
φύλλοις ἔβαλλον, οἱ δὲ πληροῦσιν πυράν,
κορμοὺς φέροντες πευκίνους, ὁ δ᾽ οὐ φέρων   575
πρὸς τοῦ φέροντος τοιάδ᾽ ἤκουεν κακά·
‘ ἕστηκας, ὦ κάκιστε, τῇ νεάνιδι
οὐ πέπλον, οὐδὲ κόσμον ἐν χεροῖν ἔχων;
οὐκ εἶ τι δώσων τῇ περίσσ᾽ εὐκαρδίῳ
ψυχήν τ᾽ ἀρίστῃ;’ τοιάδ᾽ ἀμφὶ σῆς λέγω   580
παιδὸς θανούσης· εὐτεκνωτάτην δέ σε
πασῶν γυναικῶν δυστυχεστάτην θ᾽ ὁρῶ.

ΧΟ. δεινόν τι πῆμα Πριαμίδαις ἐπέζεσε
πόλει τε τῇμῇ· θεῶν ἀναγκαῖον τόδε.

ΕΚ. ὦ θύγατερ, οὐκ οἶδ᾽ εἰς ὅ τι βλέψω κακῶν,   585
πολλῶν παρόντων· ἢν γὰρ ἅψωμαί τινος,
τόδ᾽ οὐκ ἐᾷ με, παρακαλεῖ δ᾽ ἐκεῖθεν αὖ
λύπη τις ἄλλη διάδοχος κακῶν κακοῖς.
καὶ νῦν τὸ μὲν σὸν ὥστε μὴ στένειν πάθος
οὐκ ἂν δυναίμην ἐξαλείψασθαι φρενός·   590
τὸ δ᾽ αὖ λίαν παρεῖλες, ἀγγελθεῖσά μοι
γενναῖος. οὔκουν δεινόν, εἰ γῆ μὲν κακὴ
τυχοῦσα καιροῦ θεόθεν εὖ στάχυν φέρει,

χρηστὴ δ᾽ ἁμαρτοῦσ᾽ ὧν χρεὼν αὐτὴν τυχεῖν
κακὸν δίδωσι καρπόν, ἀνθρώποις δ᾽ ἀεὶ   595
ὁ μὲν πονηρὸς οὐδὲν ἄλλο πλὴν κακός,
ὁ δ᾽ ἐσθλὸς ἐσθλός, οὐδὲ συμφορᾶς ὕπο
φύσιν διέφθειρ᾽, ἀλλὰ χρηστός ἐστ᾽ ἀεί;
ἆρ᾽ οἱ τεκόντες διαφέρουσιν, ἢ τροφαί;
ἔχει γε μέντοι καὶ τὸ θρεφθῆναι καλῶς   600
δίδαξιν ἐσθλοῦ· τοῦτο δ᾽ ἤν τις εὖ μάθῃ,
οἶδεν τό γ᾽ αἰσχρόν, κανόνι τοῦ καλοῦ μαθών.
καὶ ταῦτα μὲν δὴ νοῦς ἐτόξευσεν μάτην·
σὺ δ᾽ ἐλθὲ καὶ σήμηνον Ἀργείοις τάδε,
μὴ θιγγάνειν μοι μηδέν᾽, ἀλλ᾽ εἴργειν ὄχλον   605
τῆς παιδός. ἔν τοι μυρίῳ στρατεύματι
ἀκόλαστος ὄχλος ναυτική τ᾽ ἀναρχία
κρείσσων πυρός, κακὸς δ᾽ ὁ μή τι δρῶν κακόν.
σὺ δ᾽ αὖ λαβοῦσα τεῦχος, ἀρχαία λάτρι,
βάψασ᾽ ἔνεγκε δεῦρο ποντίας ἁλός,   610
ὡς παῖδα λουτροῖς τοῖς πανυστάτοις ἐμὴν
νύμφην τ᾽ ἄνυμφον παρθένον τ᾽ ἀπάρθενον
λούσω προθῶμαι θ᾽· ὡς μὲν ἀξία, πόθεν;
οὐκ ἂν δυναίμην· ὡς δ᾽ ἔχω· τί γὰρ πάθω;
κόσμον γ᾽ ἀγείρασ᾽ αἰχμαλωτίδων πάρα,   615
αἵ μοι πάρεδροι τῶνδ᾽ ἔσω σκηνωμάτων
ναίουσιν, εἴ τις τοὺς νεωστὶ δεσπότας
λαθοῦσ᾽ ἔχει τι κλέμμα τῶν αὑτῆς δόμων.
ὦ σχήματ᾽ οἴκων, ὦ ποτ᾽ εὐτυχεῖς δόμοι,
ὦ πλεῖστ᾽ ἔχων κάλλιστά τ᾽, εὐτεκνώτατε   620
Πρίαμε, γεραιά θ᾽ ἥδ᾽ ἐγὼ μήτηρ τέκνων,
ὡς ἐς τὸ μηδὲν ἥκομεν, φρονήματος

τοῦ πρὶν στερέντες. εἶτα δῆτ᾽ ὀγκούμεθα
ὁ μέν τις ἡμῶν πλουσίοις ἐν δώμασιν,
ὁ δ᾽ ἐν πολίταις τίμιος κεκλημένος.   625
τὰ δ᾽ οὐδέν· ἄλλως φροντίδων βουλεύματα,
γλώσσης τε κόμποι. κεῖνος ὀλβιώτατος,
ὅτῳ κατ᾽ ἦμαρ τυγχάνει μηδὲν κακόν.

ΧΟ. ἐμοὶ χρῆν συμφορὰν,   στρ.
   ἐμοὶ χρῆν πημονὰν γενέσθαι,   630
   Ἰδαίαν ὅτε πρῶτον ὕλαν
   Ἀλέξανδρος εἰλατίναν
   ἐτάμεθ᾽, ἅλιον ἐπ᾽ οἶδμα ναυστολήσων
   Ἑλένας ἐπὶ λέκτρα, τὰν καλλίσταν ὁ χρυσο-
      φαὴς   635, 6
   Ἅλιος αὐγάζει.
   πόνοι γὰρ καὶ πόνων   ἀντ.
   ἀνάγκαι κρείσσονες κυκλοῦνται.
   κοινὸν δ᾽ ἐξ ἰδίας ἀνοίας   640
   κακὸν τᾷ Σιμουντίδι γᾷ
   ὀλέθριον ἔμολε, συμφορά τ᾽ ἀπ᾽ ἄλλων.
   ἐκρίθη δ᾽ ἔρις, ἃν ἐν Ἴ-
   δᾳ κρίνει τρισσὰς μακάρων   645
   παῖδας ἀνὴρ βούτας,
   ἐπὶ δορὶ καὶ φόνῳ καὶ ἐμῶν μελάθρων λώβᾳ·   ἐπῳδ.
   στένει δὲ καί τις ἀμφὶ τὸν εὔροον Εὐρώταν   650
   Λάκαινα πολυδάκρυτος ἐν δόμοις κόρα,
   πολιόν τ᾽ ἐπὶ κρᾶτα μάτηρ
   τέκνων θανόντων τίθεται χέρα,
   δρύπτεταί τε παρειὰν,   655
   δίαιμον ὄνυχα τιθεμένα σπαραγμοῖς.

ΘΕΡΑΠΑΙΝΑ.

γυναῖκες, Ἑκάβη ποῦ ποθ᾽ ἡ παναθλία,
ἡ πάντα νικῶσ᾽ ἄνδρα καὶ θῆλυν σποράν
κακοῖς, ἵν᾽ οὐδεὶς στέφανον ἀνθαιρήσεται;   660

ΧΟ. τί δ᾽, ὦ τάλαινα σῆς κακογλώσσου βοῆς;
ὡς οὔποθ᾽ εὕδει λυπρά σου κηρύγματα.

ΘΕ. Ἑκάβῃ φέρω τόδ᾽ ἄλγος· ἐν κακοῖσι δὲ
οὐ ῥᾴδιον βροτοῖσιν εὐφημεῖν στόμα.

ΧΟ. καὶ μὴν περῶσα τυγχάνει δόμων ὕπερ   665
ἥδ᾽, ἐς δὲ καιρὸν σοῖσι φαίνεται λόγοις.

ΘΕ. ὦ παντάλαινα, κἄτι μᾶλλον ἢ λέγω,
δέσποιν᾽, ὄλωλας, οὐκέτ᾽ εἶ, βλέπουσα φῶς,
ἄπαις, ἄνανδρος, ἄπολις, ἐξεφθαρμένη.

ΕΚ. οὐ καινὸν εἶπας, εἰδόσιν δ᾽ ὠνείδισας.   670
ἀτὰρ τί νεκρὸν τόνδε μοι Πολυξένης
ἥκεις κομίζουσ᾽, ἧς ἀπηγγέλθη τάφος
πάντων Ἀχαιῶν διὰ χερὸς σπουδὴν ἔχειν;

ΘΕ. ἥδ᾽ οὐδὲν οἶδεν, ἀλλά μοι Πολυξένην
θρηνεῖ, νέων δὲ πημάτων οὐχ ἅπτεται.   675

ΕΚ. οἲ ᾽γὼ τάλαινα, μῶν τὸ βακχεῖον κάρα
τῆς θεσπιῳδοῦ δεῦρο Κασάνδρας φέρεις;

ΘΕ. ζῶσαν λέλακας, τὸν θανόντα δ᾽ οὐ στένεις
τόνδ᾽. ἀλλ᾽ ἄθρησον σῶμα γυμνωθὲν νεκροῦ,
εἴ σοι φανεῖται θαῦμα καὶ παρ᾽ ἐλπίδας.   680

ΕΚ. οἴμοι, βλέπω δὴ παῖδ᾽ ἐμὸν τεθνηκότα
Πολύδωρον, ὅν μοι Θρῇξ ἔσῳζ᾽ οἴκοις ἀνήρ.
ἀπωλόμην δύστηνος, οὐκέτ᾽ εἰμὶ δή.
ὦ τέκνον,

αἰαῖ, κατάρχομαι νόμον   685
βακχεῖον, ἐξ ἀλάστορος
ἀρτιμαθὴς κακῶν.

ΘΕ. ἔγνως γὰρ ἄτην παιδός, ὦ δύστηνε σύ;

ΕΚ. ἄπιστ᾽ ἄπιστα, καινὰ καινὰ δέρκομαι.
ἕτερα δ᾽ ἀφ᾽ ἑτέρων κακὰ κακῶν κυρεῖ·   690
οὐδέποτ᾽ ἀστένακτον, ἀδάκρυτον ἀμέρα μ᾽ ἐπισχήσει.

ΧΟ. δείν᾽, ὦ τάλαινα, δεινὰ πάσχομεν κακά.

ΕΚ. ὦ τέκνον, τέκνον ταλαίνας ματρός,   695
τίνι μόρῳ θνῄσκεις, τίνι πότμῳ κεῖσαι; πρὸς τίνος
ἀνθρώπων;

ΘΕ. οὐκ οἶδ᾽. ἐπ᾽ ἀκταῖς νιν κυρῶ θαλασσίαις.

ΕΚ. ἔκβλητον, ἢ πέσημα φοινίου δορός,
ἐν ψαμάθῳ λευρᾷ;   700

ΘΕ. πόντου νιν ἐξήνεγκε πελάγιος κλύδων.

ΕΚ. ὤμοι, αἰαῖ, ἔμαθον ἔνυπνον ὀμμάτων
ἐμῶν ὄψιν, οὔ με παρέβα φά-
σμα μελανόπτερον   705
ἃν ἐσεῖδον ἀμφί σ᾽,
ὦ τέκνον, οὐκέτ᾽ ὄντα Διὸς ἐν φάει.

ΧΟ. τίς γάρ νιν ἔκτειν᾽; οἶσθ᾽ ὀνειρόφρων φράσαι;

ΕΚ. ἐμὸς ἐμὸς ξένος, Θρήκιος ἱππότας,   710
ἵν᾽ ὁ γέρων πατὴρ ἔθετό νιν κρύψας.

ΧΟ. ὤμοι, τί λέξεις; χρυσὸν ὡς ἔχῃ κτανών;

ΕΚ. ἄρρητ᾽, ἀνωνόμαστα, θαυμάτων πέρα,
οὐχ ὅσι᾽, οὐδ᾽ ἀνεκτά. ποῦ δίκα ξένων;   715
ὦ κατάρατ᾽ ἀνδρῶν, ὡς διεμοιράσω
χρόα, σιδαρέῳ τεμὼν φασγάνῳ

μέλεα τοῦδε παιδὸς, οὐδ' ᾤκτισω. 720

ΧΟ. ὦ τλῆμον, ὥς σε πολυπονωτάτην βροτῶν
δαίμων ἔθηκεν, ὅστις ἐστί σοι βαρύς.
ἀλλ' εἰσορῶ γὰρ τοῦδε δεσπότου δέμας
Ἀγαμέμνονος, τοὐνθένδε σιγῶμεν, φίλαι. 725

ΑΓΑΜΕΜΝΩΝ.

Ἑκάβη, τί μέλλεις παῖδα σὴν κρύπτειν τάφῳ
ἐλθοῦσ', ἐφ' οἷσπερ Ταλθύβιος ἤγγειλέ μοι
μὴ θιγγάνειν σῆς μηδέν' Ἀργείων κόρης;
ἡμεῖς μὲν οὖν εἰῶμεν οὐδ' ἐψαύομεν·
σὺ δὲ σχολάζεις, ὥστε θαυμάζειν ἐμέ. 730
ἥκω δ' ἀποστελῶν σε· τἀκεῖθεν γὰρ εὖ
πεπραγμέν' ἐστίν, εἴ τι τῶνδ' ἐστὶν καλῶς.
ἔα· τίν' ἄνδρα τόνδ' ἐπὶ σκηναῖς ὁρῶ
θανόντα Τρώων; οὐ γὰρ Ἀργεῖον, πέπλοι
δέμας περιπτύσσοντες ἀγγέλλουσί μοι. 735

ΕΚ. δύστην', ἐμαυτὴν γὰρ λέγω λέγουσα σὲ,
Ἑκάβη, τί δράσω; πότερα προσπέσω γόνυ
Ἀγαμέμνονος τοῦδ', ἢ φέρω σιγῇ κακά;

ΑΓ. τί μοι προσώπῳ νῶτον ἐγκλίνασα σὸν
δύρει, τὸ πραχθὲν δ' οὐ λέγεις, τίς ἔσθ' ὅδε. 740

ΕΚ. ἀλλ' εἴ με δούλην πολεμίαν θ' ἡγούμενος
γονάτων ἀπώσαιτ', ἄλγος ἂν προσθείμεθ' ἄν.

ΑΓ. οὔτοι πέφυκα μάντις, ὥστε μὴ κλύων
ἐξιστορῆσαι σῶν ὁδὸν βουλευμάτων.

ΕΚ. ἆρ' ἐκλογίζομαί γε πρὸς τὸ δυσμενὲς 745
μᾶλλον φρένας τοῦδ', ὄντος οὐχὶ δυσμενοῦς;

ΑΓ. εἴ τοί με βούλει τῶνδε μηδὲν εἰδέναι,

ἐς ταὐτὸν ἥκεις· καὶ γὰρ οὐδ' ἐγὼ κλύειν.

ΕΚ. οὐκ ἂν δυναίμην τοῦδε τιμωρεῖν ἄτερ
τέκνοισι τοῖς ἐμοῖσι. τί στρέφω τάδε;   750
τολμᾶν ἀνάγκη, κἂν τύχω κἂν μὴ τύχω.
'Αγάμεμνον, ἱκετεύω σε τῶνδε γουνάτων
καὶ σοῦ γενείου δεξιᾶς τ' εὐδαίμονος.

ΑΓ. τί χρῆμα μαστεύουσα; μῶν ἐλεύθερον
αἰῶνα θέσθαι; ῥᾴδιον γάρ ἐστί σοι.   755

ΕΚ. [οὐ δῆτα· τοὺς κακοὺς δὲ τιμωρουμένη,
αἰῶνα τὸν ξύμπαντα δουλεῦσαι θέλω.

ΑΓ. καὶ δὴ τίν' ἡμᾶς εἰς ἐπάρκεσιν καλεῖς;]

ΕΚ. οὐδέν τι τούτων ὧν σὺ δοξάζεις, ἄναξ.
ὁρᾷς νεκρὸν τόνδ', οὗ καταστάζω δάκρυ;   760

ΑΓ. ὁρῶ· τὸ μέντοι μέλλον οὐκ ἔχω μαθεῖν.

ΕΚ. τοῦτόν ποτ' ἔτεκον κἄφερον ζώνης ὕπο.

ΑΓ. ἔστιν δὲ τίς σῶν οὗτος, ὦ τλῆμον, τέκνων;

ΕΚ. οὐ τῶν θανόντων Πριαμιδῶν ὑπ' Ἰλίῳ.

ΑΓ. ἦ γάρ τιν' ἄλλον ἔτεκες ἢ κείνους, γύναι;   765

ΕΚ. ἀνόνητά γ', ὡς ἔοικε, τόνδ' ὃν εἰσορᾷς.

ΑΓ. ποῦ δ' ὢν ἐτύγχαν', ἡνίκ' ὤλλυτο πτόλις;

ΕΚ. πατήρ νιν ἐξέπεμψεν, ὀρρωδῶν θανεῖν.

ΑΓ. ποῖ τῶν τότ' ὄντων χωρίσας τέκνων μόνον;

ΕΚ. ἐς τήνδε χώραν, οὗπερ ηὑρέθη θανών.   770

ΑΓ. πρὸς ἄνδρ', ὃς ἄρχει τῆσδε Πολυμήστωρ χθονός;

ΕΚ. ἐνταῦθ' ἐπέμφθη πικροτάτου χρυσοῦ φύλαξ.

ΑΓ. θνήσκει δὲ πρὸς τοῦ καὶ τίνος πότμου τυχών;

ΕΚ. τίνος γ' ὑπ' ἄλλου; Θρῇξ νιν ὤλεσε ξένος.

ΑΓ. ὦ τλῆμον, ἦ που χρυσὸν ἠράσθη λαβεῖν;   775

ΕΚ. τοιαῦτ', ἐπειδὴ ξυμφορὰν ἔγνω Φρυγῶν.

ΑΓ. ηὗρες δὲ ποῦ νιν, ἢ τίς ἤνεγκεν νεκρόν;
ΕΚ. ἥδ᾽, ἐντυχοῦσα ποντίας ἀκτῆς ἔπι.
ΑΓ. τοῦτον ματεύουσ᾽, ἢ πονοῦσ᾽ ἄλλον πόνον;
ΕΚ. λουτρ᾽ ᾤχετ᾽ οἴσουσ᾽ ἐξ ἁλὸς Πολυξένῃ.   780
ΑΓ. κτανών νιν, ὡς ἔοικεν, ἐκβάλλει ξένος.
ΕΚ. θαλασσόπλαγκτόν γ᾽, ὧδε διατεμὼν χρόα.
ΑΓ. ὦ σχετλία σὺ τῶν ἀμετρήτων πόνων.
ΕΚ. ὄλωλα, κοὐδὲν λοιπόν, Ἀγάμεμνον, κακῶν.
ΑΓ. φεῦ φεῦ· τίς οὕτω δυστυχὴς ἔφυ γυνή;   785
ΕΚ. οὐκ ἔστιν, εἰ μὴ τὴν τύχην αὐτὴν λέγοις.
    ἀλλ᾽ ὧνπερ οὕνεκ᾽ ἀμφὶ σὸν πίπτω γόνυ,
    ἄκουσον. εἰ μὲν ὅσιά σοι παθεῖν δοκῶ,
    στέργοιμ᾽ ἄν· εἰ δὲ τοὔμπαλιν, σύ μοι γενοῦ
    τιμωρὸς ἀνδρὸς ἀνοσιωτάτου ξένου,   790
    ὃς οὔτε τοὺς γῆς νέρθεν οὔτε τοὺς ἄνω
    δείσας δέδρακεν ἔργον ἀνοσιώτατον,
    κοινῆς τραπέζης πολλάκις τυχὼν ἐμοί,
    [ξενίας τ᾽ ἀριθμῷ πρῶτα τῶν ἐμῶν φίλων·
    τυχὼν δ᾽ ὅσων δεῖ καὶ λαβὼν προμηθίαν,]   795
    ἔκτεινε, τύμβου δ᾽, εἰ κτανεῖν ἐβούλετο,
    οὐκ ἠξίωσεν, ἀλλ᾽ ἀφῆκε πόντιον.
    ἡμεῖς μὲν οὖν δοῦλοί τε κἀσθενεῖς ἴσως·
    ἀλλ᾽ οἱ θεοὶ σθένουσι χὠ κείνων κρατῶν
    νόμος· νόμῳ γὰρ τοὺς θεοὺς ἡγούμεθα,   800
    καὶ ζῶμεν ἄδικα καὶ δίκαι᾽ ὡρισμένοι·
    ὃς ἐς σ᾽ ἀνελθὼν εἰ διαφθαρήσεται,
    καὶ μὴ δίκην δώσουσιν οἵτινες ξένους
    κτείνουσιν ἢ θεῶν ἱρὰ τολμῶσιν φέρειν,
    οὐκ ἔστιν οὐδὲν τῶν ἐν ἀνθρώποις ἴσον.   805

ταῦτ' οὖν ἐν αἰσχρῷ θέμενος αἰδέσθητί με,
οἴκτειρον ἡμᾶς, ὡς γραφεύς τ' ἀποσταθεὶς
ἰδοῦ με κἀνάθρησον οἷ' ἔχω κακά.
τύραννος ἦν ποτ', ἀλλὰ νῦν δούλη σέθεν,
εὔπαις ποτ' οὖσα, νῦν δὲ γραῦς ἄπαις θ' ἅμα,   810
ἄπολις, ἔρημος, ἀθλιωτάτη βροτῶν.
οἴμοι τάλαινα, ποῖ μ' ὑπεξάγεις πόδα;
ἔοικα πράξειν οὐδέν· ὦ τάλαιν' ἐγώ.
τί δῆτα θνητοὶ τἆλλα μὲν μαθήματα
μοχθοῦμεν ὡς χρὴ πάντα καὶ μαστεύομεν,   815
πειθὼ δὲ τὴν τύραννον ἀνθρώποις μόνην,
οὐδέν τι μᾶλλον ἐς τέλος σπουδάζομεν
μισθοὺς διδόντες μανθάνειν, ἵν' ἦν ποτε
πείθειν ἅ τις βούλοιτο, τυγχάνειν θ' ἅμα;
πῶς οὖν ἔτ' ἄν τις ἐλπίσαι πράξειν καλῶς;   820
οἱ μὲν γὰρ ὄντες παῖδες οὐκέτ' εἰσί μοι,
αὐτὴ δ' ἐπ' αἰσχροῖς αἰχμάλωτος οἴχομαι·
καπνὸν δὲ πόλεως τόνδ' ὑπερθρώσκονθ' ὁρῶ.
καὶ μὴν ἴσως μὲν τοῦ λόγου κενὸν τόδε,
Κύπριν προβάλλειν· ἀλλ' ὅμως εἰρήσεται·   825
πρὸς σοῖσι πλευροῖς παῖς ἐμὴ κοιμίζεται
ἡ φοιβὰς ἣν καλοῦσι Κασάνδρα Φρύγες.
ποῦ τὰς φίλας δῆτ' εὐφρόνας δείξεις, ἄναξ,
ἢ τῶν ἐν εὐνῇ φιλτάτων ἀσπασμάτων
χάριν τίν' ἕξει παῖς ἐμή, κείνης δ' ἐγώ;   830
[ἐκ τοῦ σκότου γὰρ τῶν τε νυκτέρων πάνυ
φίλτρων μεγίστη γίγνεται βροτοῖς χάρις.]
ἄκουε δή νυν· τὸν θανόντα τόνδ' ὁρᾷς;
τοῦτον καλῶς δρῶν ὄντα κηδεστὴν σέθεν

δράσεις. ἑνός μοι μῦθος ἐνδεὴς ἔτι.   835
εἴ μοι γένοιτο φθόγγος ἐν βραχίοσι
καὶ χερσὶ καὶ κόμαισι καὶ ποδῶν βάσει,
ἢ Δαιδάλου τέχναισιν ἢ θεῶν τινος,
ὡς πάνθ' ὁμαρτῇ σῶν ἔχοιτο γουνάτων
κλαίοντ', ἐπισκήπτοντα παντοίους λόγους·   840
ὦ δέσποτ', ὦ μέγιστον Ἕλλησιν φάος,
πιθοῦ, παράσχες χεῖρα τῇ πρεσβύτιδι
τιμωρόν, εἰ καὶ μηδέν ἐστιν, ἀλλ' ὅμως.
ἐσθλοῦ γὰρ ἀνδρὸς τῇ δίκῃ θ' ὑπηρετεῖν
καὶ τοὺς κακοὺς δρᾶν πανταχοῦ κακῶς ἀεί.   845
ΧΟ. δεινόν γε, θνητοῖς ὡς ἅπαντα συμπίτνει,
καὶ τὰς ἀνάγκας οἱ νόμοι διώρισαν,
φίλους τιθέντες τούς τε πολεμιωτάτους,
ἐχθρούς τε τοὺς πρὶν εὐμενεῖς ποιούμενοι.
ΑΓ. ἐγὼ σὲ καὶ σὸν παῖδα καὶ τύχας σέθεν,   850
Ἑκάβη, δι' οἴκτου χεῖρά θ' ἱκεσίαν ἔχω,
καὶ βούλομαι θεῶν θ' οὕνεκ' ἀνόσιον ξένον
καὶ τοῦ δικαίου τήνδε σοι δοῦναι δίκην,
εἴ πως φανείη γ' ὥστε σοί τ' ἔχειν καλῶς,
στρατῷ τε μὴ δόξαιμι Κασάνδρας χάριν   855
Θρῄκης ἄνακτι τόνδε βουλεῦσαι φόνον.
ἔστιν γὰρ ᾗ ταραγμὸς ἐμπέπτωκέ μοι·
τὸν ἄνδρα τοῦτον φίλιον ἡγεῖται στρατός,
τὸν κατθανόντα δ' ἐχθρόν· εἰ δ' ἐμοὶ φίλος
ὅδ' ἐστί, χωρὶς τοῦτο κοὐ κοινὸν στρατῷ.   860
πρὸς ταῦτα φρόντιζ'· ὡς θέλοντα μέν μ' ἔχεις
σοὶ ξυμπονῆσαι καὶ ταχὺν προσαρκέσαι,
βραδὺν δ', Ἀχαιοῖς εἰ διαβληθήσομαι.

ΕΚ. φεῦ·
  οὐκ ἔστι θνητῶν ὅστις ἔστ' ἐλεύθερος·
  ἢ χρημάτων γὰρ δοῦλός ἐστιν ἢ τύχης,   865
  ἢ πλῆθος αὐτὸν πόλεος ἢ νόμων γραφαὶ
  εἴργουσι χρῆσθαι μὴ κατὰ γνώμην τρόποις.
  ἐπεὶ δὲ ταρβεῖς τῷ τ' ὄχλῳ πλέον νέμεις,
  ἐγώ σε θήσω τοῦδ' ἐλεύθερον φόβου.
  ξύνισθι μὲν γὰρ, ἤν τι βουλεύσω κακὸν   870
  τῷ τόνδ' ἀποκτείναντι, συνδράσῃς δὲ μή.
  ἢν δ' ἐξ Ἀχαιῶν θόρυβος ἢ 'πικουρία
  πάσχοντος ἀνδρὸς Θρῃκὸς οἷα πείσεται
  φανῇ τις, εἶργε μὴ δοκῶν ἐμὴν χάριν.
  τὰ δ' ἄλλα θάρσει· πάντ' ἐγὼ θήσω καλῶς.   875
ΑΓ. πῶς οὖν; τί δράσεις; πότερα φάσγανον χερὶ
  λαβοῦσα γραίᾳ φῶτα βάρβαρον κτενεῖς,
  ἢ φαρμάκοισιν, ἢ 'πικουρίᾳ τίνι;
  τίς σοι ξυνέσται χείρ; πόθεν κτήσει φίλους;
ΕΚ. στέγαι κεκεύθασ' αἵδε Τρῳάδων ὄχλον.   880
ΑΓ. τὰς αἰχμαλώτους εἶπας, Ἑλλήνων ἄγραν;
ΕΚ. ξὺν ταῖσδε τὸν ἐμὸν φονέα τιμωρήσομαι.
ΑΓ. καὶ πῶς γυναιξὶν ἀρσένων ἔσται κράτος;
ΕΚ. δεινὸν τὸ πλῆθος, ξὺν δόλῳ τε δύσμαχον.
ΑΓ. δεινόν· τὸ μέντοι θῆλυ μέμφομαι γένος.   885
ΕΚ. τί δ'; οὐ γυναῖκες εἷλον Αἰγύπτου τέκνα,
  καὶ Λῆμνον ἄρδην ἀρσένων ἐξῴκισαν;
  ἀλλ' ὡς γενέσθω· τόνδε μὲν μέθες λόγον,
  πέμψον δέ μοι τήνδ' ἀσφαλῶς διὰ στρατοῦ
  γυναῖκα. καὶ σὺ, Θρῃκὶ πλαθεῖσα ξένῳ,   890
  λέξον, 'καλεῖ σ' ἄνασσα δή ποτ' Ἰλίου

Ἑκάβη, σὸν οὐκ ἔλασσον ἢ κείνης χρέος,
καὶ παῖδας· ὡς δεῖ καὶ τέκν' εἰδέναι λόγους
τοὺς ἐξ ἐκείνης.' τὸν δὲ τῆς νεοσφαγοῦς
Πολυξένης ἐπίσχες, Ἀγάμεμνον, τάφον,　　　895
ὡς τώδ' ἀδελφὼ πλησίον μιᾷ φλογί,
δισσὴ μέριμνα μητρί, κρυφθῆτον χθονί.

ΑΓ. ἔσται τάδ' οὕτως· καὶ γὰρ εἰ μὲν ἦν στρατῷ
πλοῦς, οὐκ ἂν εἶχον τήνδε σοι δοῦναι χάριν·
νῦν δ', οὐ γὰρ ἵησ' οὐρίους πνοὰς θεός,　　　900
μένειν ἀνάγκη πλοῦν ὁρῶντας ἥσυχον.
γένοιτο δ' εὖ πως· πᾶσι γὰρ κοινὸν τόδε,
ἰδίᾳ θ' ἑκάστῳ καὶ πόλει, τὸν μὲν κακὸν
κακόν τι πάσχειν, τὸν δὲ χρηστὸν εὐτυχεῖν.

ΧΟ. σὺ μὲν, ὦ πατρὶς Ἰλιάς,　　　　στρ. α'. 905
τῶν ἀπορθήτων πόλις οὐκέτι λέξει·
τοῖον Ἑλλάνων νέφος ἀμφί σε κρύπτει
δορὶ δὴ δορὶ πέρσαν.
ἀπὸ δὲ στεφάναν κέκαρσαι　　　　　　910
πύργων, κατὰ δ' αἰθάλου
κηλῖδ' οἰκτροτάταν κέχρωσαι,
τάλαιν', οὐκέτι σ' ἐμβατεύσω.
μεσονύκτιος ὠλλύμαν,　　　　　　ἀντ. α'.
ἦμος ἐκ δείπνων ὕπνος ἡδὺς ἐπ' ὄσσοις　　　915
κίδναται, μολπᾶν δ' ἄπο καὶ χοροποιῶν
θυσιᾶν καταπαύσας
πόσις ἐν θαλάμοις ἔκειτο,
ξυστὸν δ' ἐπὶ πασσάλῳ,　　　　　　920
ναύταν οὐκέθ' ὁρῶν ὅμιλον
Τροίαν Ἰλιάδ' ἐμβεβῶτα.

ἐγὼ δὲ πλόκαμον ἀναδέτοις   στρ. β'.
μίτραισιν ἐρρυθμιζόμαν
χρυσέων ἐνόπτρων   925
λεύσσουσ' ἀτέρμονας εἰς αὐγάς,
ἐπιδέμνιον ὡς πέσοιμ' ἐς εὐνάν.
ἀνὰ δὲ κέλαδος ἔμολε πόλιν·
κέλευσμα δ' ἦν κατ' ἄστυ Τροίας τόδ'· 'ὦ
παῖδες Ἑλλάνων, πότε δὴ πότε τὰν   930
Ἰλιάδα σκοπιὰν
πέρσαντες ἥξετ' οἴκους;'
λέχη δὲ φίλια μονόπεπλος   ἀντ. β'.
λιποῦσα, Δωρὶς ὡς κόρα,
σεμνὰν προσίζουσ'   935
οὐκ ἤνυσ' Ἄρτεμιν ἁ τλάμων·
ἄγομαι δὲ θανόντ' ἰδοῦσ' ἀκοίταν
τὸν ἐμὸν ἅλιον ἐπὶ πέλαγος,
πόλιν τ' ἀποσκοποῦσ', ἐπεὶ νόστιμον
ναῦς ἐκίνησεν πόδα καί μ' ἀπὸ γᾶς   940
ὥρισεν Ἰλιάδος,
τάλαιν', ἀπεῖπον ἄλγει·
τὰν τοῖν Διοσκόροιν Ἑλέναν   ἐπῳδ.
κάσιν, Ἰδαῖόν τε βούταν
αἰνόπαριν κατάρᾳ διδοῦσ', ἐπεί με γᾶς   945, 6
ἐκ πατρίας ἀπώλεσεν ἐξ-
ῴκισέν τ' οἴκων
γάμος, οὐ γάμος, ἀλλ' ἀλάστορός τις οἰζύς·
ἂν μήτε πέλαγος ἅλιον ἀπαγάγοι πάλιν,   950, 1
μήτε πατρῷον ἵκοιτ' ἐς οἶκον.

ΠΟΛΥΜΗΣΤΩΡ.

[ὦ φίλτατ' ἀνδρῶν Πρίαμε, φιλτάτη δὲ σύ,]
Ἑκάβη, δακρύω σ' εἰσορῶν πόλιν τε σὴν,
τήν τ' ἀρτίως θανοῦσαν ἔκγονον σέθεν.   955
φεῦ·
οὐκ ἔστιν οὐδὲν πιστὸν οὔτ' εὐδοξία
οὔτ' αὖ καλῶς πράσσοντα μὴ πράξειν κακῶς.
φύρουσι δ' αὐτὰ θεοὶ πάλιν τε καὶ πρόσω,
ταραγμὸν ἐντιθέντες, ὡς ἀγνωσίᾳ
σέβωμεν αὐτούς, ἀλλὰ ταῦτα μὲν τί δεῖ   960
θρηνεῖν, προκόπτοντ' οὐδὲν ἐς πρόσθεν κακῶν;
σὺ δ' εἴ τι μέμφει τῆς ἐμῆς ἀπουσίας,
σχές· τυγχάνω γὰρ ἐν μέσοις Θρῄκης ὅροις
ἀπών, ὅτ' ἦλθες δεῦρ'· ἐπεὶ δ' ἀφικόμην,
ἤδη πόδ' ἔξω δωμάτων αἴροντί μοι   965
ἐς ταὐτὸν ἥδε συμπίτνει δμωὶς σέθεν,
λέγουσα μύθους ὧν κλύων ἀφικόμην.
ΕΚ. αἰσχύνομαί σε προσβλέπειν ἐναντίον,
Πολυμῆστορ, ἐν τοιοῖσδε κειμένη κακοῖς.
ὅτῳ γὰρ ὤφθην εὐτυχοῦσ', αἰδώς μ' ἔχει,   970
ἐν τῷδε πότμῳ τυγχάνουσ', ἵν' εἰμὶ νῦν,
κοὐκ ἂν δυναίμην προσβλέπειν ὀρθαῖς κόραις.
ἀλλ' αὐτὸ μὴ δύσνοιαν ἡγήσῃ σέθεν,
Πολυμῆστορ· ἄλλως δ' αἴτιόν τι καὶ νόμος,
γυναῖκας ἀνδρῶν μὴ βλέπειν ἐναντίον.   975
ΠΟΛΥΜ. καὶ θαῦμά γ' οὐδέν. ἀλλὰ τίς χρεία σ' ἐμοῦ;
τί χρῆμ' ἐπέμψω τὸν ἐμὸν ἐκ δόμων πόδα;
ΕΚ. ἴδιον ἐμαυτῆς δή τι πρὸς σὲ βούλομαι
καὶ παῖδας εἰπεῖν σούς· ὀπάονας δέ μοι

χωρὶς κέλευσον τῶνδ' ἀποστῆναι δόμων.			980

ΠΟΛΥΜ. χωρεῖτ'· ἐν ἀσφαλεῖ γὰρ ἤδ' ἐρημία.
φίλη μὲν εἶ σύ, προσφιλὲς δέ μοι τόδε
στράτευμ' Ἀχαιῶν. ἀλλὰ σημαίνειν σε χρῆν
τί χρὴ τὸν εὖ πράσσοντα μὴ πράσσουσιν εὖ
φίλοις ἐπαρκεῖν· ὡς ἕτοιμός εἰμ' ἐγώ.			985

ΕΚ. πρῶτον μὲν εἰπὲ παῖδ' ὃν ἐξ ἐμῆς χερὸς
Πολύδωρον ἔκ τε πατρὸς ἐν δόμοις ἔχεις,
εἰ ζῇ· τὰ δ' ἄλλα δεύτερόν σ' ἐρήσομαι.

ΠΟΛΥΜ. μάλιστα· τοὐκείνου μὲν εὐτυχεῖς μέρος.

ΕΚ. ὦ φίλταθ', ὡς εὖ κἀξίως σέθεν λέγεις.		990

ΠΟΛΥΜ. τί δῆτα βούλει δεύτερον μαθεῖν ἐμοῦ;

ΕΚ. εἰ τῆς τεκούσης τῆσδε μέμνηταί τί μου.

ΠΟΛΥΜ. καὶ δεῦρό γ' ὡς σὲ κρύφιος ἐζήτει μολεῖν.

ΕΚ. χρυσὸς δὲ σῶς, ὃν ἦλθεν ἐκ Τροίας ἔχων;

ΠΟΛΥΜ. σῶς, ἐν δόμοις γε τοῖς ἐμοῖς φρουρούμενος.

ΕΚ. σῶσόν νυν αὐτόν, μηδ' ἔρα τῶν πλησίον.		996

ΠΟΛΥΜ. ἥκιστ'· ὀναίμην τοῦ παρόντος, ὦ γύναι.

ΕΚ. οἶσθ' οὖν ἃ λέξαι σοί τε καὶ παισὶν θέλω;

ΠΟΛΥΜ. οὐκ οἶδα· τῷ σῷ τοῦτο σημανεῖς λόγῳ.

ΕΚ. ἔστ', ὦ φιληθεὶς ὡς σὺ νῦν ἐμοὶ φιλεῖ,—	1000

ΠΟΛΥΜ. τί χρῆμ', ὃ κἀμὲ καὶ τέκν' εἰδέναι χρεών;

ΕΚ. χρυσοῦ παλαιαὶ Πριαμιδῶν κατώρυχες.

ΠΟΛΥΜ. ταῦτ' ἔσθ' ἃ βούλει παιδὶ σημῆναι σέθεν;

ΕΚ. μάλιστα, διὰ σοῦ γ'· εἶ γὰρ εὐσεβὴς ἀνήρ.

ΠΟΛΥΜ. τί δῆτα τέκνων τῶνδε δεῖ παρουσίας;		1005

ΕΚ. ἄμεινον, ἢν σὺ κατθάνῃς, τούσδ' εἰδέναι.

ΠΟΛΥΜ. καλῶς ἔλεξας τῇδε καὶ σοφώτερον.

ΕΚ. οἶσθ' οὖν Ἀθάνας Ἰλίας ἵνα στέγαι;

ΠΟΛΥΜ. ἐνταῦθ᾽ ὁ χρυσός ἐστι; σημεῖον δὲ τί;

ΕΚ. μέλαινα πέτρα γῆς ὑπερτέλλουσ᾽ ἄνω.   1010

ΠΟΛΥΜ. ἔτ᾽ οὖν τι βούλει τῶν ἐκεῖ φράζειν ἐμοί;

ΕΚ. σῶσαί σε χρήμαθ᾽ οἷς συνεξῆλθον θέλω.

ΠΟΛΥΜ. ποῦ δῆτα, πέπλων ἐντὸς ἢ κρύψασ᾽ ἔχεις;

ΕΚ. σκύλων ἐν ὄχλῳ ταῖσδε σώζεται στέγαις.

ΠΟΛΥΜ. ποῦ δ᾽; αἵδ᾽ Ἀχαιῶν ναύλοχοι περιπτυχαί.

ΕΚ. ἴδιαι γυναικῶν αἰχμαλωτίδων στέγαι.   1016

ΠΟΛΥΜ. τἄνδον δὲ πιστὰ, κἀρσένων ἐρημία;

ΕΚ. οὐδεὶς Ἀχαιῶν ἔνδον, ἀλλ᾽ ἡμεῖς μόναι.
    ἀλλ᾽ ἕρπ᾽ ἐς οἴκους· καὶ γὰρ Ἀργεῖοι νεῶν
    λῦσαι ποθοῦσιν οἴκαδ᾽ ἐκ Τροίας πόδα·   1020
    ὡς πάντα πράξας, ὧν σε δεῖ, στείχῃς πάλιν
    ξὺν παισὶν οὗπερ τὸν ἐμὸν ᾤκισας γόνον.

ΧΟ. οὔπω δέδωκας, ἀλλ᾽ ἴσως δώσεις δίκην,
    ἀλίμενόν τις ὡς ἐς ἄντλον πεσὼν   1025
    λέχριος ἐκπεσεῖ φίλας καρδίας,
    ἀμέρσας βίον. τὸ γὰρ ὑπέγγυον
    δίκᾳ καὶ θεοῖσιν οὐ ξυμπίτνει, ὀλέθριον κακόν. 1030, 1
    ψεύσει σ᾽ ὁδοῦ τῆσδ᾽ ἐλπὶς, ἥ σ᾽ ἐπήγαγε
    θανάσιμον πρὸς Ἀΐδαν, ἰὼ τάλας·
    ἀπολέμῳ δὲ χειρὶ λείψεις βίον.

ΠΟΛΥΜ. ὤμοι, τυφλοῦμαι φέγγος ὀμμάτων τάλας. 1035

ΧΟ. ἠκούσατ᾽ ἀνδρὸς Θρῃκὸς οἰμωγὴν, φίλαι;

ΠΟΛΥΜ. ὤμοι μάλ᾽ αὖθις, τέκνα, δυστήνου σφαγῆς.

ΧΟ. φίλαι, πέπρακται καίν᾽ ἔσω δόμων κακά.

ΠΟΛΥΜ. ἀλλ᾽ οὔτι μὴ φύγητε λαιψηρῷ ποδί·
    βάλλων γὰρ οἴκων τῶνδ᾽ ἀναρρήξω μυχούς. 1040

ΧΟ. ἰδοὺ, βαρείας χειρὸς ὁρμᾶται βέλος.

βούλεσθ᾽ ἐπεσπέσωμεν; ὡς ἀκμὴ καλεῖ
Ἑκάβῃ παρεῖναι Τρωάσιν τε συμμάχους.

ΕΚ. ἄρασσε, φείδου μηδὲν, ἐκβάλλων πύλας·
οὐ γάρ ποτ᾽ ὄμμα λαμπρὸν ἐνθήσεις κόραις, 1045
οὐ παῖδας ὄψει ζῶντας, οὓς ἔκτειν᾽ ἐγώ.

ΧΟ. ἦ γὰρ καθεῖλες Θρῆκα καὶ κρατεῖς ξένου,
δέσποινα, καὶ δέδρακας οἷάπερ λέγεις;

ΕΚ. ὄψει νιν αὐτίκ᾽ ὄντα δωμάτων πάρος
τυφλὸν, τυφλῷ στείχοντα παραφόρῳ ποδὶ, 1050
παίδων τε δισσῶν σώμαθ᾽ οὓς ἔκτειν᾽ ἐγὼ
ξὺν ταῖς ἀρίσταις Τρῳάσιν· δίκην δέ μοι
δέδωκε· χωρεῖ δ᾽, ὡς ὁρᾷς, ὅδ᾽ ἐκ δόμων.
ἀλλ᾽ ἐκποδὼν ἄπειμι κἀποστήσομαι
θυμῷ ζέοντι Θρῃκὶ δυσμαχωτάτῳ. 1055

ΠΟΛΥΜ. ὤμοι μοι ἐγώ,
πᾶ βῶ, πᾶ στῶ, πᾶ κέλσω;
τετράποδος βάσιν θηρὸς ὀρεστέρου
τιθέμενος ἐπὶ χεῖρα κατ᾽ ἴχνος; ποίαν,
[ἢ] ταύταν ἢ τάνδ᾽, ἐξαλλάξω 1060
τὰς ἀνδροφόνους μάρψαι χρῄζων
Ἰλιάδας, αἵ με διώλεσαν;
τάλαιναι κόραι τάλαιναι Φρυγῶν,
ὦ κατάρατοι, ποῖ καί με φυγᾷ
πτώσσουσι μυχῶν; 1065
εἴθε μοι ὀμμάτων αἱματόεν βλέφαρον
ἀκέσαι᾽ ἀκέσαιο τυφλὸν, Ἅλιε,
φέγγος ἀπαλλάξας.
ἀᾶ.
σῖγα, κρυπτὰν βάσιν αἰσθάνομαι

τάνδε γυναικῶν. πᾷ πόδ᾽ ἐπᾴξας   1070
σαρκῶν ὀστέων τ᾽ ἐμπλησθῶ,
θοίναν ἀγρίων θηρῶν τιθέμενος
ἀρνύμενος λώβαν,
λύμας ἀντίποιν᾽ ἐμᾶς; ὦ τάλας.
ποῖ, πᾷ φέρομαι τέκν᾽ ἔρημα λιπὼν   1075
βάκχαις Ἅιδου διαμοιρᾶσαι,
σφακτὰν κυσί τε φοινίαν δαῖτ᾽ ἀνή-
μερόν τ᾽ οὐρείαν ἐκβολάν;
[πᾷ βῶ,] πᾷ στῶ, πᾷ κάμψω,
ναῦς ὅπως ποντίοις πείσμασι λινόκροκον   1080, 1
φᾶρος στέλλων, ἐπὶ τάνδε συθεὶς
τέκνων ἐμῶν φύλαξ
ὀλέθριον κοίταν.

ΧΟ. ὦ τλῆμον, ὥς σοι δύσφορ᾽ εἴργασται κακά·   1085
δράσαντι δ᾽ αἰσχρὰ δεινὰ τἀπιτίμια
[δαίμων ἔδωκεν, ὅστις ἐστί σοι βαρύς.]

ΠΟΛΥΜ. αἰαῖ, ἰὼ Θρῄκης
λογχοφόρον, ἔνοπλον,
εὔιππον *τ᾽ Ἄρει τε* κάτοχον γένος.   1090
ἰὼ ᾽Αχαιοί, ἰὼ ᾽Ατρεῖδαι,
βοὰν ἀυτῶ, βοάν·
ἴτ᾽ ἴτε, μόλετε πρὸς θεῶν.
κλύει τις, ἢ οὐδεὶς ἀρκέσει; τί μέλλετε;
γυναῖκες ὤλεσάν με,   1095
γυναῖκες αἰχμαλώτιδες.
δεινὰ δεινὰ πεπόνθαμεν·
ὤμοι ἐμᾶς λώβας.
ποῖ τράπωμαι, ποῖ πορευθῶ;

ἀμπτάμενος οὐράνιον   1100
ὑψιπετὲς
ἐς μέλαθρον, Ὠρίων
ἢ Σείριος ἔνθα πυρὸς φλογέας ἀφίη-
σιν ὄσσων αὐγὰς, ἢ τὸν ἐς Ἅιδα
μελάγχρωτα πορ-   1105
θμὸν ᾄξω τάλας;

ΧΟ. ξυγγνῶσθ', ὅταν τις κρείσσον' ἢ φέρειν κακὰ
πάθῃ, ταλαίνης ἐξαπαλλάξαι ζόης.

ΑΓ. κραυγῆς ἀκούσας ἦλθον· οὐ γὰρ ἥσυχος
πέτρας ὀρείας παῖς λέλακ' ἀνὰ στρατὸν   1110
Ἠχὼ, διδοῦσα θόρυβον. εἰ δὲ μὴ Φρυγῶν
πύργους πεσόντας ᾖσμεν Ἑλλήνων δορὶ,
φόβον παρέσχεν οὐ μέσως ὅδε κτύπος.

ΠΟΛΥΜ. ὦ φίλτατ', ἠσθόμην γὰρ, Ἀγάμεμνον, σέθεν
φωνῆς ἀκούσας, εἰσορᾷς ἃ πάσχομεν;   1115

ΑΓ. ἔα·
Πολυμῆστορ ὦ δύστηνε, τίς σ' ἀπώλεσε;
τίς ὄμμ' ἔθηκε τυφλὸν, αἱμάξας κόρας,
παῖδάς τε τούσδ' ἔκτεινεν; ἢ μέγαν χόλον
σοὶ καὶ τέκνοισιν εἶχεν, ὅστις ἦν ἄρα.

ΠΟΛΥΜ. Ἑκάβη με σὺν γυναιξὶν αἰχμαλωτίσιν   1120
ἀπώλεσ', οὐκ ἀπώλεσ', ἀλλὰ μειζόνως.

ΑΓ. τί φῄς; σὺ τοὔργον εἴργασαι τόδ', ὡς λέγει;
σὺ τόλμαν, Ἑκάβη, τήνδ' ἔτλης ἀμήχανον;

ΠΟΛΥΜ. ὤμοι, τί λέξεις; ἦ γὰρ ἐγγύς ἐστί που;
σήμηνον, εἰπὲ ποῦ 'σθ', ἵν' ἁρπάσας χεροῖν   1125
διασπάσωμαι καὶ καθαιμάξω χρόα.

ΑΓ. οὗτος, τί πάσχεις;

4—2

ΠΟΛΥΜ.   πρὸς θεῶν σε λίσσομαι,
μέθες μ' ἐφεῖναι τῆδε μαργῶσαν χέρα.

ΑΓ. ἴσχ'· ἐκβαλὼν δὲ καρδίας τὸ βάρβαρον,
λέγ', ὡς ἀκούσας σοῦ τε τῆσδέ τ' ἐν μέρει   1130
κρίνω δικαίως, ἀνθ' ὅτου πάσχεις τάδε.

ΠΟΛΥΜ. λέγοιμ' ἄν. ἦν τις Πριαμιδῶν νεώτατος
Πολύδωρος, Ἑκάβης παῖς, ὃν ἐκ Τροίας ἐμοὶ
πατὴρ δίδωσι Πρίαμος ἐν δόμοις τρέφειν,
ὕποπτος ὢν δὴ Τρωικῆς ἁλώσεως.   1135
τοῦτον κατέκτειν'· ἀνθ' ὅτου δ' ἔκτεινά νιν,
ἄκουσον, ὡς εὖ καὶ σοφῇ προμηθίᾳ.
ἔδεισα μὴ σοὶ πολέμιος λειφθεὶς ὁ παῖς
Τροίαν ἀθροίσῃ καὶ ξυνοικίσῃ πάλιν,
γνόντες δ' Ἀχαιοὶ ζῶντα Πριαμιδῶν τινα   1140
Φρυγῶν ἐς αἶαν αὖθις ἄρειαν στόλον,
κἄπειτα Θρῄκης πεδία τρίβοιεν τάδε
λεηλατοῦντες, γείτοσιν δ' εἴη κακὸν
Τρώων, ἐν ᾧπερ νῦν, ἄναξ, ἐκάμνομεν.
Ἑκάβη δὲ παιδὸς γνοῦσα θανάσιμον μόρον,   1145
λόγῳ με τοιῷδ' ἤγαγ', ὡς κεκρυμμένας
θήκας φράσουσα Πριαμιδῶν ἐν Ἰλίῳ
χρυσοῦ· μόνον δὲ σὺν τέκνοισί μ' εἰσάγει
δόμους, ἵν' ἄλλος μή τις εἰδείη τάδε.
ἵζω δὲ κλίνης ἐν μέσῳ κάμψας γόνυ·   1150
πολλαὶ δὲ χειρὸς αἱ μὲν ἐξ ἀριστερᾶς,
αἱ δ' ἔνθεν, ὡς δὴ παρὰ φίλῳ, Τρώων κόραι
θάκους ἔχουσαι κερκίδ' Ἠδωνῆς χερὸς,
ᾔνουν, ὑπ' αὐγὰς τούσδε λεύσσουσαι πέπλους·
ἄλλαι δὲ κάμακα Θρηκίαν θεώμεναι   1155

γυμνόν μ' ἔθηκαν διπτύχου στολίσματος.
ὅσαι δὲ τοκάδες ἦσαν, ἐκπαγλούμεναι
τέκν' ἐν χεροῖν ἔπαλλον, ὡς πρόσω πατρὸς
*γένοιτο, διαδοχαῖς ἀμείβουσαι χερῶν.
κᾆτ' ἐκ γαληνῶν πῶς δοκεῖς προσφθεγμάτων 1160
εὐθὺς λαβοῦσαι φάσγαν' ἐκ πέπλων ποθὲν
κεντοῦσι παῖδας, αἱ δὲ πολεμίων δίκην
ξυναρπάσασαι τὰς ἐμὰς εἶχον χέρας
καὶ κῶλα· παισὶ δ' ἀρκέσαι χρῄζων ἐμοῖς,
εἰ μὲν πρόσωπον ἐξανισταίην ἐμὸν,   1165
κόμης κατεῖχον, εἰ δὲ κινοίην χέρας,
πλήθει γυναικῶν οὐδὲν ἤνυον τάλας.
τὸ λοίσθιον δὲ, πῆμα πήματος πλέον,
ἐξειργάσαντο δείν'· ἐμῶν γὰρ ὀμμάτων,
πόρπας λαβοῦσαι, τὰς ταλαιπώρους κόρας   1170
κεντοῦσιν, αἱμάσσουσιν· εἶτ' ἀνὰ στέγας
φυγάδες ἔβησαν· ἐκ δὲ πηδήσας ἐγὼ
θὴρ ὣς διώκω τὰς μιαιφόνους κύνας,
ἅπαντ' ἐρευνῶν τοῖχον, ὡς κυνηγέτης,
βάλλων, ἀράσσων. τοιάδε σπεύδων χάριν   1175
πέπονθα τὴν σὴν, πολέμιόν τε σὸν κτανὼν,
Ἀγάμεμνον. ὡς δὲ μὴ μακροὺς τείνω λόγους,
εἴ τις γυναῖκας τῶν πρὶν εἴρηκεν κακῶς,
ἢ νῦν λέγων τίς ἐστιν, ἢ μέλλει λέγειν,
ἅπαντα ταῦτα συντεμὼν ἐγὼ φράσω·   1180
γένος γὰρ οὔτε πόντος οὔτε γῆ τρέφει
τοιόνδ'· ὁ δ' ἀεὶ ξυντυχὼν ἐπίσταται.
ΧΟ. μηδὲν θρασύνου, μηδὲ τοῖς σαυτοῦ κακοῖς
τὸ θῆλυ συνθεὶς ὧδε πᾶν μέμψῃ γένος·

[πολλαὶ γὰρ ἡμῶν αἱ μὲν εἴσ' ἐπίφθονοι,   1185
αἱ δ' εἰς ἀριθμὸν τῶν κακῶν πεφύκαμεν.]

ΕΚ. Ἀγάμεμνον, ἀνθρώποισιν οὐκ ἐχρῆν ποτε
τῶν πραγμάτων τὴν γλῶσσαν ἰσχύειν πλέον.
ἀλλ' εἴτε χρήστ' ἔδρασε, χρήστ' ἔδει λέγειν,
εἴτ' αὖ πονηρά, τοὺς λόγους εἶναι σαθρούς,   1190
καὶ μὴ δύνασθαι τἄδικ' εὖ λέγειν ποτέ.
σοφοὶ μὲν οὖν εἴσ' οἱ τάδ' ἠκριβωκότες,
ἀλλ' οὐ δύναιντ' ἂν διὰ τέλους εἶναι σοφοί,
κακῶς δ' ἀπώλοντ'· οὔτις ἐξήλυξέ πω.
καί μοι τὸ μὲν σὸν ὧδε φροιμίοις ἔχει·   1195
πρὸς τόνδε δ' εἶμι, καὶ λόγοις ἀμείψομαι,
ὃς φῂς Ἀχαιῶν πόνον ἀπαλλάσσων διπλοῦν
Ἀγαμέμνονός θ' ἕκατι παῖδ' ἐμὸν κτανεῖν.
ἀλλ', ὦ κάκιστε, πρῶτον οὔποτ' ἂν φίλον
τὸ βάρβαρον γένοιτ' ἂν Ἕλλησιν γένος,   1200
οὐδ' ἂν δύναιτο. τίνα δὲ καὶ σπεύδων χάριν
πρόθυμος ἦσθα; πότερα κηδεύσων τινά,
ἢ ξυγγενὴς ὤν, ἢ τίν' αἰτίαν ἔχων;
ἢ σῆς ἔμελλον γῆς τεμεῖν βλαστήματα
πλεύσαντες αὖθις; τίνα δοκεῖς πείσειν τάδε;   1205
ὁ χρυσός, εἰ βούλοιο τἀληθῆ λέγειν,
ἔκτεινε τὸν ἐμὸν παῖδα καὶ κέρδη τὰ σά.
ἐπεὶ δίδαξον τοῦτο· πῶς, ὅτ' ηὐτύχει
Τροία, πέριξ δὲ πύργος εἶχ' ἔτι πτόλιν,
ἔζη τε Πρίαμος, Ἕκτορός τ' ἤνθει δόρυ,   1210
τί δ' οὐ τότ', εἴπερ τῷδ' ἐβουλήθης χάριν
θέσθαι, τρέφων τὸν παῖδα κἀν δόμοις ἔχων
ἔκτεινας, ἢ ζῶντ' ἦλθες Ἀργείοις ἄγων;

ἀλλ' ἡνίχ' ἡμεῖς οὐκέτ' ἐσμὲν ἐν φάει,
καπνῷ δ' ἐσήμην' ἄστυ πολεμίων ὕπο,　　　1215
ξένον κατέκτας σὴν μολόντ' ἐφ' ἑστίαν.
πρὸς τοῖσδέ νυν ἄκουσον ὡς φανῇς κακός.
χρῆν σ', εἴπερ ἦσθα τοῖς Ἀχαιοῖσιν φίλος,
τὸν χρυσὸν ὃν φῇς οὐ σὸν, ἀλλὰ τοῦδ' ἔχειν,
δοῦναι φέροντα πενομένοις τε καὶ χρόνον　　　1220
πολὺν πατρῴας γῆς ἀπεξενωμένοις·
σὺ δ' οὐδὲ νῦν πω σῆς ἀπαλλάξαι χερὸς
τολμᾷς, ἔχων δὲ καρτερεῖς ἔτ' ἐν δόμοις.
καὶ μὴν τρέφων μὲν ὥς σε παῖδ' ἐχρῆν τρέφειν
σώσας τε τὸν ἐμὸν εἶχες ἂν καλὸν κλέος·　　　1225
ἐν τοῖς κακοῖς γὰρ ἀγαθοὶ σαφέστατοι
φίλοι· τὰ χρηστὰ δ' αὔθ' ἕκαστ' ἔχει φίλους.
εἰ δ' ἐσπάνιζες χρημάτων, ὁ δ' ηὐτύχει,
θησαυρὸς ἄν σοι παῖς ὑπῆρχ' οὑμὸς μέγας·
νῦν δ' οὔτ' ἐκεῖνον ἄνδρ' ἔχεις σαυτῷ φίλον, 1230
χρυσοῦ τ' ὄνησις οἴχεται παῖδές τέ σοι,
αὐτός τε πράσσεις ὧδε. σοὶ δ' ἐγὼ λέγω,
Ἀγάμεμνον, εἰ τῷδ' ἀρκέσεις, κακὸς φανεῖ·
οὔτ' εὐσεβῇ γὰρ οὔτε πιστὸν οἷς ἐχρῆν,
οὐχ ὅσιον, οὐ δίκαιον εὖ δράσεις ξένον·　　　1235
αὐτὸν δὲ χαίρειν τοῖς κακοῖς σε φήσομεν
τοιοῦτον ὄντα· δεσπότας δ' οὐ λοιδορῶ.

ΧΟ. φεῦ φεῦ· βροτοῖσιν ὡς τὰ χρηστὰ πράγματα
χρηστῶν ἀφορμὰς ἐνδίδωσ' ἀεὶ λόγων.

ΑΓ. ἀχθεινὰ μέν μοι τἀλλότρια κρίνειν κακά·　　　1240
ὅμως δ' ἀνάγκη· καὶ γὰρ αἰσχύνην φέρει
πρᾶγμ' ἐς χέρας λαβόντ' ἀπώσασθαι τόδε.

ἐμοὶ δ', ἵν' εἰδῇς, οὔτ' ἐμὴν δοκεῖς χάριν
οὔτ' οὖν Ἀχαιῶν ἄνδρ' ἀποκτεῖναι ξένον,
ἀλλ' ὡς ἔχῃς τὸν χρυσὸν ἐν δόμοισι σοῖς.　1245
λέγεις δὲ σαυτῷ πρόσφορ', ἐν κακοῖσιν ὤν.
τάχ' οὖν παρ' ὑμῖν ῥᾴδιον ξενοκτονεῖν·
ἡμῖν δέ γ' αἰσχρὸν τοῖσιν Ἕλλησιν τόδε.
πῶς οὖν σε κρίνας μὴ ἀδικεῖν φύγω ψόγον;
οὐκ ἂν δυναίμην. ἀλλ' ἐπεὶ τὰ μὴ καλὰ　1250
πράσσειν ἐτόλμας, τλῆθι καὶ τὰ μὴ φίλα.

ΠΟΛΥΜ. οἴμοι, γυναικὸς, ὡς ἔοιχ', ἡσσώμενος
δούλης, ὑφέξω τοῖς κακίοσιν δίκην.

ΕΚ. οὔκουν δικαίως, εἴπερ εἰργάσω κακά;　1254
ΠΟΛΥΜ. οἴμοι τέκνων τῶνδ' ὀμμάτων τ' ἐμῶν, τάλας.
ΕΚ. ἀλγεῖς· τί δ' ἡμᾶς; παιδὸς οὐκ ἀλγεῖν δοκεῖς;
ΠΟΛΥΜ. χαίρεις ὑβρίζουσ' εἰς ἔμ', ὦ πανοῦργε σύ.
ΕΚ. οὐ γάρ με χαίρειν χρή σε τιμωρουμένην;
ΠΟΛΥΜ. ἀλλ' οὐ τάχ', ἡνίκ' ἄν σε ποντία νοτὶς
ΕΚ. μῶν ναυστολήσῃ γῆς ὅρους Ἑλληνίδος;　1260
ΠΟΛΥΜ. κρύψῃ μὲν οὖν πεσοῦσαν ἐκ καρχησίων.
ΕΚ. πρὸς τοῦ βιαίων τυγχάνουσαν ἁλμάτων;
ΠΟΛΥΜ. αὐτὴ πρὸς ἱστὸν ναὸς ἀμβήσει ποδί.
ΕΚ. ὑποπτέροις νώτοισιν, ἢ ποίῳ τρόπῳ;
ΠΟΛΥΜ. κύων γενήσει πύρσ' ἔχουσα δέργματα.　1265
ΕΚ. πῶς δ' οἶσθα μορφῆς τῆς ἐμῆς μετάστασιν;
ΠΟΛΥΜ. ὁ Θρῃξὶ μάντις εἶπε Διόνυσος τάδε.
ΕΚ. σοὶ δ' οὐκ ἔχρησεν οὐδὲν ὧν ἔχεις κακῶν;
ΠΟΛΥΜ. οὐ γάρ ποτ' ἂν σύ μ' εἷλες ὧδε σὺν δόλῳ.
ΕΚ. θανοῦσα δ' ἢ ζῶσ' ἐνθάδ' ἐκπλήσω βίον;　1270
ΠΟΛΥΜ. θανοῦσα· τύμβῳ δ' ὄνομα σῷ κεκλήσεται

ΕΚ. μορφῆς ἐπῳδὸν, ἢ τί, τῆς ἐμῆς ἐρεῖς;

ΠΟΛΥΜ. κυνὸς ταλαίνης σῆμα, ναυτίλοις τέκμαρ.

ΕΚ. οὐδὲν μέλει μοι, σοῦ γέ μοι δόντος δίκην.

ΠΟΛΥΜ. καὶ σὴν δ᾽ ἀνάγκη παῖδα Κασάνδραν θανεῖν.

ΕΚ. ἀπέπτυσ᾽· αὐτῷ ταῦτά σοι δίδωμ᾽ ἔχειν.   1276

ΠΟΛΥΜ. κτενεῖ νιν ἡ τοῦδ᾽ ἄλοχος, οἰκουρὸς πικρά.

ΕΚ. μήπω μανείη Τυνδαρὶς τοσόνδε παῖς.

ΠΟΛΥΜ. καὐτόν σε τοῦτον, πέλεκυν ἐξάρασ᾽ ἄνω.

ΑΓ. οὗτος σύ, μαίνει, καὶ κακῶν ἐρᾷς τυχεῖν;   1280

ΠΟΛΥΜ. κτεῖν᾽, ὡς ἐν Ἄργει φόνια σ᾽ ἀμμένει.

ΑΓ. οὐχ ἕλξετ᾽ αὐτόν, δμῶες, ἐκποδὼν βίᾳ;

ΠΟΛΥΜ. ἀλγεῖς ἀκούων;   ΑΓ. οὐκ ἐφέξετε στόμα;

ΠΟΛΥΜ. ἐγκλῇετ᾽· εἴρηται γάρ.

ΑΓ.   οὐχ ὅσον τάχος

νήσων ἐρήμων αὐτὸν ἐκβαλεῖτέ που,   1285
ἐπείπερ οὕτω καὶ λίαν θρασυστομεῖ;
Ἑκάβη, σὺ δ᾽, ὦ τάλαινα, διπτύχους νεκροὺς
στείχουσα θάπτε· δεσποτῶν δ᾽ ὑμᾶς χρεὼν
σκηναῖς πελάζειν, Τρῳάδες· καὶ γὰρ πνοὰς
πρὸς οἶκον ἤδη τάσδε πομπίμους ὁρῶ.   1290
εὖ δ᾽ ἐς πάτραν πλεύσαιμεν, εὖ δὲ τὰν δόμοις
ἔχοντ᾽ ἴδοιμεν, τῶνδ᾽ ἀφειμένοι πόνων.

ΧΟ. ἴτε πρὸς λιμένας σκηνάς τε, φίλαι,
τῶν δεσποσύνων πειρασόμεναι
μόχθων· στερρὰ γὰρ ἀνάγκη.   1295

NOTES.

[1—58. *Prologue*, contains an outline of the plot. The ghost of Polydorus appears, explains his own miserable murder by his host Polymestor, prince of Thracian Chersonese, the demand of the shade of Achilles for the sacrifice of his sister Polyxena and his own appearance in a dream to his unhappy mother, Hecuba.]

'Εκάβη—appears in Lat. as *Hecuba*: so κυνὸς corresponds to *canis*, κύλιξ to *calix*, μυδάω to *madeo*.

1. ἥκω—prob. a dialectical variety of ἵκω, in most of its tenses means 'I am here', equiv. to ἐλήλυθα.

σκότου—The masc. form is now always read in Trag. and Comedy; occasionally however a form τὸ σκότος is found even in Attic, e.g. in Xen. and Demosth.

2. "Αιδης—(ἀ priv. and √ιδ see), the god of the unseen world, called by euphemism, Ploutôn.

ᾤκισται—'has his home', lit. 'was and is established'. χωρὶς θεῶν—cf. *Il.* 20. 65 οἰκία σμερδαλέ', εὐρώεντα, τά τε στυγέουσι θεοί περ.

3. παῖς γεγ. τῆς Κ.—(sc. θυγατρός) 'by birth a son of H. daughter of Kisseus'. H. was according to Hom. (*Il.* 16. 718) daughter of Dymas, a Phrygian, the only daughter of Kisseus known to him being Theano, wife of Antenor (*Il.* 6. 299). Κισσίας, a local name, was therefore suggested by some ancient critics to reconcile the two accounts. Vergil follows Eur. and Lat. poets generally, except Ovid who calls her *Dymantis*. Polydorus himself is in Hom. son of Priam and Laothoë and is slain by Achilles.

γεγὼς—formed from obsolete poetical γάω collat. form of γίγνομαι: so βέβαα.

4. **Φρυγῶν πόλιν**—The Phrygians were a branch of the great Thracian family, which may account for the familiarity of Priam and Polymestor. In eιrly times they occupied the N.W. coast of Asia and were not, as we see them now in maps, localised inland.

5. **πεσεῖν**—not fut. which would be πεσεῖσθαι, but aor., the peculiar force of which is to regard the fall as momentary not protracted. Perhaps we may consider the phrase as substantival = τοῦ πεσεῖν, 214 n. **δορί**—δόρει would here be inadmissible, which does away with the theory that it is the only allowable form in iambics. **Ἑλληνικῷ**—strictly an anachronism, for Hom. never calls the united Greeks ,by the name ῎Ελληνες, nor indeed any of them except Achilles' followers from Phthiotis, who were the original Hellenes.

6. **ὑπεξέπεμψε**—'sent me secretly (ὑπό = sub = furtim of Verg. *Aen.* 3. 50) away from'. In *Androm.* 47 a stronger phrase, ὑπεκπέμπω λάθρα, is used. Τρω. χθονός is governed by ἐκ in the verb.

7. **ξένου**—'a guest-friend'.

8. **τήνδε Χερσ. πλάκα**—'This steppe of Chersonese'. The Thracian Chers. is a narrow strip of land running along the N. of the Hellespont. τήνδε of Hermann is more graphic than the usual τήν. Χερσ. is the form introduced by Brunck and subsequent editors because the old form χερρ. is nowhere found in tragedy. πλάκα conn. with *lanx.* Cf. πλύνω, *lavo.* The general idea is that of breadth and flatness, akin to πλατύς, *planus,* flat, πλακοῦς, *placenta.*

9. **φίλιππον λαόν**—'a warrior people'. *Il.* 13. 4, νόσφιν ἐφ᾽ ἱπποπόλων Θρῃκῶν καθορώμενος αἶαν where the schol. explains it as equal to 'warrior'. Thrace was celebrated for horses and cavalry in days of Eur. See Thuc. 2. 98. **δορί**—not 'sceptre', though that was the heroic badge of royalty, but ' spear', to indicate the warlike character of the Thracians.

10. **ἐκπέμπει**—hist. present, i.e. stands for aorist: hence εἴη in 12, contrary to the strictly grammatical sequence of tenses.

11. **Ἰλίου**—so called from its founder Ilus; Troy after his father Tros.

12. **μή**—is better taken with εἴη than with σπάνις (= 'sufficiency'), though the neg. *after* the verb is awkward. The

same question occurs *Or.* 942, ὡς τῆς γε τόλμης οὐ σπάνις γενήσεται.

13. We find in *Il.* 20. 408 that Polydorus is youngest son and forbidden to fight; but contrary to orders he joined in the battle and was slain by Achilles. τὸν δ᾽ οὔτι πατὴρ εἴασκε μάχεσθαι | οὔνεκά οἱ μετὰ πᾶσι νεώτατος ἔσκε γόνοιο | καί οἱ φίλτατος ἔσκε.

ὅ = δι᾽ ὅ—'wherefore'. Pors. says 'which fact' (τὸ εἶναι νεώτατον), but ὑπεξέπεμψε would be almost a ridiculous word in this connection.

14. ὅπλα—defensive, as ἔγχος is offensive, armour. Cf. use of *arma* in Lat.

15. οἷός τε—'able'. The τε has no very obvious force; it may be classed under the head of τε epexegetic or explanatory.

16. ὁρίσματα—'the flanking walls', by which the circuit of a city is defined, as Paley explains. It would naturally mean the 'boundaries' or 'landmarks', which an enemy would of course remove: Scaliger suggested ἐρείσματα to which ἔκειτο would more naturally apply. The word occurs in *Hipp.* 1459, ὦ κλεῖν᾽ Ἀθηνῶν Παλλάδος θ᾽ ὁρίσματα.

ἔκειτο—little more than ἦν.

18. ηὐτύχει—form preferred to εὐτύχει by Porson, though Herodian the grammarian (2nd cent. A.D.) tells us that εὐ does not augment, αὐ does to ηὐ.

20. 'I grew up like some sapling, to my sorrow'. This recalls *Il.* 18. 56, ὁ δ᾽ ἀνέδραμεν ἔρνεϊ ἶσος. ηὐξόμην—there are alternative forms αὔξω and αὐξάνω, Eur. uses αὔξω in all but three places. τάλας √τλα. Cf. *latum*, ἔτλην. Most words from this root have a twofold signification, as τλήμων, τλημοσύνη, τλησικάρδιος, τλητός, viz. (1) enduring, persistent, sometimes in bad sense, (2) wretched.

21, 22. ἀπόλλυται...κατεσκάφη—the change of tense (as in 266) may sometimes be accounted for by the wish to make incidents expressed by the present more vivid. But the tragedians often varied the tense for variety's sake. Here the pres. may signify the enduring character of the result.

23. αὐτός—sc. πατήρ (Priam) implied in πατρῴα: so Soph. *Trach.* 259, ἔρχεται πόλιν | τὴν Εὐρυτείαν, τόνδε γὰρ κ.τ.λ. Cic.

(quoting Pacuvius) *de Or.* 2. 46, *neque paternum adspectum es veritus*, QUEM &c. θεοδμήτῳ, 'consecrated', built for the gods, not by them. One of the scholia θειῶς καὶ θαυμαστῶς κτισθέντι is tame. The altar referred to in βωμῷ is that of Zεὺς Ἑρκεῖος, as we see from *Tro.* 483, κατασφάγεντ' ἐφ' ἑρκείῳ πυρᾷ and Vergil *Aen.* 2. 550 speaks of Priam, *altaria ad ipsa trementem*.

24. παιδὸs—Neoptolemus or Pyrrhus.

25. κτείνει...κτανὼν—such repetition is frequent, especially in Eur. Cf. *H. Fur.* 33, κτείνει Κρέοντα καὶ κτανὼν ἄρχει χθονός.

27. μεθῆχ', ἵν'...ἔχῃ—'flung me into the billowy sea in order himself to have the gold in his house'. The subj. anomalously follows an hist. tense to shew that the result still abides. [ἔχῃ, however, may fairly depend on κτείνει in 25.] According to Verg., Polymestor buried the corpse, but Ov. *Met.* 13. 438 follows Eur. *exanimum e scopulo subiectas misit in undas.*

28. ἐπ' ἀκτῆς. So the best MS.—There is a variant ἀκταῖς, perhaps from 36. √ΑG break, like ῥηγμίν from √ΡΑΓ, 'place where waves break'. ἄλλοτ'—it is usual though not necessary to understand another ἄλλοτε in preceding clause, as in Soph. *El.* 752, φορούμενος πρὸς οὖδος, ἄλλοτ' οὐρανῷ | σκέλη προφαίνων, and Verg. *Aen.* 5. 830, *sinistros* | nunc *dextros solvere sinus.*

29. 'Carried about by many revolutions in the waves, (now up now down)'. *Not* 'ebb and flow of tide', for there was no tide properly speaking in Hellespont, which in view of the ancients was a river, [hence its epithet πλατύς]. δίαυλοι—strictly the limbs of a race-course; the chariots raced up one, turned at the post, κάμπτήρ, and then passed down the other limb to the finish. Aesch. *Agam.* 344 uses the same figure—κάμψαι διαύλου θάτερον κῶλον πάλιν, i.e. the Greeks have done only half their journey; the other half, the return, remains to be done. φορούμενος—frequentative form, *huc illuc iactatus.*

30. ἄκλαυστος, ἄταφος—an echo of *Il.* 22. 386, ἄκλαυστος ἄθαπτος, the words occur Soph. *Antig.* 29, where, as here, their order is disputed. Cf. *Aen.* 11. 372, *inhumata infletaque turba.* ὑπὲρ—'because of', 'for the sake of', not = ὑπεράνω, 'above', for if, as is the case, the ghost is visible (see 52), this interpretation would involve his being in two places at once, unless indeed we consider his statement in 31 sqq. a merely general

one. There is throughout some confusion between P.'s spirit and his corpse.

31. ἀίσσω—like *ruo*, is used of any active movement up or down and is both trans. and intrans. In *Ody.* 10. 495, τοὶ δὲ σκιαὶ ἀίσσουσιν, it is appropriately used of the *flitting of* ghosts. The form in Attic poets is usually a dissyllable which gave rise to the variant ἀνάσσω in this place.

32. 'Now for three days' space have I hovered aloft, all such time as my illstarred mother', &c. τριταῖον—the term -αιος='of so many days' standing', e.g. τεταρταῖος, S. John xi. 39, 'a corpse of four days'. But cf. Hdt. 4. 113, τῇ δευτεραίᾳ, 'on the 2nd day', and in this passage τριταῖον is equivalent to τρίτον, as in *Hipp.* 277, πῶς δ' οὐ, τριταίαν γ' οὖσ' ἄσιτος ἡμέραν.

34. πάρα = πάρεστιν—i.e. the prep. is intensified in meaning and then suffers *anastrophe*.

35. ναῦς ἔχοντες = κατέχοντες—'with their ships brought to, sit idle'. πάντες Ἀχ. = Hom. παναχαιοὶ Ἀχ. strictly applies to the main tribe of Greeks at Troy whose head-quarters were in Thessaly, but whose offshoots had spread to Peloponnese, Ithaca and Crete.

39. 'Homeward guiding their sea-dipt oars'. εὐθύνοντας, plural words agree with a sing. collective, especially when used of living beings, and then take their right gender. Cf. Aesch. *Agam.* 575, Τροίαν ἑλόντες...στόλος. Eur. *Rhes.* 46, στρατὸς... ἐφιέμενοι.

πλάτην—the 'blade', then the whole oar. Grimm's law tells us that πλάτη is connected with Engl. *flat:* while *blade* is etym. connected with φύλλον, *folium*.

41. τύμβῳ—a locative, like οἴκοι, κύκλῳ, &c. [Or, *a dat. commodi*, 'an acceptable sacrifice and special honour for his tomb'.]

43. ἡ πεπρωμένη—sc. μοῖρα or τύχη.

45. δυοῖν...δύο—these juxtapositions, which are notable in tragedians in the case of numbers (see 896), are due partly to the love of distinctness and clearness, but still more to rhetorical effect. Such are μόνος μόνοις, *mortali immortalitatem non arbitror contemnendam*, 'faith unfaithful kept him falsely true' (Tennyson).

49. ἐξητησάμην—'I asked for myself and won'. Cf. Lat. *exoro.* A double accus. (for τυμβ. κυρῆσαι is virtually a substantive) as in Lat. is used with verbs of asking.

51. τοὐμὸν μὲν οὖν, κ.τ.λ.—'For my part, then, all that I wished to get will result'. τυχεῖν here has an accus.; so λαγχάνω usually and κυρῶ in 697 [or τοὐμὸν is subject of ἔσται].

53. περᾷ...πόδα—cf. *Alk.* 1153, νόστιμον δ' ἔλθοις πόδα. Verbs denoting motion of the body may be followed by a dat. or acc. of the part of the body in motion, e.g. βαίνειν πόδα, χαίνειν στόμα. In πόδα ἐπάσσειν, 1070, the prep. accounts for the transitive force. ὑπὸ σκηνῆς—'from under the tent'= ὑπέκ. There is no occasion to alter this reading: yet πρὸ, ἀπὸ have been suggested, and Porson adopts Musgrave's ὑπὲρ σκήνην, 'past or beyond the tent'. The constr. with gen. is justified by Hom. ὑπὸ ζύγου, Hes. ὑπὸ χθονός, &c.

54. Ἀγαμ.—H. in 'Troades' falls to lot of Odysseus: here of Agam.

55. ἥτις=*quippe quae.* 'Since in exchange for a royal home, thou hast seen a day of slavery'. ἐκ. So in *Tro.* 494, κἄν πέδῳ κοίτας ἔχειν | ῥυσοῖσι νώτοις βασιλικῶν ἐκ δεμνίων.

56. πράσσεις κακῶς—'farest ill' must be carefully distinguished from ποιεῖς κακῶς, 'behavest ill'.

57. ἀντισηκώσας—'some god is ruining thee, and has given thee compensation for thy former blessedness'. ἀντι-implies *counter* balancing, and governs the gen. which follows. The word ἀντισηκ. is intrans. in Aesch. *Pers.* 437, ὡς τοῖσδε καὶ δὶς ἀντισηκῶσαι ῥοπῇ, but if a trans. signf. seems necessary, φθορὰν may be supplied from φθείρει. [The idea of compensation is thoroughly Greek, and in its theological aspect is known as the doctrine of Nemesis.]

[59—99. *An interlude.* Enter Hecuba, supported by Trojan ladies; she describes herself as troubled with presentiment of disaster, with nightly visions of a fawn torn by a wolf and dragged from her knees. She longs for Helenus or Kasandra to interpret the dream. Achilles too has appeared above his tomb and demanded the gift of a Trojan maid; may the gods avert the omen from her daughter!]

[As to *metre*, see appendix. The *dialect* of lyric passages is Doric, but the Doric forms are not very consistently used by the different tragic writers. Its chief characteristics are the frequent use of a broad and rough ā for η and ω, and for -ου the gen. of 1st declension. Two letters are used where other Greeks employed a double consonant as σδ for ζ, e.g. μελίσδεται. The most eminent writers in old Doric were *Tyrtaeus* (the lame schoolmaster who encouraged the Spartans during the Messenian war), *Alkman* (about 630 B.C. chief Spartan lyric poet), *Theognis* (elegiac and gnomic poet born about 570), *Epicharmus* (comic poet of Kos and Sicily b. 540)].

59. δόμων—tents of Achæan camp.

60. ὀρθοῦσαι—'supporting'.

τὴν—the reading of all MSS., more vigorous, lifelike, and better Gk. than νῦν which Pors. reads, and which perhaps crept in as an amplification.

64. μου γεραιᾶς, κ.τ.λ.—'taking me by my aged arm'. This gen. comes under class *partitive*, and its use is analogous to that with ἔχομαι (398) and other verbs of seizing, grasping, holding, which have a gen. of the object. We say 'by' or 'on'; so Theocr. 4. 35, τὸν ταῦρον...ἆγε πιάξας | τᾶς ὁπλᾶς, 'seized it by the hoof'.

γεραιᾶς—obs. quantity of -αι. Cf. *El.* 497, παλᾰιόν τε θησαύ-ρισμα, see 82, n. Pors. suggests without reading γραιᾶς. προσ-λαζ.—if any force is to be assigned to πρός it must be that of taking *to* oneself. λαζύμαι is the form preferred by Attic poets especially Eur. to λάζομαι, Ep. and Ion. collateral form of λαμβάνω.

65 sqq. 'And I propping myself on a bent arm as on a staff will hasten the crawling motion of my limbs setting one foot before the other'. H.'s own arm, linked (διὰ) with that of her ladies, forms her stick: the epithet 'bent' is transferred from the stick to the arm; observe that Greek usage limits by an adj. a metaphor which seems too strong: e.g. Aesch. calls vultures Ζηνὸς κύνες, but corrects the metaphor at once by adding ἀκραγεῖς, 'dogs, but not *barking* dogs'. So here Eur. calls an arm σκίπωνα, but adds σκολιόν, because real sticks are straight, not crooked. The gen. thus used is called a *definitive* gen. [Two other interpretations are given, (1) a real stick. Cf. Cic. *de div.* 1. 30, *incurvum et leviter a summo* INFLEXUM BACILLUM: then χερὸς means 'by my hand' and προτιθεῖσα may govern σκίπωνα supplied from σκίπωνι, (2) 'supporting myself by

my hand on a bent stick', i.e. on *shoulders* of her attendants:
but this is scarcely consistent with προσλαΐ. χερός above.]
σκίπων—same root as σκῆπτρον, Lat. *scipio:* for interchange of
e and *i,* cf. χθές, χθιΐός, πέντε, *quinque:* ἵππος, *equus.*

67. ἄρθρων—strictly the socket of a joint (√ΑΡ, cf. *artus,*
arms), and is generally joined with other more specific words,
as ἄρθρα ποδοῖν, ἄρθρα τῶν κύκλων, 'the eyes', ἄρθρα στόματος,
'mouth', &c.

68. ὦ στερ. Διός—'O flashing light of day'. A similarly
strong phrase is used by Soph., *Trach.* 99, λαμπρᾷ στεροπᾷ
φλεγέθων, of the sun. So 709, Διὸς φάος.

69. 'Why, O why am I excited thus?' ποτε as *tandem* in
Lat., of strong appeals. This is a rather unusual sense of
αἴρομαι equivalent to μετεωρίΐομαι. ἔννυχος—the Greeks prefer
the adjectival form to τῇ νυκτί: it is a poetic form, more usually
ἐννύχιος which is of three terminations, ἔννυχος of only two.

70. 'O sovereign earth, mother of darkwinged dreams' (i.e.
illomened, 705). Pors. wished to transpose this with ὦ σκοτ.
νύξ, 68, but χθών includes the nether world whence dreams
come. πότνια—one of the very few fem. trisyllables in -ιἄ [cf.
ὄμπνια], a poetical title of honour used in Hom. of persons
only, but in tragic poets often used as an epithet of earth.

72. ἀποπέμπομαι—'I deprecate'. Lat. *abominor.*

73. ἄν—τἀν is suggested *metri gratia* to make final syllable
of ὄψιν long. σωΐομένου—an instance of tragic irony; for the
audience knew that her son was dead.

76. ἐδάην—'I noticed and understood' if we retain ὄψιν
ἔμαθον. This means she took particular heed to the dream: its
interpretation she knew not, for she wishes to consult Helenus
or Kasandra. ἐδάην—is aor. pass. from √δα, δάω not being
found: it is only used in the *Chorus* of Attic poetry.

79. ὦ χθον. θεοί—'ye nether gods', see 70; better than
'gods of the country', with which cf. Lat. *dii indigetes,* more
appropriate but with less authority. σώσατε—notice the dis-
tinction between the momentary aorist and the continuous
present τοῦ σωΐομένου.

80. ἄγκυρ' ἅτ' ἐμῶν—this is the excellent emendation of
Pors. after Reiske, ἅτε being a particle of comparison. Other

readings are ἔτ᾽ ἀγκ. ἀμῶν, ἐπ᾽ ἐμῶν, for the original ἀγκυρά τ᾽ ἐμῶν which is objectionable from the position of τε, yet we have a parallel in 426, and in the position of *que* in elegiac verse, e.g. Tib. 1. 3. 56, *Messallam terra dum sequiturque mari*, and even in prose as Cic. *inter nosque*. [The metaphor in ἄγκυρα is common in all languages; perhaps H. refers to Polyd. in these strong and at first sight exaggerated terms (for Helenus and Kas. were still alive) because he was the only child still at liberty].

81. χιονώδη—most words in -οειδής remain uncontracted, as κερατοειδής, μονοειδής, -οει should strictly be contracted into οι as δηλοῖς for δηλόεις, but θεοειδής contracts into θεουδής. Θρῄκην, Ep. and Ion. form of Θρᾴκην preferred by tragedians, though in other cases they choose the Doric as 'Αθάνα. κατέχει, 'dwells in'.

82. πατρίου—so the best MS. Old reading was πατρῴου which involved a difficulty in quantity. φυλακαῖσιν—Greek idiom uses the plural in many words where we use the sing: e.g. πλοῦτοι, γέλωτες, ἔνδειαι, κρέα, πυροί, κριθαί, ἅλες, 265, n.

83. τι νέον—'Some new sorrow will hap'. νέον, like *novae res*, usually implies something untoward.The Greeks made great use of their neuts. sing. and plur. as in such phrases as μῶρα φρονεῖν, καλὸν ἀείδειν, μαχητέον (-τέα) ἐστίν.

85. ἀλίαστος—'at no other time does my soul thus unceasingly shudder and quail'. The der. is √κλιν, cf. νέφος and κνέφας, χλαῖνα and *lana*, and its general sense is 'unbending' as we see in Hom. who uses it of war, battle, lamentation. *Il.* 24. 549, μηδ᾽ ἀλίαστον ὀδύρεο, 'mourn not incessantly'.

86. φρίσσει, ταρβεῖ—asyndeton, usual in agitation.

87. ποῦ ποτε—'where ever'. So τί ποτε, 69. θείαν—'inspired', hence 'divining' =μαντικήν. Cf. *Aen.* 3. 373 (of Helenus) *canit* divino *ex ore sacerdos*. *Helenus*, son of Priam and Hec.; later traditions say that he was the only grown son of Priam who survived the Trojan war, and that he deserted the Trojans and married Andromache after Neoptolemus' death. *Kasandra* was endowed with prophetic powers by Apollo, but no one would believe her. On the taking of Troy, Agam. won her and took her home to Mykenæ, when his wife Klytemnestra murdered her from jealousy; see 1275.

88. **ἐσίδω**—conj. deliberativus [unless we call it like ἴδωμαι a Homeric fut.]. Goodwin, § 213. 2. **Κασάνδρας**—this reading instead of Κάσανδραν removes the difficulty which was felt about Ἐλ. **ψυχάν** as though Hel. were already dead and only his soul could be spoken of; the phrase is equivalent to Ἑλένον simply.

89. **κρίνωσιν**—if, when two or more substs. are joined by ἤ = 'or', the verb applies indifferently to both, it is put in the plur. e.g. *Alk.* 367, καὶ μ' οὔθ' ὁ Πλούτωνος κύων | οὔθ' οὐπὶ κώπῃ ψυχοπομπὸς ἂν Χάρων | ἔσχον. There is therefore no need to read καὶ for ἤ in 88.

90. **γάρ**—the inferential force here is *nil*, and the particle merely introduces the dream.

βαλιάν—'dappled' √βαλ- same word as *varius*. Eur. himself explains the word *Iph. Aul.* 221 (of the horses of Eumelus), λευκοστίκτῳ τριχὶ βαλιάν.

91. **σφαζομέναν...σπασθ.**—79, n. **ἀνοίκτως**, the excellent reading of Pors., see metrical note.

92. **τόδε**—viz. what follows, so in Thuc., τάδε ἔλεγον commences, ταῦτα ἔλεγον ends a speech.

96. **ᾔτει**—'was urgent in asking', notice force of imperf. **γέρας**, a gift of honour, strictly that called also ἐξαιρετόν, which the chiefs received before division of the spoil.

99. **ἀπο...πέμψατε**—by tmesis for ἀποπέμψατε, 'avert'.

100—154. **πάροδος**—The chorus of Trojan captive women, 15 in number, enter the orchestra from the side, and marching either in ranks (κατὰ ζυγὰ) or files (κατὰ στοίχους), muster round the θυμέλη, the raised altar of Dionysus in the centre of the orchestra, whence the κορυφαῖος would direct its movements. They say, 'We have left our master's tents not to lighten your sorrow, but as heralds of woe. Achilles has asked for a victim, and the Greeks in conclave have resolved to offer your daughter. In the debate, Agam. from regard to Kasandra, advocated your cause, but the opposition urged that Achilles' spear was worth more than Kasandra's bed. Odysseus turned the scale, with the plea that none should stand up among the dead and reproach Greeks for thanklessness to Greeks. He will be here anon to seize your daughter—supplicate the gods: so you will save yourself bereavement, or else you must see your daughter die'.

100. σπουδῇ—is on the point of being 'petrified' into an adverb. The dat. is one of manner, so βίᾳ, σιγῇ, ἔργῳ, ἰδίᾳ, δρόμῳ, κύκλῳ, ὀργῇ. ἐλιάσθην—'I came away to thee'=Lat. secessi, 85, n.

101. δεσποσύνους—'of my master'. Attributive adjectives are used in Gk. and Lat. where we employ a preposition, e.g. Τελαμώνιε παῖ, son of Telamon, Ἀχίλεια λόγχη, 131, filius erilis, 'master's son'. Sullanus exercitus, 'Sulla's army'.

102. ἵν' ἐκλήρ.—'to which I was apportioned by lot', with this sense of motion implied in ἵνα, cf. Thuc. 4. 48. 6, ἐς τὴν Σικελίαν, ἵνα περ τὸ πρῶτον ὥρμηντο, ἀποπλεύσαντες. There is a constant interchange of ποῦ and ποῖ and such adverbs, just as we use 'where' and 'whither' rather loosely. [The captives would stand round: each warrior's κλῆρος, marked, would be put into a helmet, a maiden would step forward, the helmet be shaken and the girl assigned to him whose lot leaped out].

104. λογχ. αἰχ. δοριθήρ.—'captured at the spear's point'. This is a pleonasm, especially dear to tragedians, e.g. 66, Phoen. 328, ἄπεπλος φάρεων, El. 310, ἀνέορτος ἱερῶν.

106, 7. 'In no respect lightening thee of thy calamities, but having taken on myself a heavy weight of tidings'. οὐδὲν—is an adverb, as appears from the use of ἀποκουφ. in Or. 1341, σε is easily supplied. The gen. is one of separation. ἀράμενη—the long ᾱ is accounted for by the fact that αἴρω is contracted from ἀείρω.

109. 'For in full conclave of the Achs. it is said that it was resolved to make thy daughter a sacrifice to Achilles'. δοκέω, a legal t. t. especially of public resolutions, e.g. ἔδοξε τῇ βουλῇ, τῷ δήμῳ, so senatui placere in Lat.

111. τύμβ. ἐπιβάς—'mounted the tomb'. ἐπί means 'to-wards', and denotes the action of alighting upon.

112. οἶσθ' ὅτε=meministi quum, see 239 for this sense of οἶσθα, there is a conjecture ὅτι which is decidedly weaker, and Schaefer observes that the Greeks used a particle of time quite unnecessarily, e.g. 307, ὅταν almost=ἐάν. χρυσέοις—'armour inlaid with gold', unless this epithet apply to it as made by a god, after the epic manner. σὺν ὅπλ.—is a usual Homeric mode of expression, 'with his armour on'.

113. 'Stayed the ships from going to sea, though their sails were braced on the halyards,' i.e. ready to start. ποντ.—

a usual epithet of ships: here it adds point to ἔσχε, and becomes almost proleptic. σχεδ.—properly rafts for the nonce. Thuc. 1. 10 conjectures from Homer's statement the size of the ships which went to Troy, the largest holding 120 men, the smallest 50.

114. προτ.—is more properly the sheet which held the mast in its place, fastened to the prow. λαίφη—is acc. of ref. προτ. dat. of instrument, unless ἐπερειδ. have a transitive sense, as in L. and S. Cf. Hor. *Sat.* 1. 6. 74, *laevo suspensi loculos tabulamque lacerto*, and 910.

115. θωΰσσων—'by this loud chiding', perhaps strictly of the cry of an animal, akin to θώς a lynx through √krug = 'to cry'. It is used as a hunting term, κυσὶ θωύξαι, *Hippol.* 219, and when applied to men denotes a loud impulsive shout. Soph. uses it of the cry of Ajax (*Aj.* 308, 335).

116. 'Whither then set ye forth?'—δή like δῆτα strongly emphasizes a question. Δαναοί—according to Mr Gladstone is a purely *military* denomination; historically or politically the Greeks could not be so called in the heroic age.

118—121. 'Then clashed there waves of frequent strife, and through the warrior Hellenic host there 'gan to pass two diverse streams of opinion, some minded to present a sacrifice at the tomb, some not'. ξυνέπαισε,—intrans. as in Aesch. *Prom.* 885, θολεροὶ δὲ λόγοι παίουσ' εἰκῆ | στυγνῆς πρὸς κύμασιν ἄτης. The MS. reading ξυνέπεσε is unmetrical. τύμβῳ—locative. Cf. 31 n. δοκοῦν—acc. absol. see 506. This construction is confined to neut. participles, mostly some simple word or compound of εἰμί, e. g. ἐνόν, παρόν, ἐξόν, δόξαν, δέον.

122. 'Eagerly advancing thy interest, constant in honour to the bed of the inspired prophetess', i.e. Kasandra. ἀνέχων—so Soph. *Aj.* 212, ἐπεί σε λέχος δουριάλωτον | στέρξας ἀνέχει θούριος Αἴας.

125. τὼ Θησ.—Demophoon and Akamas his sons by Phaedra. ὄζω—'two scions' 20 n.

126. δισσῶν—'two', not dissonant, which would be διπλῶν. We have in Soph. *Aj.* 57, δισσοὶ Ἀτρεῖδαι. The rhetorical opposition δισσῶν...μιᾷ is quite Euripidean, 45 n., 896.

128. στεφανοῦν—double idea of 'crowning' and 'honouring' as schol. says, comes from crowning victors at games. Cf. Soph. *Ant.* 431, χοαῖσι τρισπόνδοισι τὸν νέκυν στέφει.

129. χλωρῷ—(χλοή, tender grass), 'fresh, young'. ἀ-κραιφνές, 537, conveys same idea.

130. 'They declared they would never set K.'s couch before A.'s spear', or rather 'the warrior Achilles'. See 101 n.

132. 'Now well-nigh equal was the zeal for the hotly-contended arguments, till the wily-minded, bullying, sweet-tongued people-courtier', &c. κατατειν. The κατά is intensi-tive. ποικιλόφρων—an echo of Homer's epithet ποικιλομήτης, which however is an epithet of honour. κόπις—practically same as κοπίς 'an axe or chopper'. The Schol. explains 'orator' but the idea of κόπτω requires to be brought out. Possibly 'incisive' as Paley suggests; but there is a pointed antithesis: Odys. would be bully or fawner to serve his pur-pose. Eur. was perhaps thinking of Hyperbolus, or Kleophon the demagogue, or some contemporary.

135. πείθει—ἔπεισε would be the true grammatical sequence after πρίν, but that would imply that the effect of the principal verb had altogether passed: the present tense brings the result on to the time of the speaker's remark.

137. δούλων σφαγίων—=δουλίων. Cf. στρατὸν αἰχμήτην 120, δούλης γυναικός 1253, servum pecus. Hor.

141. 'Who have died for the sake of'.

143. 'Now Odys. will be here almost immediately to drag away', &c. ὅσον οὐκ—so ὅτι μή, ὅσαν οὔπω (Thuc.). Lat. tantum non. ἀφέλξων—corresponds rather to supine in -um than to fut. participle, to detractum rather than detracturus.

144. πῶλον—the young of any animal, men included; so μόσχον, of a young girl, 526, πῶλος, of a youth, Phoen. 954.

146. ναοὺς—supply πρὸς from latter part of sentence; so Hel. 863, Τροίας δὲ σωθεὶς κἀπὸ βαρβάρου χθονός.

148. κήρυσσε—'loudly call upon', 'hail', as we speak of hailing a ship. The ancients looked with suspicion on silent prayer.

149. γαῖαν—the reading of MSS., corrected to γαίας by Pors. for sake of metre. But -αν is lengthened in the pause, see 83, metrical note.

151. ὀρφανὸν—in Att. sometimes of two terminations. Cf. 296, 592.

152 sqq. 'Or thou must see thy virgin prostrate before the tomb, incarnadined with blood as it runs in dark-gleaming flow from her gold-decked throat'. τύμβου—depends on προ- in προπετῆ. Two MSS. read τύμβῳ locative. χρυσοφόρου— refers to usual adornment of maidens. Cf. *Il.* 2. 872 (of a young warrior) ὃs καὶ χρυσὸν ἔχων πολέμονδ᾽ ἴεν, ἠΰτε κούρη, though by the analogy of *Suppl.* 1054 the adorning may be for sacrifice. νασμ. μελαν.—in apposition with αἵματι.

[155—443. *First Episode.* After Hecuba's monody, a series of expressions of woe, and the attempts of Polyxena to console her, which conclude with a lament that she cannot share her mother's slavery, and a noble expression of disregard for her own life (155, 215), the action of the play continues. Odys. enters: Hec. appeals to him for protection on the score of past favours shown. Odys. urges the extreme necessity of not neglecting due honours to the brave, and the scene closes with the removal of Polyx. H. faints.]

156. ἀχώ—Doric for ἠχώ.

157. δειλαία γήρως—'forlorn because of'. This is analogous to the gen. of exclamation, as τοῦ χασμήματος, 'what a swallow!' Goodwin, § 173. 3.

159. φερτᾶς—poetical form of φορητῆς, i.e. verbal from φέρω, not φόρεω.

160. 'Who is my helper? what child? what city?' ποία— differs but little from τίς. γέννα—[This word can lengthen the final syllable, as in *Iph. Taur.* 159, like τόλμᾱ in Pindar; γενεά is read by Pors. to avoid the difficulty;] the word may fairly mean either 'child' or 'people' just as Eur. uses Σπάρτων γέννα, Φρυγῶν γέννα, Κενταύρων γέννα.

162. φροῦδος—'is dead', lit. 'gone'; so οἴχομαι, βέβηκα. The der. is πρὸ-ὁδός, cf. φροίμιον, φρούριον.

164. ποῖ δ᾽ ἤσω;—strictly an acc. is required as with ὁρμάω and verbs of sending; many amendments have been proposed. Schol. reads ἤσω from ἴημι=eo for which there is no evidence. Musgrave, ποῖ δ᾽ ἤσω πόδα; τίς.

166. 'O daughters of Troy that have brought evil tidings'. Τρῳάδες—like *Troiugenae* and *Aeneadae*, &c. Reference is to 107.

169. 'No more to me is life in this light of day object of desire'. βίος ἐν φάει—little more than βίος. Hom. *Odys.* 10. 498, ἔτι ζώειν καὶ ὁρᾶν φάος ἠελίοιο.

172. αὐλάν—the tent where Polyx. is.

172 sqq. See introd. for bearing of this passage on the date of play.

176. φάμαν—'tidings'. √FA cf. φημί, *fama, fari*.

179. καρύξασ'—We should rather have expected the fut. for H. as yet had announced little or nothing. ὥστ'—Ep. particle of comparison, but found in 204 of this play.

180. ἐξέπταξας—Dor.=ἐξέπτηξας, 'startled me from the tents'. πτήσσω is usually intrans. 'crouch', except perhaps in *Il.* 14. 40, πτῆξε δὲ θυμὸν ἐνὶ στήθεσσιν Ἀχαιῶν.

182. φρ. μοι κακά—'a sad prelude methinks'. μοι, ethical dat.

184. ἐξαύδα—κρύψῃς—Notice change in tense: latter makes a more definite request: the line is copied from *Il.* 1. 363, ἐξαύδα μὴ κεῦθε νόῳ, ἵνα εἴδομεν ἄμφω.

185. δειμ....ἀναστένεις—an elliptical mode of speech. 'I fear (and fearing doubt) why thou liftest up (ἀνα) thy voice in lament'.

189 sqq. 'A public decree of the Argives unanimously aims at thy slaughter at the tomb in honour of Peleus' son'. πρὸς τύμβον—acc. implies the process of dragging her to the tomb. Πηλείᾳ γέννᾳ—this reading avoids the difficulty which is found in the common reading Πηλείδα γέννᾳ, for that would be Neoptolemus, not Achilles. [The variants are (1) Πηλείδα γέννα, and dat. κοινᾷ γνώμᾳ, 'the child of P. intends by common decree;' (2) Ἀργ. γέννα might=Ἀργεῖοι, like more common γένος; (3) γέννα may be voc. 'O my child'].

193. ἀμέγαρτα κακῶν—'how utterest thou most unenviable woes'=ἀφθόνητα, some have preferred the idea of ἄφθονος, 'unstinted', 'numerous'. The neut. plur. thus joined with a gen. is very common; and is imitated by Hor. *amara curarum, dura navis* (gen.).

197. μοι—dat. eth.; notice the elegance of its position. These lines are at first sight weak after 189—191, but the repetition is full of pathos.

199. δυστ. μᾶτερ βιοτᾶς—Take these words together and make δ. β. gen. of quality, so 211. Observe that Eur. is very fond of repeating a word or phrase in choral parts.

203. **παῖς ὅδ'**—'I thy child here', like *hic*, ὅδε is used of a speaker indicating himself.

205. **μόσχον**—142 n.

207. **"Αιδạ**—'to Hades', dat. of motion is not common, it recalls Hom. *Il.* 1. 3, "Αϊδι προῒαψεν. So in Lat. *it clamor caelo* (Verg.), *nigro compulerit gregi* (Hor.).

213. 'But my life, its outrage and its shame, I weep not after' (μετά), i.e. she does not regret the loss of life. Cf. *Med.* 996, μεταστένομαι δὲ σὸν ἄλγος. Other translations are (1) therewith, at same time, (2) too late, after the event, (3) with a notion of change, i.e. from death to life.

214. **θανεῖν**=τὸ θανεῖν.

216. **καὶ μην**—'and lo', usual formula for introducing a new person on stage, as in oratory it begins a new argument, and in description a new incident.

[217—250. Enter Odysseus. He reminds H. of the decree and says that he has come to take away her daughter; he advises submission and deprecates all violence. H. in reply mourns that she did not die before, and asks leave to put a question, if a slave may be allowed to address a freeman. She recalls his visit as a spy to Troy, her discovery and concealment of him, his urgent entreaties for life, and her saving of him.]

218. **γύναι**—'lady', a title of respect.

219. **κρανθεῖσαν**—'ratified'.

221. **πρὸς ὀρθ. χῶμα**—190 n.

224. **ἔπεσται**—This is the excellent cmend. of Nauck for usual ἐπέστη which is tame after ἐπιστάτης.

225. **οἶσθ' οὖν ὃ δρᾶσον**—'dost thou know what to do? neither be torn from her by violence nor come to any conflict of blows with me'. This curious phrase which means properly 'do, dost thou know what?' recurs often in Eur., Soph. and Aristoph.

227. 'Know thy powers', i.e. thy real powerlessness. Cf. Xen. *Anab.* 1. 6. 7, ὅποτ' αὖ ἔγνως τὴν σεαυτοῦ δύναμιν.

228. ''Tis wise, I ween, even in troubles, to have wise thoughts'. τοι gnomic, i.e. its province is to introduce a proverb or sentiment.

234. 'But if a slave may ask questions of the free, neither grievous nor vexing to the heart, then it is befitting that thy speech indeed should have been spoken but that thou shouldst hear me when I ask these questions'. [Prof. Paley follows a scholiast in making σοί = πρὸς σέ, "'tis to thee our speech must be addressed', but this loses the force of the tense. Weil, objecting that Odysseus had finished speaking and that Hecuba did not wish him to cease entirely, conjectures σὲ μὲν ἐρωτᾶσθαι χρεών.]

235. μή—not οὐ, because the statement is general, 237. Hec. speaks of herself in the plur. and the rule is that in such cases the masc. must be used.

238. χρόνου—*causal* gen. after verb of envying. 'I do not grudge thee on the count of time'. Goodwin, § 173. 1.

239. οἶσθα—'dost remember?'

240. 'And from thy eyes gouts of blood dripped down upon thy chin'. The allusion is not to his weeping 'tears of blood', but to his general ghastly appearance when he entered Troy as a spy and had mutilated himself, pretending that the Greeks had maltreated him. The story is told by Hom. *Od.* 4. 244 sqq., where *Helen* not Hecuba recognises him: as the schol. remarks, Hec. would hardly have let him go. φόβου and δόλου have been conjectured, and if adopted, then σταλ. would refer only to 'tears'.

242. 'Yes, for it did not touch merely the surface of my heart', i.e. it cut deep. The gen. is *partitive*.

244. μεμν...ἐλθόντες—the participle is regularly used after vbs. of emotion. 397. The constr. is imitated by Verg. *Aen.* 2. 377, *sensit...delapsus in hostis*, i.e. *se delapsum fuisse*.

246. 'Yea, till my hand grew numbed within thy robes'. The γε confirms the previous speaker's assertion and adds a new feature.

247. δῆτα—'prithee'.

[251—295. Hecuba to Odys. 'You owe me gratitude not unkindness. I hate you orators who speak to please, careless what injury you inflict. Why was my daughter to die, a *human* sacrifice, where a beast would have served? Achilles has no grudge against *her;* Helen, alike as the cause of mischief and as the loveliest, would have been the best victim. Such is the plea of equity. For you, I claim your gratitude:

give me a life for a life: you have power I know, but use it not unlawfully; go, urge the Greeks to change the decree; ye did not always kill women; your law is to care alike for slave and free—and *your* prestige would persuade them even against their interests'.]

251. βουλεύμασιν—'because of these schemes', causal dat.

252. ἔπαθες—'didst experience'.

253. δύνῃ = δύνασαι—there is no occasion to regard this as a subj.: indeed, though there are occasional instances of such use, yet more properly ἄν should be inserted to complete the constr. δύνᾳ, which Pors. preferred, is condemned by Herm. as a Doric form.

254. 'All the sort of you who affect a speaker's fame'. Eur. has clearly in mind some reference to a contemporary: he had an intense dislike of mere oratory apart from principle, as we see from *Or.* 907, ὅταν γὰρ ἡδὺς τοῖς λόγοις, φρονῶν κακῶς | πείθῃ τὸ πλῆθος, τῇ πόλει κακὸν μέγα. Aristoph.'s savage attacks upon him in this respect are most unfair.

258. 'But pray what policy did they find in this—that they determined upon a vote of death against this my daughter'.

260. τὸ χρῆν—poet. form of χρῆναι. The suggestion χρεών is unnecessary. σφε is used of all genders sing. and plur.

263. τείνει φόνον—'aims death', metaphor from a bow.

264. εἴργασται—'has done him no hurt'. This middle sense of perf. pass. is found more especially in words meaning doing or performing. This particular word is in Soph. always middle. Cf. ἦρμαι, γέγραμμαι, παρεσκεύασμαι.

265. προσφάγματα—there is not much additional point in the plur. and there is a variant πρόσφαγμά τι. We find an analogy in 616 σκηνώματα. Soph. *Antig.* 568, νυμφεῖα = νύμφην, see 82 n.

266. ὤλεσεν...ἄγει—for change of tense see 21 n.

268. οὐχ ἡμῶν τόδε—'this is not our concern'. H. means that on the score of beauty as well as of just vengeance Helen was the more suitable victim.

269. ἐκπρεπεστάτη—'supereminent'. The MSS. vary between this and εὐπρεπεστάτη.

271. 'On score of justice this is my contention and argument'. The phrase = τήνδε τὴν ἄμιλλαν λόγου ἀμιλλῶμαι. She wishes to contrast the plea of equity with her *personal* appeal to gratitude of Odys.

274. γραίας—Valckenaer's correction for the unmetrical γεραιᾶς, but see 64 n.

275. σου—partitive gen. after τῶν αὐτῶν, 'the same parts of thee', i.e. hand and cheek.

280. ἡ δὲ—'for she'.

282. τοὺς κρατοῦντας—plur. used to prevent too direct a reference to Odys. ἃ μὴ χρεών 'in unlawful things'. μὴ is used because the whole class of things unlawful is included. Cf. *Bacch.* 515, ὅτι γὰρ μὴ χρεών οὗτοι χρεών παθεῖν. χρεών is indeclinable. Cf. Shakespeare, *Measure for Measure*, 'it is excellent | to have a giant's strength, but tyrannous | to use it like a giant'.

283. πράξειν is properly referred back to τοὺς κρατ. as subject.

284. ἦν ποτ'—implying that it is so no more. Cf. *fuimus Troes* (Verg.), [perhaps εὐτυχοῦσα may be supplied].

285. Double acc. is used after verbs of depriving. Goodwin, § 164. This may be explained as a combination of direct and indirect accusatives 'robbed me as to'.

286. ὦ φίλ. γέν.—here she takes him by the beard.

288. παρηγόρησον—'counsel them to change' (παρά). The words introduced by ὡς (=nam) are the comment of H., not the words which Odys. is to use in council. φθόνος equivalent to νέμεσις, i.e. it excites the anger of the gods.

291. δὲ—'for'. Here Eur. refers to heroic times the custom of his own age. Demosth. *in Mid.* p. 529 gives us the law of ὕβρις or outrage, and says that slaves and free were treated alike.

293—5. 'Thy prestige, though it speak but ill, will persuade them: for the same speech has not the same weight when it comes from the insignificant as (when it comes) from those of repute'. λέγῃ—is the MS. reading, and cannot be the same in sense as λέγῃς which is substituted for it. There is no doubt some violence to language in saying that 'his prestige speaks', but ἀξίωμα is the personification of an abstraction. Cf. *Hipp.* 11, ἁγνοῦ Πίτθεως παιδεύματα. [κακῶς— is sometimes interpreted 'against their interest', under the idea that Odys. as a notable speaker would not be disparaged by any accusation of indifferent pleading.]

295. τῶν δοκούντων—a recognised phrase = εὐδοκίμων, hence perhaps the use of the article: cf. *Troades,* 609, where τὰ δοκοῦντα and τὰ μηδὲν ὄντα are contrasted.

296. στερρός—151 n.

297. ἥτις = ὥστε—'as not to shed a tear'. So also the simple relative ὅς. *Hel.* 501, ἀνὴρ γὰρ οὐδεὶς ὧδε βάρβαρος φρένας | ὃς ὄνομ' ἀκούσας τοὐμὸν οὐ δώσει βοράν. Cf. Scott, Lay,

> 'Breathes there the man with soul so dead,
> *Who* never to himself hath said,
> This is my own, my native land!'

[299—331. Odys. to Hec. 'You personally I can save: but I cannot gainsay my promise to give your daughter to the bravest warrior we had. To do so would be bad in principle: for states would suffer if their champions were not duly honoured : no one would take the field if he thought his bravery would not command respect. I myself should like to have honour paid to my tomb, however little might suffice me in life. And do not imagine yourself alone in suffering; we, too, have aged widows. So endure: we will take the consequences of our reverence of our warriors : you barbarians may do as you will, and reap the proper fruits of your conduct'.]

299. 'Be advised and do not by reason of thy anger regard in thy mind thy good counsellor as a foe'. διδάσκου—(mid.) usu. = 'get some one taught'. τῷ θυμουμένῳ—article and neut. participle equal a subst.; a constr. very common in Thucydides. δυσμενῆ is the predicate.

301. τὸ μὲν σὸν σῶμα—'thy person'. So Soph. *Ant.* 675, τῶν δ' ὀρθουμένων | σώζει τὰ πολλὰ σώμαθ' ἡ πειθαρχία.

302. κοὐκ ἄλλως λέγω—'and not idly do I speak'.

307. πρόθυμος—'ready '.

308. φέρηται—'wins for himself no more than his inferiors'. Cf. Soph. *Ant.* 637, ἐμοὶ γὰρ οὐδεὶς ἀξιώσεται γάμος | μεῖζον φέρεσθαί σου καλῶς ἡγουμένου.

309. ἡμῖν—'at our hands'. Almost a dative of the agent.

311. 'Is not this shame to us if we make use of a friend while he lives, but when he is dead no longer treat him

in friendly wise?' There is a double sense here of χρῶμαι—
(1) to make use of a person, as in Xen. *Anab.* 1. 4. 8, καὶ ἐρεῖ
οὐδεὶς ὡς ἐγὼ, ἔως μὲν ἂν παρῇ τις, χρῶμαι, ἐπειδὰν δὲ ἀπιέναι
βούληται κ.τ.λ. (2) = *uti amico*, 'to treat as a friend'. [Cobet,
Obs. Criticae, suggests ἐχρώμεθ', bringing into more striking
contrast the different times, past and present.] βλέποντι is
used as οἱ βλέποντες, 'the living'. Cf. Ter. *Eun.* 73, *vivus
vidensque pereo.*

312. ὄλωλε—the MS. reading, softened down by some to
ἄπεστι.

315. φιλοψυχήσομεν—'play the coward'. Observe that
this line is spoken by Odys. as his own sentiment: if he
had put it into the mouth of anyone else, the conjunctive
would have been used.

317. καὶ μὴν—'and look you', 216 n. καθ' ἡμέρ.—con-
nect closely with the words which follow, 'if with but small
supply day by day'. καὶ εἰ states an imaginary or reluctantly
admitted, εἰ καὶ an actual case.

319. 'But my tomb I should like to see deemed worthy of
honour'. ὁρᾶσθαι—mid. but probably in poetry = active.

320. διὰ μακρ.—'for long lasting is the reward'. The sentiment is like that which Antigone expresses (Soph. *Ant.* 76),
where she refuses to please the living rather than the dead,
ἐκεῖ γὰρ ἀεὶ κείσομαι.

323. ἠδὲ—Epic form common enough in Aesch. but otherwise of doubtful tragic usage.

324. νυμφίων τητ.—Goodwin, § 174.

325. κεύθει—act. in sense whereas the perf. κέκευθα is
often intrans. 'is buried', cf. ἐρείπω, ἤριπον, ἵστημι, ἔστηκα.

326 seq. 'If our custom of honouring the dead is a mis-
taken one we shall (willingly) incur the charge of folly, but
do ye barbarians neither regard your friends as friends, nor
admire those who have bravely died, that so Hellas may
prosper and ye may win reward to match your thoughts'
(i. e. may suffer because you refuse to honour the dead).
[κακῶς may be, but not so well, taken with τιμᾶν.]

326. τόλμα τάδ'—'endure this'.

327. ὀφλ.—strictly, 'to lose a lawsuit'. Cf. Soph. *Ant.*
470, σχεδόν τι μωρῷ μωρίαν ὀφλισκάνω, and *debeo* in Hor. *Od.*
1. 14. 15, *tu nisi ventis | debes ludibrium, cave.*

330. ὡς ἂν—'that so'. It is difficult to see that any change is effected by introd. of ἂν which in Hom. and Hdt. is used with opt. as well as subj. Goodwin, § 216, 1. n. 2. [Herm. says = *dummodo*, 'provided that'.]

[332—341. The Chor. laments slavery as an evil. Hec. appeals to her daughter to attempt Odys. with all sweet notes of woe: for he, too, has children, and will pity her fate.]

332. 'Slavery, what an evil is it ever, and it tolerates indignities under tyranny of force'. The reading adopted in the text is that given by Stobaeus (flor. about 500 A. D. quotes more than 500 passages of Eur.) and is simple and consistent. τολμᾶν and πεφυκέναι which are variants also go well together. νικώμενον is also read for κρατούμενον.

334. οὑμοὶ—by crasis from οἱ ἐμοί.

335. φροῦδοι—supply εἰσιν, which is usually omitted in this connection. ματ. ῥιφθ.—'cast idly to the winds'. The tragedians prefer this fuller form to ῥιφέντες.

337, 8. 'By uttering every note which comes from the nightingale's throat'. πάσας = παντοίας. ἱεῖσα, (the ι is common). ὥστε = ὡς, see 179 n. [The common epithets of the nightingale, λίγεια, λιγύφωνος, *flebilis*, *querula*, illustrate the appropriateness of the comparison. Polyx. had need of a tongue like that of the much-wronged Philomela.]

338. μὴ στερ.—in prose τοῦ μὴ would be required: it shows very clearly the relation of cause and effect.

340. πρόφασιν—'a plea', often though not necessarily a *false* plea. πεῖθε—'try to persuade'. The definite act of persuading would have been expressed by aor. For appeal made on the score of children, cf. *Alk.* 275 (Admetus to Alk. on point of death) μὴ πρὸς παίδων οὓς ὀρφανιεῖς.

[342—378. Polyxena sees Odysseus showing signs of shrinking from her appeal and assures him that she is willing to follow him to death. For slavery is abominable to her, a king's daughter and once sought in marriage by princes, a rival of the gods, save in being mortal. She shrinks from menial offices or degrading alliance with a slave. If she is to die, let her die *free*. She urges her mother to accept the position.]

342. ὁρῶ σε κρύπτοντα = ὅτι κρύπτεις: verbs of *perception* usually take a participial construction not an object clause. Goodwin, § 280. δεξιάν—the right hand and beard were seized

by suppliants, who were watched over and avenged by Ζεὐs
ἱκέσιος.

344. γενειάδος—gen. of the object aimed at. Goodwin,
§ 171.

345. ἰκέσιον Δία—'thou hast escaped my suppliant Zeus',
i.e. his vengeance [or Polyxena regards Zeus as her colleague
in entreaty, identifying him with her cause].

346. ὡς—'be sure that'. γε strongly emphasizes ἕψομαι:
'not only shall I not seek to avoid but will even court death'.

347. βουλήσομαι—the fut. with εἰ shows that she can still
avail herself of the choice.

348. φιλόψυχος—'cowardly', cf. 315. S. John xii. 25, ὁ
φιλῶν τὴν ψυχὴν αὐτοῦ ἀπολέσει αὐτήν.

349. The tragedians often express a negative by an interrogative. 'What call have I to live?' is equivalent to, but
livelier than, 'I have no, &c.' γάρ—referring to a suppressed
thought.

ζῆν—other verbs which contract into η not α are διψάω,
πεινάω, σμάω, χράω, χράομαι, and sometimes κνάω and ψάω.

μὲν—answered by δέ, 354.

350. πρῶτον βίου—'this is the glory of my life'.

352. 'A bride for kings, with no mean rivalry for my nup-
tials, to whose hearth and home I shall come'. γάμων = περὶ
γάμων. Thuc. 1. 140, τὸ τῶν Μεγαρέων ψήφισμα, 'the decree
about the Megareans'.

353. ἀφίξομαι—for more usual optative, Polyxena reverting
for a moment in thought to the time when the choice still lay
open to her.

δῶμα ἑστίαν τε—almost a hendiadys, the hearth being with
all Aryan nations the most sacred and central part of the δῶμα.
Ἑστία—*Vesta*, was the only deity common to Greeks and
Romans.

354. δ'—'for'. ἡ δύστ.—'articulus insignis', as Bengel
calls it.

Ἴδα—the mountain which overhung Troy: cf. 631 note.

355. The caesura in this line is not complete. ἀπόβλεπτος—'conspicuous'; so Vergil G. 3. 17, *victor Tyrio conspectus*
(=*conspiciendus*) *in ostro*.

E. H. 6

ἀπό denotes that men look *from* others to her. μέτα with dative is mainly an epic usage. Goodwin, § 191. vi. 3. Kirchhoff boldly reads παρθένων.

356. πλήν—adverb. τὸ κατθανεῖν—acc. of respect.

357. νῦν δ'—'but as things are'. τοὔνομα—'the name (of slave) by its strangeness makes me in love with death'.

358. εἰωθὸς ὄν—such a combination of two participles is rare: cf. Hom. *Il.* 19. 80, ἐπιστάμενόν περ' ἐόντα. Aristoph. *Frogs* 721, οὔτε γὰρ τούτοισιν οὖσιν οὐ κεκιβδηλευμένοις.

359. ἄν...ἄν—the repetition of ἄν is emphatic. Soph. *Ant.* 69 (Antigone is indignantly refusing her sister's aid), οὔτ' ἄν κελεύσαιμ' οὔτ' ἄν εἰ θέλοις ἔτι | πράσσειν, ἐμοῦ γ' ἄν ἡδέως δρῴης μέτα.

ὠμῶν φρένας—'of savage heart', acc. of specification, Goodwin, § 160.

360. δεσποτῶν ὅστις—a like combination of sing. and pl. occurs *Med.* 220, βροτῶν | ὅστις στυγεῖ. ὠνήσεται—cf. ἀφίξομαι, 352 note. ἀργύρου—gen. of price, Goodwin, § 178.

362. 'Imposing upon me the harsh service of making bread at home and of sweeping the house and standing over the loom,' harshly will he use me'. κερκίς—in the ἰστός or upright loom is the 'rod' or in later times 'comb' by which the threads of the woof were driven home so as to make the web even and close. It is probably derived from κρέκω (an onomatopoetic word='to strike') and was probably held in the hands. σαίρειν—including all menial offices. [σέσηρα and tenses formed from it mean 'to snarl', 'to sneer'.]

ἐφεστάναι—similar short forms of the perf. inf. used by Attic writers are τεθνάναι, βεβάναι, τετλάναι, δεδειπνάναι, ἡριστάναι. λυπρὸς and λυπηρὸς are collateral but distinct forms: it must not be thought that one is a contracted form of the other. ἀναγκάσει—following so soon after ἀνάγκην is to us ill-sounding, but cf. e.g. 223, ἐπιστάτης, ἐπέσται.

366. τυράννων ἤξ.—'deemed worthy of princes'. [The Greek τύραννος (Doric form of κοίρανος, a ruler) might or might not be 'a tyrant', being a despot who had gained his power by force or fraud, whether he exercised it ill or well. The early tyrants did as a rule govern well, but the words of the Corinthians at Sparta (B.C. 509), when dissuading the Spartans from

replacing Hippias in Athens by force, show the hateful excesses into which they might fall, Hdt. 5. 92.]

367. οὐ δῆτα—'no indeed', δῆτα strongly emphasizing the word after which it stands; cf. τί δῆτα; πῶς δῆτα; how pray? cf. notes on 247, 623. φέγγος—a Greek loved the light, and all dying addresses (e.g. those of Ajax, and Alkestis, and Dido, Vergil *Aeneid* 4 copied from the *Ajax*) bid a loving farewell to the sun and his light. ἐλεύθερον—freedom was a passion with the Greek. We should have expected ἐλευθέρα and some editors read ἐλευθέρων; but it is one of the many instances of transferred epithets.

369. ἄγ' οὖν μ'—Porson's correction after an old commentator for ἄγου μ'. ἄγων—the present participle is rather loosely used.

370. ἐλπίς is distinguished from δόξα as being better grounded. Plato contrasts δόξα mere 'opinion' or 'seeming' with ἐπιστήμη, 'certain knowledge'. του=τινος is contracted from the Ionian form τεο found in Homer, and is only found in Attic. It is similarly placed Aesch. *Prom.* 21, ἵν' οὔτε φωνὴν οὔτε του μορφὴν βροτῶν | ὄψει.

372. μῆτερ, σὺ δ'—in suddenly addressing a new person first comes the vocative, then the pronoun, then the particle. 1287, Ἑκάβη σὺ δ' ὦ κ.τ.λ.

373. λέγουσα μήτε δρῶσα—'neither by word nor act', supply μήτε before λέγουσα. [Some MSS. and editors read μηδέ, but λ. μηδὲ δρῶσα='saying but not doing'.] συμβούλου, 'join in wishing for my death'. Beware of confusing βούλομαι and its compounds with βουλεύω.

374. θανεῖν—substantive, object of συμβούλου.

375. Stobaeus quoting this passage reads πόνων, 378 ἐν κακοῖς, 380 πλεῖστον.

377. μᾶλλον εὐτυχέστερος—double comparatives are occasionally met with. Eur. *Hippolytus* 485, μᾶλλον ἀλγίων, Soph. *Antig.* 1210, μᾶλλον ἆσσον, Shakespeare, *Tempest*, 1. 2, 'more better'.

378. Nauck suspects this verse, perhaps with reason. On the one hand it is just such a verse as copyists would insert, on the other hand Euripides often ends with such saws.

μὴ καλῶς—'if with dishonour', μὴ adding a hypothetic touch.

379. 'Marvellous and notable among men is the stamp of noble birth and rises to higher repute of nobility'.

χαρακτήρ—a metaphor from the stamping of money. Milton (with whom Euripides was a great favourite) may have borrowed hence, 'Reason's mintage | charactered in the face'. ἐσθλῶν—gen. of origin, Soph. *Ant.* 38, εἴτ' εὐγενὴς πέφυκας εἴτ' ἐσθλῶν κακή. Euripides had a high opinion of the value of good birth, but it must be accompanied by nobility of nature. κἀπὶ μεῖζον ἔρχεται—Soph. *Phil.* 258, ἡ δ' ἐμὴ νόσος | ἀεὶ τέθηλε κἀπὶ μεῖζον ἔρχεται. ὄνομα, acc., the nom. would require τοὔνομα in strict Greek.

[382. *Hecuba.* Let me be substituted for Polyxena; I am the mother of that Paris who slew Achilles. *Odysseus.* Nay it is Polyxena whom Achilles demands. *Hecuba.* Let us die together: nothing shall avail to separate us, I will cling to her as ivy to the oak.]

382. εἶπας—the quick Greek uses the aorist in order to revert to the precise moment, so ἀπέπτυσα I loathe, ἐπῄνεσα I praise, ἐδεξάμην I accept.

383. 'But to that good is added pain'.

τῷ Πηλέως—a spondaic caesura is allowable in the fifth foot when the first part of it is a monosyllable capable of beginning a sentence, or the second part a monosyllable incapable of beginning one.

384. ψόγον—'the blame' of not honouring the brave.

386. ἄγοντες—cf. ἄγων, 369 note. ἡμᾶς—'me only'. Cf. 237 note.

391. ἀλλά—'at any rate'. This use of ἀλλά is due to an ellipse, ὑμεῖς δὲ, εἰ μὴ μόνην με βούλεσθε φονεῦσαι, ἀλλὰ θυγατρὶ συμφονεύσατε.

392. Eur. *Troades* 381, οὐδὲ πρὸς τάφους | ἔσθ' ὅστις αὐτοῖς αἷμα γῇ δωρήσεται. The earth is endowed with life and sense.

πῶμα—the correction of Porson for πόμα of MSS., this not being an Attic form.

394. εἰς, the reading of the best MS., is better than σῆς of most editors. 'We must not add one death to another, would that the obligation even of this death were spared us'. μηδὲ (not οὐδέ) is used because ὠφείλομεν expresses an unattainable wish. The aorist is more usual than the imperfect, and often in the form εἴθ' ὤφελον. Supply προσφέρειν from προσοιστέος.

396. γε (condemned by Hermann) is forcible.

397. 'How? for I am not aware that I have masters'. κεκτημένος—this participle (nom. because it refers to the subject of the clause) is the regular construction after οἶδα and ἐπίσταμαι. Cf. 244 note. δεσπότας—for the strong sense of this word cf. *Hippol.* 88, where the attendant calls Hippolytus ἄναξ, adding θεοὺς γὰρ δεσπότας καλεῖν χρεών, 'for the gods alone may I style lords'.

398. If one could go so far as to declare the verse corrupted by the intrusion of a gloss τῆσδε, the line might be re-written thus:—ὅπως; ὁποῖα κισσὸς ἕξομαι δρυός. 'Dost ask how? like ivy to an oak will I cling.' The τῆσδε would be manifestly understood from θυγατρί in 396. [This is Dr Kennedy's view. Other ways of taking the passage are (1) 'Know that I will cling to her as ivy to an oak', supplying before ὅπως some such word as ἴσθι. (2) A double comparison may be intended, 'I, like ivy, will cling to her as to an oak'.] δρυός—cf. 64 note.

399. οὔκ—'No!' Thus emphatically used accented. ἤν γε—'that is, if'. [Aldus reads οὐ μὴν γε, but οὐ μήν is never immediately followed by γε.]

400. ὡς—'know that'=ἴσθι ὡς. Soph. *Aj.* 39, ὡς ἔστιν ἀνδρὸς τοῦδε τἄργα ταῦτα σοι, 'know that in him thou hast the doer of these deeds'. The phrase is a formula 'fortiter affirmantis' (Elmsley).

401. οὐ μήν—formula of emphatic denial. αὐτοῦ—gen. of place.

[**402—443.** *Polyx.* 'Mother resist not, it is unseemly'. Polyxena exchanges a tearful farewell with her mother and is led off with veiled head by Odysseus.]

402. Λαερτίου—the name of Laertius (father of Odysseus and king of Ithaca) is variously spelt by the tragedians Λαέρτιος, Λάρτιος, Λαέρτης.

403. χάλα—'give way to'. τοκεῦσιν—vague plural alluding to Hecuba, as 404 κρατοῦσι to Odysseus. This plural is often used instead of a definite name which it might be inconvenient to give.

406. πρὸς βίαν—'with violence', so πρὸς ἡδονήν, 'willingly'; πρὸς χάριν, 'pleasingly'; πρὸς τάχος, 'quickly'.

407. ἐκ—'by'.

408. πείσει—future from πάσχω. The form πείσῃ is not

rightly read in Euripides. μὴ σύ γ'—a formula of fond entreaty. Supply from the context some such words as οὕτω ποίησον.

410. προσβαλεῖν—object of δός.

411. Soph. *Aj.* 857, καὶ τὸν διφρευτὴν ἥλιον προσεννέπω, | πανύστατον δὴ κοὔποτ' αὖθις ὕστερον (Ajax's dying speech).

413. δή strengthens τέλος (as πανύστατον in the passage from the *Ajax*). Cf. Eur. *Herakl.* 573, προσειποῦσ' ὕστατον πρόσφθεγμα δή.

414. ἄπειμι—often used as an euphemism for dying: so οἴχομαι.

415. ἡμεῖς—'I', as in 386.

416. ὧν—supply ὑμεναίων from ἀνυμέναιος.

418. ἐκεῖ—a constant euphemism for ἐν Ἅιδου (sc. δόμοις), which here occurs by its side. κείσομαι—especially of lying among the dead. There is some confusion between the body lying in the dead and the spirit in Hades.

419. ποῖ τελευτήσω—'to what end shall I bring my life?' This construction is called *pregnant* = 'whither shall I (carry and) end my life?' Cf. *Troad.* 1029, ἵν' εἰδῇς οἱ τελευτήσω λόγον.

420. πατρὸς οὖσα—gen. of origin, which is taken by εἰμί, γίγνομαι, and πέφυκα. Cf. 380 note.

421. According to Homer these 50 children were those of Priam, 19 (or 38) of them by Hecuba. Verg. *Aen.* 2. 503, *quinquaginta illi thalami spes tanta nepotum.* ἄμμοροι τ.—'bereft of', gen. of separation. [The old reading was ἡμεῖς δὲ πεντήκοντ' ἄμοιροι δὴ τέκνων, a verse which Eur. cannot have written. Cf. 383 n.]

422. σοι—ethic dative. **Hektor**—his eldest son. εἴπω—deliberative conjunctive. Goodwin, § 256.

425. ἀθλία—This is Markland's suggestion for ἀθλίας. Two epithets for τύχης would be very awkward, and the whole sentence would be jerky and uncomfortable.

426. For position of τε cf. 80 n.

427. χαίρουσιν—'others fare well, but this is not thy mother's lot'. Polyxena had said 'farewell', and Hecuba plays upon the words. The same pun is found in Sophokles, Euripides, Plautus, &c. ἔστιν—emphatic, and so accented. τόδε—sc. τὸ χαίρειν. The variant χαρά is clearly an explanatory gloss.

430. θανούσης...σὸν—θαν. agrees with σου supplied from σόν. Cf. Ov. Her. 5. 45, et flesti et nostros vidisti flentis ocellos.

ὄμμα συγκλῄειν—'to shut the eyes', i.e. attend to her at her death. Verg. Aen. 9. 487, nec te tua funera mater | produxi, pressive oculos, aut volnera lavi. [The form -κλῄειν is more Attic than -κλείειν of old editions.]

432. ἀμφιθεὶς κάρα πέπλοις virtually form one word, hence follows the accusative με.

433. ἐκτέτηκα—Contrast this intransitive usage of the 2nd (or strong) perfect with the transitive meaning of ἐκτήκω 434. So ἔαγα='I am broken', from ἄγνυμι, 'I break'; ὄλωλα 'I am destroyed', from ὄλλυμι, 'I destroy'. καρδίαν—acc. of respect or specification. Goodwin, § 160. 1.

435. 'O light! for I may yet invoke thy name, but have no share of thee save for so long as I pass hence to the sword and pyre of Achilles'. [ὄνομα—a plausible suggestion ὄμμα has been made, but ὄνομα is more appropriate, implying that although Polyxena could invoke the name, she could not enjoy the reality.]

438. προλείπω—'I faint'. Cf. Alk. 401, τί δρᾷς; προλείπω. λύεται—'are failing me'. Herakl. 602, ὦ παῖδες, οἰχόμεσθα, λύεται μέλη | λύπῃ. In Attic, λύω, ἔλυον, λύσω, ἔλυσα: but λέλυκα.

441—443. These verses are spurious. For they cannot be spoken by Hecuba, who has fainted; they are more than awkward as beginning a stasimon; they are in themselves feeble.

ὡς—'in this plight', i.e. a slave. [ὡς would =utinam.]

Διοσκόροι—Castor and Pollux were born at a birth with Helen. The form διόσκουροι (whence Latin Dioscūri) is not Attic.

Ἑλένην—There is a play on this word and εἷλε 443 (which =καθεῖλε); cf. αἰνόπαριν 945.

[444—483. First Stasimon, στάσιμον (μέλος), or ode by the entire chorus after taking up their position at the thymele. The term itself appears to involve two notions—that of the chorus in position at the thymele—and that of an ode unbroken by dialogue or anapaests. Cho. 'Ocean breeze, to whose house wilt thou waft me a slave? To Doris, or Phthia, or Delos, or Athens? My city smoulders in ruins, I am a slave'.]

441. ποντιάς—adjectives in -άς are usually (but not of necessity) joined with fem. words. *Phoen.* 1025, φοιτάσι πτεροῖς.

445. ποντοπόρους, θοάς—fixed Epic epithets.

446. ἀκάτους—an exclusively poetical word, the usual prose equivalent being ναῦς, and ἀκάτιον is a mere skiff.

447. πορεύω—'I make to go', πορεύομαι—'I go'.

448. τῷ; = τίνι; κτηθεῖσα—rarely used passive as here.

450. Δωρὶς αἶα—the Peloponnese.

451. Phthia—in Thessaly.

453. ὑδάτων πατέρα—So Eur. *Med.* 573 praises the Haliakmon.

454. Apidanus—a tributary of the Peneus, and one of the few rivers, says Herodotus 7. 196, which Xerxes did not drink dry. γύας—restored by Hermann for the gloss πέδια.

455. νάσων—connected with ποῖ, 447.

456. πεμπομέναν—governed by πορεύσεις, 447.

458. The palm is said to have been first born at Delos, because it gained its eminence among trees from its connection with Apollo who was there born. δῖος is often used of things glorious [from same root as *dies, divus*, &c.], but the epithet here alludes probably to the fact that Latona's travail brought forth gods, viz. Apollo and Artemis [or that they were the children of Zeus]. Delos was in Olympiad 88. 3 (B.C. 426, cf. Thuc. 3. 104) solemnly purified by the Athenians. Plutarch tells us that Nikias, the Athenian general, took pains to make this celebration a success by providing splendid chorus and uniting Delos to the islet of Rheneia. [This is one of the contemporary allusions which help to fix the date of the play.]

465. ἄμπυξ—'a head-band', so called because it ἀμπέχει (surrounds) the hair.

466. Παλλάδος πόλις—Athens.

467. θεᾶς ναίουσ'—Nauck's emendation for the unmetrical 'Αθαναίας.

καλλιδίφρου—Athene is represented in her chariot fighting against the Titans. Compounds of καλ- are formed from the subst. κάλλος, not the adj. καλός. [Porson reads καλλιδίφροι', but the elision is impossible.]

468. πέπλος—the sacred vestment of Athene on which was depicted the goddess doing battle with the giants. It was carried

in solemn procession at the greater Panathenaea once every Olympiad.

470. δαιδαλεαῖσι—used by Homer of stone or metal working, but here referring clearly to embroidery. ' Shall I yoke?' of course means 'shall I represent by embroidery the yoking of the steeds?'

471. ἀνθόκροκος—perhaps merely variegated (ἄνθος) and saffron-coloured (κρόκος). πήνη—'thread', pl. 'the web', Latin *tela.* From the same root comes the Latin *pannus,* a patch.

472. **Titans**—the sons of Ouranos and Gaia, who rebelled against Zeus after he had conquered them and Kronos their king. Later poets add largely to their numbers, Aeschylus including Prometheus, while in the Latin poets *Titan* = the sun-god.

473. τὰν = ἥν. ἀμφιπύρῳ—used by Sophokles of Artemis holding torches in both hands.

475. τεκέων—Goodwin, § 173. 3.

478. δορίκτητος Ἀργείων—a possessive genitive.

480. κέκλημαι—more forcible than εἰμί, which it often means. A Greek hated the *name* as much as the reality of slavery. Cf. 552.

482. See the translation of the entire ode. The old translation was 'having left Asia the handmaid of Europe, having by exchange become the bride of Hades' (which of course was absurd, as they had not to die): or 'having changed death's chambers (for slavery)', which is harsh. But the fatal objection brought forward by Hartung is that Eur. often uses θέραπνα in the sense of 'a habitation', never in that of 'a handmaid', which would be θεράπαινα.

"Breeze, ocean breeze, that carriest swift sea-bound barques o'er the swelling flood, whither wilt thou waft me the forlorn one? To whose house gotten for a slave shall I come? Shall it be to a harbour in the land of Doris, or of Phthia, where they say that Apidanus, father of fairest waters, fattens the furrows? Or to what isle wilt thou bring me, hapless one, sped by the sea-sweeping oar, spending a piteous life in the house,—to that one where the palm there first created and the bay tree raised their sacred shoots for dear Leto, to grace her divine travail? And shall I praise with Delian maidens the golden fillet and bow of Artemis? Or shall I, dwelling in the city of Pallas of the fair chariot, yoke young steeds on her saffron robe, embroidering them on the rich wrought flower-decked web, or [embroidering] the race of the Titans which Zeus, Kronos' son, with flashing flame hushes to rest? Woe is me for my children, for my fathers, for my country, which, smoke-defiled, lies in ruin won by the Argives' spear. And I in a strange land am called a slave, having left Asia and taken in exchange an abode in Europe (which is to me) the bridal-chamber of Hades."

[484—517. *Enter Talthybius.* Is there a god in heaven, or does chance rule all? Yonder lies one erewhile a queen, now a wretched slave. Lady, arise. *Hecuba.* Who art thou? *T.* I am Talthybius, sent by Agamemnon for thee. *H.* What? Am I too to die? Blessed news! *T.* Nay, thou art to bury thy daughter. *H.* Tell me how ye did the cruel deed.]

484. δή ποτε (to be written separately)—'lately'. But Pflugk prefers to give δή the sense which it has with superlatives.

485. ἐξεύροιμι ἄν—a modified future, a tense avoided by the Greeks where possible, an example of their softening down.

486. νῶτ' ἔχουσα—Hecuba is lying huddled up. The position has been objected to as undignified, but it is for this very reason that Euripides introduces it to heighten the pity of the audience.

488. 'Zeus, what am I to say? that thou regardest men or that they have idly and to no purpose this false opinion, thinking that there is a race of gods, whereas chance watches over all things among mortals'. The change of subject is harsh, that of ὁρᾶν being σέ, that of κεκτῆσθαι being ἀνθρώπους. ἄλλως μ. ψ.—This piling up of the agony is quite in the tragic vein, and v. 490, condemned by several editors, appears quite genuine. δοκοῦντας—epexegetic of τήνδε δόξαν. Euripides was a pupil of the great philosopher Anaxagoras and averse to popular mythology, but Aristophanes' strictures on him are unjust.

492. ἥδε—pointing at her.

494. πᾶσ' ἀνέστηκεν—'is utterly destroyed'. The position of πᾶσα shows that it closely qualifies ἀνέστηκεν. [Remember that the present, imperfect, future and 1st aorist of ἵστημι and its compounds are transitive, the rest intransitive.]

495. αὐτή—'and *she*', the correction of Elmsley for αὕτη.

496. κεῖται—'is grovelling', the word used of Achilles in his rage and grief after the taking away of Briseis (*Il.* 2. 688), of Ajax when he recovered his senses and realised his shame (Soph. *Aj.* 206). κόνει φύρ.—lit. 'caking with dust her head', always a sign of mourning. Cf. Catullus 64. 224, *canitiem terra atque infuso pulvere foedans.*

497. Talthybius means 'I have but little life left to enjoy, (this little being on that account the more precious,) but I would surrender that', &c.

498. περιπίπτω—usually of 'coming across' a disaster.

500. παλ-λευκον—a favourite compound with Euripides, e.g. 196, 212, 411, 528, 657, 667.

501. τίς οὗτος οὐκ ἐᾷς—Hecuba, looking up for the first time, 'Who art thou that sufferest me not, &c.?' For construction cf. Hom. *Il.* 10, 82, τίς δ' οὗτος κατὰ νῆας ἀνὰ στράτον ἔρχεαι οἶος; σῶμα τοὐμόν—a periphrasis for ἐμέ.

502. He ought to have respected her grief.

503. Δαναϊδῶν—Peoples are often designated by patronymics, so *Dardanidae, Aeneadae.*

504. πέμψαντος—supply ἐμέ. μέτα—i.e. μεταπέμψαντος. This *cutting* words asunder is called tmesis.

506. δοκοῦν—'because it is decided', acc. abs. Cf. 121 n. We should have expected the aorist δόξαν: cf. ἄγων, 369 note.

507. ἐγκονέω—said to be connected with κόνις = 'raise dust by bustling'. ἡγοῦ μοι—cf. 383 note.

509. μετασείχων—'seeking for thee', not 'to seek for thee', which would be future. For the force of μετά in composition cf. 213 note.

510. Ἀτρεῖδαι—the two sons of Atreus, Agamemnon king of Mykenae, and Menelaüs king of Sparta. λ. Ἀχαιϊκὸς—a democratic anachronism. In those early times the people would have little voice in the matter.

511. τί λέξεις;—'what art thou about to say?' Hecuba fears still worse remains to hear, it is incorrect therefore to say that it = τί λέγεις;

ἄρα—'it would seem', the lightest of the inferential particles. ὡς θανουμένους—'for death'. ὡς with the future participle gives the avowed cause whether really meant or not.

514. τὸ ἐπί σε—'with regard to thee' (Polyxena). Many editors have considered that σ'=σοί, *which however never suffers elision,* and would give a wrong sense, 'as far as depends upon thee'.

ἡμεῖς—cf. 386 note. Notice how she becomes singular and feminine at the same time.

515. πῶς καί;—'how in fact?' (1) τίς (ποῖ, ποῦ, ποῖος, πῶς) καί asks for real information, the καί adding vigour=τίς δή. Cf. 1064. (2) καί τίς (ποῖ, ποῦ, ποῖος, πῶς) is a formula of contradiction, the question being a sneering one. νιν=αὐτήν. μιν, a corresponding dialectical form, is not found in tragedy. 'How in fact did ye despatch her? with reverence, or came ye to the dread deed butchering her as a foe?'

[518—582. *Talthybius.* All the Greek host were in attendance. Neoptolemus set the maid on the tomb, poured a libation, and prayed for a safe return. The maiden at her prayer was unhanded that she a princess might die free: then tearing open her dress she bade Neoptolemus strike where he would. The blow fell; and scarce had she fallen when all vied to do her honour in collecting wood for the pyre or leaves to cover her withal, each urging his neighbour to activity in the work.]

518. 'Lady, thou wouldst have me take a double meed of tears in pity for thy daughter: for now in relating the evil tale shall I moisten this eye even as at the tomb when she was dying'. After πρὸς τάφῳ τε supply ἔτεγξα. ὤλλυτο—note the tense.

521. πᾶς...πλήρης—emphatic repetition, cf. 489 note.

522. ἐπὶ σφαγάς—'for the slaying of the maiden'. ἐπί (with acc.) denoting the direction of their attention.

523. χερὸς—'by the hand'. Goodwin, § 171.

524. ἔστησε—'set her'. ἐπ' ἄκρ. χωμ.—This was necessary: cf. Helen's directions to Elektra, *Or.* 116, καὶ στᾶσ' ἐπ' ἄκρου χώματος λέξον τάδε. πέλας δ' ἐγώ—sc. ἔστην.

525. 'And picked young men chosen from the Achaeans attended in order to restrain with their hands thy maiden's struggling'. λεκτοί and ἔκκριτοι together are awkward. μόσχου—cf. 144.

528. αἴρει—'raises on high'. [This is the reading of the best MS. and one other. All the rest read ἔρρει, but apart from the fact that the time for pouring the libation has not yet come, ῥεῖν χοάs, 'to pour libations ', is not Greek. A river might well enough be said ῥεῖν γάλα, 'to flow with milk ', but to say that a man 'flows libations' is quite another thing.]

529. σημαίνει—'signifies ', by a sign, in order to avoid ill-omened words which might mar the whole sacrifice: cf. εὔφημα φωνεῖν =silere.

531. παραστάς—'having stood forth ', Aristoph. *Knights,* 508, πρὸs τὸ θέατρον παραβῆναι. σῖγα—adv. σίγᾱ—imper. of σιγάω.

533. νήνεμον—'And I hushed the crowd into quiet', proleptic. The derivation is νή, ἄνεμος, cf. νώνυμος=νή, ὄνομα.

534. πατήρ—nominative for vocative as usual in oxytone words.

537. ἀκραιφνὲς—'virgin ', lit. 'undefiled', in sense qualifying κόρηs. Cf. *Iph. Aul.* 1574, ἄχραντον αἷμα καλλιπαρθένου δέρηs.

538. ' Show thyself kindly to us '.

539. λῦσαι—object of δόs. Note the change of construction, after δὸs ἡμῖν comes an accusative and infinitive clause.

χαλινωτήρια—sc. ὅπλα, metaphor from horses, would in prose be πρυμνήσια. As soon as a breeze sprang up these ropes from stern to shore would be cut. πρύμνας κ. χαλ.— a kind of hendiadys.

541. νόστου—from which Achilles' anger had debarred them, 113.

542. ἐπ-ηύξατο—'prayed after him ', so ἐπ-ᾴδειν.

543. ' Then by its handle he seized a knife gilt all over and was in act to draw it forth from its sheath '. κώπης— 523 n.

546. ἐφράσθη—'she noted it', passive in form, but =ἐφράσατο.

547. ' You have destroyed my city, at least let *me* die free '.

552. κεκλῆσθαι αἰσχύνομαι—The infinitive is used when a feeling of shame prevents a person from acting, the participle when that which a person does causes him shame. So αἰσχύνομαι λέγειν, 'I am ashamed to speak and so do not'; αἰσχύνομαι λέγων, ' I speak but am ashamed of it '.

553. ἐπερρόθησαν—a metaphor from the grating of the shingle on the beach when the sea is strong.

[555, 6. οἱ δ' ὡς...ἦν κράτος—probably an interpolation based upon the Homeric οὗ κράτος ἐστὶ μέγιστον, being tame, and οὗπερ misplaced.]

558. 'She seized her robes and rent them from the top of the shoulder to the middle of the waist by the navel'.

560. Every man in the audience could recall some exquisite statue. The comparison was frequent. Plato *Charmid.* 154 c, ἀλλὰ πάντες ὥσπερ ἄγαλμα ἐθεῶντο αὐτόν. Aesch. *Ag.* 242, πρέπουσα ὡς ἐν γραφαῖς.

562. τλημονέστατον—'bravest'. According to their context, words from root ΤΛΑ have an active or passive meaning.

564. παῖσον—'strike now'. More emphatic than παῖε would have been.

564. αὐχήν—'neck'.

565. λαιμός—'throat', 'gullet'.

566. Cf. Shakespeare, *Measure for Measure*, Act 2, Sc. 1, 'at war 'twixt will and will not'.

567. 'Cuts with his steel the channels of her breath', i. e. her windpipe. Southey's 'the tube which draws the breath of life'.

568. κρουνοί—sc. αἵματος. καὶ θν. ὅμως—a strong expression; such thoughts would not be expected in death.

569. εὐσχήμως—ἅπαξ λεγ. formed from εὐσχημος. Cf. Ovid, *Fasti* 2. 833, *tum quoque iam moriens ne non procumbat honeste | respicit: haec etiam cura cadentis erat.*

570. Cobet objects to the line as marring the grace of the passage. It is however copied by Ovid, *M.* 13. 479, *tum quoque cura fuit partes velare tegendas, | cum caderet, castique decus servare pudoris.*

κρύπτειν takes two accusatives, Goodwin, § 164.

571. ἀφῆκε πν.—'had given up the ghost', the Greek idiom takes the aorist where we prefer the pluperfect.

574. φύλλοις ἔβ.—'covered with leaves'. φυλλοβολία, decking with leaves, whether in life for having won in the games, or after death in token of love or respect. οἱ δὲ πλ.— 'while others heap up the funeral pile, bringing pine logs'. κορμός—short, thick log [κείρω, 'lop'].

NOTES.

576. τοιαδ' ἤκουεν κακά—'was addressed with such reproaches as these'. Cf. *Alk.* 704, εἰ δ' ἡμᾶς κακῶς | ἐρεῖς, ἀκούσει πολλὰ κού ψευδῆ κακά. Hor. *Sat.* 2. 6. 20, *matutine pater, seu Iane libentior audis.*

578. Thuc. 3. 58 (speech of the Plataeans). 'Look at the sepulchres of your fathers, whom slain by Medes and buried in our land, we were wont yearly to honour at the public expense *with garments* and all other due rites'. Verg. *Aen.* 6. 221, *purpureasque super vestes, velamina nota,* | *coniciunt.*

579. εἱ—from εἰμι, *ibo,* περισσά—neut. pl. used adverbially.

580. λέγω is Heath's correction of the MS. readings λέγον or λέγων, from which no satisfactory meaning can be got.

[583—628. *Cho.* There is a doom of the gods against the house of Priam. *Hecuba.* Daughter, thy nobleness softens my sorrow at thy fate. Is virtue inborn or can it be taught? Bid the Greeks not touch my daughter's corpse. Aged handmaid, go to the sea to fetch some lustral water, I will go to the tents to see if there be aught to honour the dead withal.]

583. ἐπέζεσε—'hath surged up against'. English has to change both tense and metaphor, as we do not speak of evil boiling over against us. Πριαμίδαις—'the house of Priam': patronymics are often loosely used.

584. ἀναγκαῖον θεῶν—'a doom of the gods'. Cf. Soph. *Aj.* 485, τῆς ἀναγκαίας τύχης, 'the fate-doomed lot.' *Il.* 16. 836, ἦμαρ ἀναγκαῖον, 'the day of doom '.

586. ἅψωμαι—'touch upon'.

587. παρακαλεῖ—'calls me aside', a frequent meaning of παρά in composition.

588. διάδοχος κ. κ.—'adding new in succession to former evils'. *Suppl.* 71, ἀγὼν ὅδ' ἄλλος ἔρχεται γόων γόοις | διάδοχος.

589. 'And now I could not wipe out thy fate from my heart so far as not to lament it'. The order is rather inverted.

591. τὸ λίαν—'excess', i.e. of grief. It is worthy of note how the Greeks utilised their neuter; here supply στένειν from the context.

592. 'Is it not then strange that poor soil if it meet with a good season at the hand of the gods brings forth corn

abundantly, and fruitful soil, should it miss what it ought to have met with, gives a poor crop; while in men at all times the corrupt is nothing but bad, and the noble noble, nor through mishap does he spoil his nature, but is ever excellent?'

595. ἀνθρώποις—'as regards men', usually ἐν ἀνθρώποις. [Some editors read ἐν βροτοῖς by conjecture.]

598. διέφθειρε—Gnomic aorist used to express a habit. Cf. Eur. *Suppl.* 227, ὁ θεὸς—διώλεσεν, 'is wont to destroy'. Hor. *Od.* 1. 34, *Fortuna sustulit.* Goodwin, § 205. [Here as elsewhere, Eur. sins against good taste in putting a rhetorical harangue on the subject εἰ διδακτὸν ἡ ἀρετή (a question discussed in the *Meno* of Plato, the decision being that it could if there were competent teachers) into the mouth of a mother mourning over the loss of her daughter.]

599. 'Is it the parents who make the difference or the bringing up?' The article before τεκόντες does duty also for τροφαί. [Or 'have the parents more weight *than*' &c. The construction διαφέρω ἤ is found.]

600. 'Yet even to have been well brought up involves teaching of good'. γε μέντοι often come together in Sophokles and Euripides, γέ τοι τι (of some editions) never.

602. κανόνι τοῦ καλοῦ—'a standard of right'. μαθών— 'having learnt it'. [Porson suggests μετρῶν, 'estimating it', which appears unnecessary.]

603. i.e. 'these things will bring me no surcease of sorrow'.

604. σὺ δ'—spoken to Talthybius; 'take to the A. this message, that they'.

605. μοι—Ethic dative, G. § 184. 3, note 2. εἴργειν— 'shut out', εἵργειν, 'shut in', acc. to Eustathius [fl. A.D. 1150] followed by Lobeck, &c. Others, however, e.g. Bekker, always read εἴργειν in Attic.

606. τῆς παιδὸς—gen. of separation after εἴργειν. G. § 174.

τοι—the usual particle in gnomes and so preferable to γάρ, which has also less MS. authority. μυρίῳ—'countless', akin to Lat. *multus.*

607. 'The lawlessness of the sailors blazes fiercer than fire'. Euripides gives a side-blow at democracy which was intimately connected with the sea. Aristotle talks of the ναυτικὸς ὄχλος as the scum of the population, *Pol.* 7. 5. κρείσσων

— cf. Soph. *Oed. Tyr.* 176, κρεῖσσον ἀμαιμακέτου πυρός, 'more quick than furious fire'.

608. μὴ—not οὐ, because it supplies a reason, *qui non faciat.*

610. ποντίας ἁλός—'some salt sea water', partitive gen.

611. After death an obol (about three-halfpence) was put in the mouth as ferry money for Charon; then the body was *washed*, anointed and dressed in a fine robe by the female attendants.

612. Polyxena was betrothed to Achilles and so not a παρθένος: but not a bride, and so ἄνυμφος. There is probably a side reference of betrothal to Hades. [This placing side by side of opposite words is called *oxymöron:* cf. Tennyson, 'His honour rooted in dishonour stood, and faith unfaithful kept him falsely true'.]

613. προθῶμαι—'lay out'. When decorated (611 n.) the corpse was *laid out* on a bed, often out of doors, the object of this formal πρόθεσις being to make sure that there had been no foul play and that death had really taken place. After the body had lain there for a day (i.e. 48 hours after death) burial took place.

'According to her deserts how can I? I cannot; but (so will I do it) as I am able'. She will consult not her wishes but her means.

614. τί γὰρ πάθω;—'what must I content myself with?' differs from τί γὰρ δρῶ in containing an idea of circumstances out of her control.

615. κόσμον—'decorations'.

616. ἔσω—'within', a sense usually borne by ἐντός.

617. τ. νεωστὶ δεσπότας—'our lately acquired masters'. For -τι cf. μεγαλωστί, ὀνομαστί. Goodwin, § 129. 18.

618. κλέμμα—a curious word for Hecuba to use, even though all they had belonged to their masters. Nauck suggests λεῖμμα, 'remnant', or κτῆμα, 'possession'.

619. ὦ σχήματ' οἴκων—'O stately halls'. The same periphrasis occurs *Alk.* 911.

620. 'O Priam, possessor of many and most excellent things, most blessed in thy children'. [Kirchhoff reads with the best MS. ὦ πλ. ἔχων κ. κεὐτεκνώτατε. Porson, ὦ πλ. ἔχων,

κάλλιστά τ' εὐτεκνώτατε, joining the two superlatives, with which cf. μέγιστον ἐχθίστη *Med.* 1323, *maxime liberalissima* Cicero, *most highest* Ps. xxi. 7 (P. Bk.).]

622. ὡς—'how'. εἰς τὸ μηδὲν—'to nought', also without the article. Soph. *El.* 1000, κἀπὶ μηδὲν ἔρχεται.

623. 'Robbed of our former pride; and forsooth are puffed up', &c.

εἶτα δῆτα—strongly sarcastic. ὀγκούμεθα—Aristoph. *Wasps* 1024, ὀγκῶσαι τὸ φρόνημα.

626. 'Yet they (wealth and honour) are but nothing, merely'.

628. 'That man is happiest who day by day chances upon no ill'. Ennius, quoted by Cic. *de Fin.* 2. 13, *nimium bonist | cui nil malist.* Plato, *Philebus* 43 D, 'Is then the absence of pain the same as pleasure?' κατ' ἦμαρ—also καθ' ἡμέραν.

[629—656. **Second Stasimon** (cf. 444 note). 'O the fatal pine with which Paris made him a ship in which to sail to Helen's bed. Then began woe for Ilion, ay and for many a Spartan maid who mourning tears her cheek'. With this chorus may be compared Horace, *Odes* 1. 15.]

629. χρῆν=ἐχρῆν: noticeable as one of the very few words which in Attic can drop their augment.

631. **Ida**—a range in Mysia, S.E. of Troy, from which in Homer the gods watched the Trojan war. 'Many fountained Ida' was famed for the 'dark tall pines that plumed the craggy ledge | high over the blue gorge' (Tennyson, *Oenone*). So Aytoun, 'On the holy mount of Ida | where the pine and cypress grow'.

632. 'Αλέξανδρος—i.e. Paris; his usual name in Homer. The accounts of him are widely inconsistent. On the one hand he is the valiant 'protector of men' ('Αλέξ-ανδρος), a kind of Romulus among the shepherds; on the other (e.g. in Horace, *Od.* 1. 15) the effeminate adulterer.

633. ἐτάμεθ'=ἐτάμετο from τέμνω.

ἐπ' οἶδμα—the acc. implies going on to and sailing on the swelling flood.

635. 'Ελένη—wife of Menelaus, king of Sparta. Cf. Tennyson's *Dream of Fair Women*, 'At length I saw a lady within call, | stiller than chiselled marble, standing there; | a daughter

of the gods divinely tall, | and most divinely fair. | Her love-
liness with shame and with surprise | froze my swift speech:
she turning on my face | the star-like sorrows of immortal
eyes, | spoke slowly in her place. | I had great beauty; ask
thou not my name: | no one can be more wise than destiny: |
many drew swords. I died. Where'er I came | I brought
calamity'.

636. τὰν = ἦν.

639. ἀνάγκαι—'dooms' of the gods, especially slavery.
Cf. ἀναγκαῖον θεῶν, 584 note.

640. κοινὸν...ἰδίας—one man's sin, many men's suffering.
The antithesis is rhetorical and occurs again 902, 3. κοινὸν in
grammar qualifies κακόν, in sense also συμφορά.

641. Σιμόεις—contracted Σιμοῦς, rises in Gargarus, a peak
of Ida, and flows N.W. into the Hellespont (Dardanelles).

643. ἄλλων—'strangers', those who were other than
Trojans. [Or='from the gods'.]

644. Eris, not being invited to the wedding of Thetis and
Peleus, avenged herself by casting a golden apple among the
goddesses with this inscription, 'For the fairest'. Hera, Atheno
and Aphrodite each claimed it, and the case was put before the
young herdsman Paris, who adjudged it to Aphrodite; with
what fatal result is known to all.

ἂν (ā) κρ. παῖδας—ἂν = ἦν is cognate acc. [or the double
accusative is similar to Aesch. *Ag.* 813—5, θεοὶ...Ἰλίου φθορὰς...
ψήφους ἔθεντο.]

645. μακάρων παῖδας—cf. a similar circumlocution, 930,
παῖδες Ἑλλάνων.

647. ἐπὶ δορὶ—'with the outcome of the spear', &c. Cf.
Herc. Fur. 881, ἐπὶ λώβᾳ. Aesch. *Sept.* 878, δόμων ἐπὶ λύμῃ. 822.

649. τις—collective.

650. Eurotas—the river on which Sparta stood: note the
alliteration in εὔροον Εὐρώταν.

651. Λάκαινα—fem. of Λάκων: so λέων, λέαινα· θεράπων,
θεράπαινα. [An allusion is very possibly meant to be understood to the capture of 292 Spartan hoplites at Sphakteria, 120
of them of the highest birth, by the Athenians. This brilliant
exploit was due to Demosthenes, B.C. 425. Cf. Thuc. 4. 1—41.]

655. δρύπτω—√δρυφ. Cf. δρέπω, 'I pluck'.

'To me was it fated that calamity, to me was it fated that
suffering should come, when first Alexandros hewed him the
pine-log of Ida to sail o'er the ocean wave to the bed of Helen,.
fairest of all on whom doth shine the golden sun. For toils
and dooms stronger than toils encircle us. And a common
evil sprung from one man's folly came fraught with death to
the land of Simois, and calamity from strangers. And the strife
was decided in which on Ida the herdsman judged the three
daughters of the blessed gods with the outcome of war and of
slaughter and of the ruin of my dwellings. And at home
beside the fair-flowing Eurotas there weeps many a Laconian
maid all bathed in tears; and the mother, her children dead,
lays hand on her hoary head, dabbling her finger-nail in the
bloody rendings of her cheek'.

658—904. Third Episode. [The discovery of the body of
the murdered Polydorus. Agam. enters to enquire the reason
of Hecuba's delay in burying her daughter, and H.; after a long
debate in her mind, appeals to him on behalf of her son for
vengeance upon the treacherous prince of Thrace. Agam.
demurs at first, half afraid of the view which the Greek army
might take of any action against their ally; H. pleads that at
any rate he will prevent any rescue, and she will take the
vengeance into her own hands.]

[658—725. Enter an aged female attendant, who had gore
to fetch water to wash Polyx.'s body, with the corpse of Polydorus. H., supposing it to be Polyx.'s, asks why it has been
brought. As she receives no answer, her idea is that it may be
Kasandra's. The body is uncovered, and H., in her lament,
lets fall an expression which provokes the question, 'Did you
know of this before?' She goes on to ask how and in what
state the corpse was found, and cries that her visions have
proved true. Then the Chor. asks, 'Can your wisdom of dreams
tell the murderer?' 'Yes', H. at once replies, 'it is the Thracian
prince', and she bursts into an indignant protest against the
violation of hospitality and the sin of mutilation.]

659. θῆλυν σπορ.—cf. τὸ θῆλυ γένος, 885. Adjectives in
-υς are often of only two terminations. Ἥρη θῆλυς ἐοῦσα, Il.
ἡδὺς ἀϋτμή, Odys., ἡμίσεος ἡμέρας, Thuc.

660. κακοῖς ἵν'—'in sorrows, wherein'. Herm.'s correction
for the abrupt κακοῖσιν, which is a dative of reference, denoting
the aspect in which the subject shows itself, the *acc.* of ref.
being used to denote a part of the subject itself. στέφανον—

'prize' (lit. garland of the victor at games). Cf. Wordsworth, *Sonnets,*

> ' "*Most wretched one!*"
> Who chose his epitaph? Himself alone
> Could thus have dared the grave to agitate
> And claim among the dead this *awful crown!*'

661. 'How! wretch, with thy ill-tongued clamour! for thy doleful messages are never quiet.' For construction cf. 211, 783. The gen. is after the analogy of the gen. of ref. with verbs of emotion.

664. εὔφημ. στόμα—'to have good-omened words in their mouth'. στόμ. is acc. of ref.: the phrase, like *favete linguis*, comes to mean silence, as though abstinence from speech were the best form of good-omened talk.

665. δόμ. ὕπερ—'from within'. MSS. vary between this (which Schol. interprets ἐπέκεινα) and ὕπο and ἄπο. There is also a conjecture πάρος. See 53 n.

668. 'No more thou livest, though thou seest the light'. This is justified by the punctuation, and is more vigorous than εἰ βλέπουσα=βλέπεις. Cf. Tennyson, 'in more of life true life no more'.

670. 'Thou sayest nothing new, but thy reproach has fallen on one who knows'. The plural is used rather vaguely. H. thinks that the attendant alludes to the death of Polyxena.

672. 'Whose burial was reported as being busily prepared at the hand of all the Achaeans'. ἀπηγγέλθη—verbs seldom have more than one aor. in regular use. ἀπηγγέλη, which some MSS. read in Eur., is not an Attic form. τάφος nearly=ταφή. διὰ χερὸς=*per*. σπουδ. ἔχειν = σπουδάζεσθαι.

674. 'She knows nothing [spoken aside], but mourns, woe's me, for Polyxena'. μοι—Eth. dat.

676. μῶν (μή, οὖν)—like *num*, expects answer 'no'. 'Surely thou art not?'

677. Κασ. κάρα—an expansion of Κασάνδραν like *caput* in Lat. for 'person': often regard or affection is expressed, as ὦ κασίγνητον κάρα 'dear brother'. See 724 n.

678. 'Thy loud lament is for one who lives'. λάσκω— only used in poetry and always of loud ringing or crashing or tearing sound; it implies therefore *loud* talking. For the turn

of the phr. equiv. to περί with a gen. cf. *Alk.* 141, καὶ ζῶσαν εἰπεῖν καὶ θανοῦσαν ἔστι σοι.

679. **γυμνωθὲν**—The attendant *uncovers* the corpse; that it was not naked we see from 734.

680. **εἰ**—'whether', i.e. 'to see if'. **ἐλπ.**—'expectations', like *spes* sometimes in Lat.

682. **οἴκοις**—*domi*, poetic dat. of place. Goodwin, § 190.

683. **οὐκέτ' εἰμὶ δή**—'now is my life o'er'.

685—7. 'I begin a frenzied strain with recent knowledge of woes sent by an avenger'. **κατάρχ.**—usually with gen., has acc. also in *Or.* 960, κατάρχομαι στεναγμόν. **ἀλάστ.** (ἀ, √λαθ)— one who does not forget wrong, and so an avenging deity, used with and without δαίμων. The ref. here is a general one, and not to the ghost of Polydorus. **κακῶν** (for which νέον is conjectured by Pors.)—is gen. of object after adjective compounded with a trans. verb. So 235, καρδίας δηκτήρια = ἃ δάκνει τὴν καρδίαν.

688. **γάρ**—'why?' 'what?' Lat. *quid enim*.

691. 'No day shall stay me from my groans and tears'. This old variant is adopted by Matthiae, who also reads ἦμαρ ἐμ'. If the adjectives be read in the nom. the force of ἐπισχήσει will be 'come upon me', 'dawn'.

696. **θνήσκεις** = ἔθανες. **κεῖσαι**—so *iaceo*. Ov. *Her.* 3. 106, *qui bene pro patria cum patriaque iacent*.

698. **νιν**—for acc. see 51 n.

699. 'A waif upon the level sand, a victim of the murderous spear'. **πέσημα** exactly = *cadaver;* **λευρᾷ**—connected with λεῖος, *lēvis*, Engl. *level*.

701. 'Cast him up from the sea'. Hdt. 1. 24, τὸν δὲ δελφῖνα λέγουσι ὑπολαβόντα ἐξενεῖκαι ἐπὶ Ταίναρον.

702. **ἔμαθον**—'I perceive'. **παρέβα**—'went by', and so 'escaped'.

706. **ἅν** refers back to ὄψιν.

708. **Διὸς ἐν φάει**—'light of day'. Cf. Hor. *sub Iove, sub divo*; 458 n.

709. **ὀνειρόφρων**—'by thy dream-wisdom', with a touch of sarcasm.

711. ἵν'—'with whom' [or ' where', for Thrace is suggested by the word Θρήκιος, as in *Andr.* 652, οὖσαν μὲν 'Ηπειρῶτιν, οὗ (= ἐν 'Ηπείρῳ)].

712. 'Alas, what art thou about to say?' ἔχῃ—so best MSS. See 27 n. The variant ἔχοι would leave the permanence of the result uncertain.

714. ἀνωνόμ.—'a deed without a name', Shakespeare, *Macbeth.*

715. οὐδ' ἀνεκτά—'and not to be borne'. A hint at vengeance. ποῦ δίκ. ξένων;—'where is the sense of right towards guests?' [or 'sense of right in hosts'], according as we consider ξένων obj. or subj. gen.

716. 'O most accursed of men, how hast thou hacked' [or 'mutilated']. A partitive gen. with positive adj. often virtually equals a superl. *Alk.* 472, ὦ φίλα γυναικῶν.

720. ᾠκτίσω—So the two best MSS., others ᾤκτισας.

722. 'Whoever he be that presses on thee'. i.e. the ἀλάστωρ.

724. 'However, since I see the form of Agam.', &c. ἀλλὰ γάρ—often separated by one word when a new comer is announced, e.g. Soph. *Ant.* 155, ἀλλ' ὅδε γὰρ δὴ βασιλεύς...χωρεῖ. 'Αγαμ. δέμας, so Or., 'Ερμιόνης δέμας='Ερμιόνην. *Iph. Aul.*, τοὐμὸν δέμας=ἐμέ: but δέμας also has a special force like Lat. idiom used six times in Verg. (virum) *corpora.* See 677 n.

[726—785. Agam. appears and chides H. for her delay in burying her daughter; he sees the body lying and asks what Trojan it is. Then H. debates in a long 'aside' whether she shall tell Agam. and ask his help, without which she can effect nothing—or bear her troubles in silence. She decides to speak. Agam. asks if she seeks a life of freedom. 'No', answers she, 'I could live a slave all my life for vengeance sake'. She then points to the body and tells him it is her son's, who was sent to Polymestor's care.]

726. μέλλ.—'delayest'.

727. 'On such terms as T. made known to me, that no Argive should lay hand on thy maid'. See 604.

729. μὲν οὖν—'well then'. εἰῶμεν...ἐψαύομεν—This is the excellent conj. of Nauck; it gets rid of the final cretic in ψαύομεν, and the addition of the impf. for ἐῶμεν makes the grammar more consistent.

731. 'I have come therefore (δὲ) to fetch thee away; for matters yonder have been well done, if aught of these things be right'. Gk. καλὸν approaches our sense of 'duty'. ἐστὶν καλῶς —not so common as ἔχειν in this conn., but cf. 532. Soph. *Ant.* 637 (MS. reading), ἀξίως ἔσται. *Hel.* 1293, καλῶς ἂν εἴη.

733. ἔα—'ha'.

734. 'For that he is not an Argive'. 'Αργεῖον—this is nearest to reading of best MS. 'Αργεῖοι, which can only be rendered 'his non-Argive dress'. There is a variant 'Αργείων 'one of the Argives', like *Iph. T.* 1207, σῶν τέ μοι σύμπεμπ' ὀπαδῶν.

736. H. speaks *aside* to 752. Agam. is meanwhile amazed, then angry at it. 'O thou poor Hecuba—ay, I speak of myself when I speak of thee—what shall I do?' δράσω follows the sense rather than the strict grammar, δράσεις would have been more natural. [The Schol. and Herm. wrongly thought that δύστην' was an appeal to Polydorus, comparing *Or.* 553, ἐμαυτὸν, ἣν λέγω | κακῶς ἐκείνην, ἐξερῶ.]

737, 8, προσπέσω...φέρω—conj. delib.

739. 'Having turned thy back upon my face'.

740. 'But dost not state the fact, who this is'. ὅστις would be more regular. δύρει—The υ is long, and so the reading ὀδύρει cannot stand. We find kindred forms μόργυμι, ὀμόργνυμι, κέλλω, ὀκέλλω, κ.τ.λ.

742. ἄν...ἄν—The double ἄν (read by the best MSS.) is by some edds. considered too emphatic in so short a sentence, and they consequently omit the last, or, with Brunck, change the first into αὖ. Herm. explains by καὶ πρὸς ἂν ἀλγήσαιμεν ἄν, but ἄν can qualify only verbs.

743. 'Know that I am not'. τοι, sententious, as usual.

744. ὁδόν—'drift'. The metaphor is more drawn out Soph. *O. T.* 68, πολλὰς δ' ὁδοὺς ἐλθόντα φροντίδος πλάνοις.

745. 'Do I take count of his feelings too much by the standard of enmity, while enemy he is not?' γε and ἐκ both add emphasis. Nauck conjectures ἆρ' εὖ λογιζόμεσθα.

748. ἐς ταὐτὸν—'thou dost but agree with me'. Supply ἐμοί, and in next clause after ἐγὼ, βούλομαι.

750. 'Why revolve I this?'

752. τῶνδε γουνάτων—This gen. of appeal (which Pors. governs by πρὸς understood) may be put under the head of causal

gen. Goodwin, § 173. Other Ionic forms found in tragedy are μοῦνος, οὔνομα, κοῦρος, δουρί, ξεῖνος, ἱρός. Inferior MSS. add many more.

755. θέσθαι—'to get thy life made free'. Pflugk can hardly be right in taking this as advice to H. to commit suicide.

756—8. Omitted in best MSS. τιμωρ—'if I take vengeance', conditional use of the participle.

758. καὶ δή—'well then', 'even so'=*fac ita esse.* τίν' εἰς ἐπ.—'to give what help?'

759. οὐδὲν—a kind of accus. of reference in connection with ἐπάρκεσιν [or μαστεύω, 'I ask for', may be supplied.]

760. 'For whom I let the tear-drop fall'. καταστάζω—used differently in 241. [Notice the break in στιχομυθία, i.e. the arrangement of lines by which in rapid dialogue each speaker replies in the same number of lines as the questioner has used. Herm. conjectures that some remark of Agam. has fallen out between 759 and 760.]

761. 'The sequel, however'.

762. 'Him I once brought forth and bare in my womb', lit. 'beneath my girdle'. A similar example of πρωθύστερον occurs *El.* 969, πῶς γὰρ κτάνω νιν ἥ μ' ἔθρεψε κάτεκεν;

766. 'Yes, but without profit, as it seems'. γε qualifies ἔτεκον supplied from 765.

767. 'Where was he as it fell out?' The idea is of *coincidence* rather than of chance. πτόλις, *metri gratia*, as in Epic. Cf. πόλεμος, πτόλεμος.

768. ὁρρ. θανεῖν—μὴ θανεῖν would be more usual.

771. Πολυμήστωρ—attracted into rel. clause; so *Hipp.* 101, τήνδ' ἢ πολαῖσι σαῖς ἐφέστηκεν Κύπρις. This is called inverse attraction and is found also in Lat. e.g. Verg. *Aen.* 1. 573, *urbem quam statuo vestra est.*

772. ἐνταῦθ'=both *illic* and *illuc.* 'In charge of most cruel gold'. This may be a transferred epithet as πικρ. should here properly belong to Polymestor. Cf. Verg. *Aen.* 1. 355, *crudeles aras.*

774. τίνος γ'—'why, at whose hand else?' Elmsley would change γε into δὲ on the ground that γε cannot occur in a question, and Pors. reads τίνος πρὸς ἄλλου;

775. ἦ που—'I suppose he lusted to get gold'.

776. τοιαῦτ'—'even so'. Aristoph. has ταῦτα in same sense.

780. ᾤχετο—virtually plupf. 'She was gone to fetch'.

782. θαλασσόπλαγκτόν γε—'yes, to be tossed on the sea, as thou beholdest'. The adj. is used *proleptically*, i.e. it anticipates the result of the action of the verb.

783. σχετλία—[√σχε which also appears in parts of ἔχω]. There is a double notion of *wretch* and *wretchedness* in the word. For gen. see 661 n.

784. 'I am undone and nought of evil remains untried'.

785, 6. δυστυχής...τύχην—for a kindred play on words cf. Milton, *Paradise Lost*, Bk. 2, 'surer to prosper than prosperity', and Trabea, quoted by Cic. *Tusc. disp.* 4. 31, *fortunam ipsam anteibo fortunis meis.* Ter. *Adelph.* 761, *ipsa si cupiat salus | servare prorsus non potest hanc familiam.*

[786—845. H. appeals to Agam. 'Hear and help me: this man was my most familiar guest-friend (ξένος) and has violated all rights of hospitality. I indeed am myself weak, but the gods are strong and the principle or law on which they act. This now devolves on you to carry out. O, have pity! contrast my former state with my present forlornness. What, will you go from me? Oh! why are we not taught persuasion's art as everything beside? I have no hope: my children are gone, my city burned. Then, too, I would urge the argument of love: this dead boy is your relation, since you have wedded Kasandra. O for a voice in every part of me to plead my cause: help, help me, 'tis a noble man's part'.]

786. ἔστιν—'exists'. Observe position of the accent. λέγοις—'unless thou shouldst mention'. λέγεις of some MSS. puts the idea rather more definitely.

787. οὕνεκ'—'on account of'. ἕνεκα usually follows its case: MSS. vary between οὕνεκα and εἵνεκα: most modern editors prefer the former.

788. ὅσια denotes the divine spirit of equity which overrides τὸ δίκαιον.

789. στέργ. ἄν—'I will be content'.

790. ἀνδρὸς—used much as French *Monsieur le*, &c. So Ajax uses it of his bitterest foe Hektor, where (says Jebb) the word gives a certain tone of distance and aversion to the mention of a well-known but hated name.

793 sqq. 'Though he had oft shared my board with me and in count of hospitality was in the first rank of my friends —yet, though he had got all that was proper and had received all consideration', &c. Vv. 794, 5 are perhaps spurious: there is a great deal of unnecessary repetition in them and they are open to two objections, (1) τυχεῖν governs an acc. unless πρῶτα be taken adverbially. Musgrave suggested ξένιά τ', *dona hospitalia.* (2) Some participle seems required. Hence Porson well conjectured πρῶτος ὤν.

795. προμηθίαν—some see here a reference to 1137, 'having taken full forethought,' but the true sense seems to be that which is given above, as more in harmony with the rest of what H. says [or, 'when he had got all that was needful (for Polydorus) and had taken him in charge'—a doubtful sense of προμηθίαν]. Variants are προμισθίαν (Musgrave), προθυμίαν (Herm.).

796, 7. P.'s crime was aggravated by his treatment of the corpse: for an unburied shade wandered about on the banks of the Styx and could get no rest for 100 years. Verg. *Aen.* 6. 324.

798. μὲν οὖν—'then', 'to sum up'. ἴσως—idiomatically used as in English, though no doubt is expressed.

799 sq. Every interpretation of this passage is attended with difficulties, so that little more can be done than to give a list of the more reasonable explanations. The passage hinges on the meaning of the ambiguous word νόμος, which may be 'principle', 'law', 'custom'; its meaning being to some extent determined by Pindar's saying νόμος ὁ πάντων βασιλεύς.

(i.) 'But the gods are strong and so is law which controls them, a law by which we deem the gods to be, whereby we live with our views of right and wrong defined: and should this law, when it has been referred to thee, be set at nought', &c. The νόμος in this case will be some high principle superior even to the gods themselves, not unlike 'Ανάγκη of which Eur. *Alk.* 978 says, καὶ γὰρ Ζεὺς ὅτι νεύσῃ | σύν σοι τοῦτο τελευτᾷ.

(ii.) νόμος='law', in its more usual sense. Eur. then says that law is superior to the gods because the state could dictate who should and who should not be worshipped. Socrates was condemned, we know, because he was accused of disallowing the state-gods. (iii.) If we substitute 'convention' for 'law' we have the sophistic theory which Eur. is generally supposed to have held. This is Paley's view.

(iv.) A schol. takes a somewhat different view. 'The gods are strong and their law which rules men: for we think that by law the gods (rule)'. Then Hec. implies that Agam. as administrator of justice is for the time being in the place of the gods.

801. ὡρισμένοι. This may be passive or middle, see 114 n. ζῶμεν—little more than ἐσμέν.

804. ἱρά...φέρειν—'violate', metaph. from carrying off plunder. Sacrilege is out of place in connexion with P.'s crime, except in so far as ξενία violated would be a sin, or religious offence, so that perhaps a reference is intended to some contemporary event. [ἱρός, connected with Sanskrit *ishira*, means 'sound', 'fresh', 'strong', as we see in relation to ἦμαρ, ὄμβρος, κῦμα, μένος. The meaning 'sacred' arises from the fact that nothing blemished or unsound could be offered to the gods.]

806. ἐν αἰσχρῷ θέμ.—'regarding these things as disgraceful', so ἐν καλῷ τίθεσθαι is used.

807. ὡς γραφ.—'as a painter stand off and look upon me and scan the miseries which I endure'. A painter would get a better idea of a picture as a whole by standing away from it.

810. οὖσα—substituted by way of variety for ἦν.

812. 'Whither stealthily (ὑπό) withdrawest thou thy foot from me?' Agam. makes a movement to go. The phrase = φεύγω and so governs an acc. Porson's rendering *quo me cogis te sequi* is forced, and Musgrave's ποῖ μετεξάγεις has no authority.

813. 'I seem likely to accomplish nought'. πράξειν—the fut. (not pres.) inf. is usual after βούλομαι, ὑπισχνέομαι and other verbs in which the object of the expectation (wish, hope, &c.) is something future.

817. ἐς τέλος—'to perfection', a sense conveyed in its derivative τέλειος.

818. ἵν' ἦν—(= ἐξῆν) 'in which case it were in our power'. This is Elmsley's conjecture for ἵν' ᾖ of some MSS. and is perhaps the original reading of the best MS. It is an instance of the peculiar usage with final conjunctions (ἵνα, ὡς, ὅπως) which are followed by past tense of indic. where the conse-

quence is in fact an impossible one. Cf. *Hipp.* 647, ἵν' εἶχον μηδὲ προσφωνεῖν τινα.

820. τις—meaning herself, as we use '*one*'. See *David Copperfield*, chap. 24. "I observed that he always spoke of himself indefinitely as 'a man' and seldom or never in the first person singular...'a man might get on very well here', &c." ἐλπίσαι, Attic writers usually adopted the Aeolic forms σειας, σειε in 2nd and 3rd sing.; but we find ἁρπαλίσαι, λέξαι (Aesch.), ἀλγύναις (Soph.), κτίσαι (Eur.), ἀκούσαις, φήσαις (Plato).

821. οἱ μὲν γὰρ ὄντες—'for my former sins.' So the best MSS. for which Weil proposes ποτ' ὄντες and many editors τοσοῦτοι after later MSS., which perhaps suggests as the true reading οἱ μὲν τότ'.

822. 'And I myself with shame perish a captive of the spear'. ἐπὶ implies the conditions: slavery involves menial and degrading services.

823. τόνδε—'yonder'.

824. καὶ μὴν introduces a fresh plea—'And look you—although this perchance is a vain part of my appeal—the plea of love, to wit'.

825. εἰρήσεται—'yet it shall be spoken'. The fut. perf. has often no perf. signification, especially in defective verbs.

827. 'K. the inspired, for so the Phrygians style her'. Κασάνδρα—this emendation for Κασάνδραν proposed by Herm. is very good, for it is idle to say that the Phrygians called her Kasandra, unless indeed she had both a Trojan and Greek name, as Alexander and Paris, Pyrrhus and Neoptolemus.

828. 'In what way, sire, I ask (δῆτα), wilt thou acknowledge thy nights of joy, or shall my daughter have any benefit of her sweetest wifely caresses, or I of her?' χάριν merely = εὔνοιαν, and the sense is that, marriage being a close connexion, H. would expect to get some benefit from the relationship.

831, 2. Spurious. πάνυ says Pors. is rare in tragedy, and Pflugk shows that τῶν νυκτ. π. φ. must be taken together, and then no sense results. [Nauck reads νυκτερησίων.]

835. 'One thing yet my speech doth lack'.

836. εἰ μοι γεν.—'would that I had', an elliptical form like εἰ γάρ, εἴθε, to express a wish. So *si* in Lat.

837. **κόμαισι**—Musgr. objects that mourners shaved their heads, and that so the word is inappropriate: but the remark applies rather to hired mourners than to the queenly Hecuba. He suggested κόραισι, 'pupils of the eyes', and even κνήμαισι, which is singularly inelegant.

ποδῶν βάσει = ποσὶ δι' ὧν βαίνω.

838. **Δαιδάλου**—the recognised master of clever engineering and mechanical appliance, and of architecture and statuary. His sculptures seemed to move and speak: thus Eur. fragm. Eurysth. τὰ Δαιδάλεια πάντα κινεῖσθαι δοκεῖ | βλέπειν τ' ἀγάλμαθ'· ὧδ' ἀνὴρ κεῖνος σοφός.

839. **ὡς ἔχοιτο**—'that weeping in concert they might cling to thy knees, urging all manner of pleadings'. ἔχοιτο, better than ἔχοιντο, of two good MSS., for where objects introduced by a neut. plur. are regarded as a united whole (and ὁμαρτῆ here combines them) a singular verb is used.

842. **παράσχες**—almost all MSS πάρασχε, which is admissible in compounds, as κατάσχε, *H. Fur.* 1210, though the simple verb always has σχές.

843. 'Although she be nought'.

844. ''Tis the part of a good man', possessive gen. Goodwin, § 169.

846 sqq. The Chor. comments on the irony of fate which makes Hec. appeal for help to a notorious enemy against her former friend. 'Wonder indeed how with men all things clash, and how their closest ties are determined by laws of circumstance which make their deadliest foes their friends!' **νόμοι**— we have a parallel in *Bacch.* 484 οἱ νόμοι δὲ διάφοροι. Musgrave's alteration χρόνοι, though it simplifies matters, is not necessary. **ἀνάγκας**, any tie of affection, or even = Lat. *necessitudo*. **διώρ.** is the gnomic aorist.

[850—904. Agam. expresses his deep pity and says that he would gladly help her but he is not a free agent : the army regard Polym. as a friend, and he cannot afford to come into ill odour with them. Hec. makes a reflection that no man is quite free; he is hampered by considerations of chance, or money, or multitude, or law. She asks Agam. at least to restrain any assistance from the Greeks, and she will do the rest. How? asks Agam. H. replies that she has many Trojan dames at hand to help, and cites the Lemnian affair and the murder by the Danaids as instances of women's power. She then sends an attendant to summon Polymestor and his children, and Agam. expresses his good wishes for the result.]

850. σέθεν = σου in Attic as well as Epic. Some grammarians class this as a sixth case, meaning 'from', as οἴκοθεν, Ἀθήνηθεν.

851. 'I regard with pity'. Similarly δι' οἴκτου λαβεῖν, *Suppl.* 194. δι' αἰσχύνης ἔχω, *I. T.* 683.

854. φανείη γ'.—'If in any way it should appear possible for thy plan to succeed, and for me to avoid appearing to the army to have planned this death against the king of Thrace for K.'s sake'. The opt. expresses A's doubt as to the possibility of keeping the matter secret. The τε should stand strictly after φαν. or else μὴ δόξαιμι be changed to ἐμέ τε στρατῷ μὴ δόξαι. [The best writers are often careless about particular words, thinking of the adjustment of the whole.]

857. ἔστιν ᾗ.—'there is one point'. ἔστιν often combines with a relative adverb to form a fresh adverb. ἔστιν ἵνα, ὅτε, 'sometimes', 'often'. So in Lat. *est ubi = interdum.*

859. 'If yonder man is friend of mine, this is a private matter, and the army has no share therein'. εἰ δ' ἐμοί—is Elmsley's conjecture, and is preferable in sense to εἰ δέ σοι.

861. πρὸς ταῦτα—'therefore'. The phrase is idiomatically used, not to express a reason but a fixed resolve. Soph. *El.* 820, πρὸς ταῦτα καινέτω τις = 'now'.

863. 'If I am to be evil·spoken of by the Achaeans'. Dat. of agent with passive verb for ὑπό with gen. From διαβάλλω comes διάβολος, 'the accuser'.

864. φεῦ—'O fie!' Expressing contempt rather than sorrow.

ὅστις—vaguer than ὅς, Lat. *qui* with subj.

866. πόλεος—a rarer form of πόλεως, a remnant of the old gen. in -ηος, which latter does not appear in tragedy till Eur. Attic generally disliked the combination -ηο. ναός, λαός, are genuine Attic forms.

867. 'Stay him so that he uses a temper not accordant to his judgment'; or 'keep him from using such temper as he would', μὴ is redundant according to the Gk. idiom which multiplies negatives; it is a little out of place on the second rendering.

868. πλέον νεμ.—*nimium tribuis*, as in *Suppl.* 243, νέμοντες τῷ φθόνῳ πλέον μέρος. Eur. was not the radical Aristoph. makes him.

869. ' I will rid thee of this fear '.

870. ξύνισθι—from ξύνοιδα. H. urges him to be accessory before the fact without taking any ostensible part in the revenge.

871. συνδράσῃς δὲ μή—' But take no active share therein'. μὴ σύνδρα, μὴ συνδράσῃς are good, μὴ συνδρᾷς (conj.), μὴ συν· δρᾶσον bad, though the latter form is very rarely found.

872. ' But if there arise on the part of the Achaeans any riot or rescue, while the man of Thrace is suffering what suffer he shall, stop it without appearing to do so for my sake'. πασχ.—gen. abs., for ἐπικουρ. would require a dat. μή, not οὐ, because the phrase = μὴ δόκει. χάριν—virtually a prep. and ἐμὴν χάριν = ἐμοῦ χάριν. Other adverbial accus. are πρόφασιν, τέλος, τρόπον, ὁδὸν, ἀρχὴν, πέρας, and δίκην.

876. οὖν—'pray', sarcastic. φάσγανον—for σφάγανον, from σφάζω, cf. θρέψω = τρέφσω.

880. ' The tents conceal a number of Trojan dames.' The perf. = a present like οἶδα, δέδοικα, πεφόβημαι, πέφυκα, ἕστηκα, ὅλωλα, κέκτημαι, κέκλημαι, μέμνημαι, πέποιθα. [Some MSS. read κεκεύθουσι a Doric form, cf. δεδοίκω, κεκλήγω, πεφύκω.]

882. φονέᾰ—In Lat. ᾰ is short, as *Orpheă*, and twice in Eur., in all other places long. It may perhaps in some places be read as one syllable, φονε͞α.

883. καὶ πῶς—'pray, how?' Cf. 515 n.

885. μέμφομαι—' I have a poor opinion of '. So μέμψιν ἔχειν, Aesch. *P. V*. 445.

886. Αἰγύπτ.—The Danaides murdered their husbands, fifty in number, sons of Aegyptus, on their wedding-night, the only one who was spared being Lynkeus, whom his wife Hypermnestra saved.

887. 'Utterly depopulated Lemnos of males '. The more usual constr. is found in 948. ἄρδην—contracted from ἀέρδην, properly means 'lifted up on high'. [When the Argonauts landed at Lemnos they found that the women had slain their own husbands, except perhaps the king Thoas (Hdt. 6, 138).]

888. ὡς γενέσθω—' so be it '. ὡς = οὕτως. γενέσθω, better than γενέσθαι of most MSS.

889. ' Send me this lady '. μοι—dat. ethic.

890. πλαθεῖσα—(not πλασθεῖσα) from πλάθω, collat. form of πελάω; this participle is chiefly confined to choral parts.

8J2. 'On thy business no less than hers'. χρέος is like χάριν in 874. So Lat. *tuam vicem.*

895. τάφον = ταφήν. Cf. 672.

896. τώδ' ἀδελφ.—'That these two, brother and sister, side by side on one pyre, twofold grief to their mother, may be buried in the earth.'

898. '(And it may be so) for if the army had been able to sail I could not have granted thee this favour: but, as it is, for the god sends not favouring breezes, remain we must, watching quietly for a chance of sailing'.

900. ἴησι—ι doubtful, as in λίαν, ἰῶμαι, ἰατρός. ὁρῶντας may refer back to στρατόν, a noun of multitude. ἥσυχον, advb., for πλοῦς ἥσυχος is a very unusual phrase. [ὁρῶντά μ., Herm.'s conj. is a decided improvement, and one MS. has -ῶντα. Dindorf adopts Hartung's ἡσύχους].

905—952. Third Stasimon. 'Thou, O my native Ilium, no more shalt count thyself as one of cities unsacked: such a cloud of Hellenes shrouds thee round and hath sacked thee with the spear, even the spear. Of thy coronal of towers art thou shorn, and with most piteous stain of smoky flame art all defiled; forlorn one, never more shall I tread (thy streets). At midnight my destruction began, when after banqueting sweet sleep is spread upon the eyes, and my lord had made me cease from song and choral sacrifice, and lay upon his bed, his spear on its peg, watching no more for the thronging sailors entering Ilian Troy. I was arranging my hair in the snood that bound it up, gazing into the mirror's vista'd light, to sink upon my cushioned bed: then through the city came a ringing shout, and down Troy's streets the cry was this, "Sons of the Hellenes, when, oh when will ye have sacked the Ilian citadel and reached your homes?" Then left I my loved bed in a single robe like some Dorian maid, but—unhappy—I gained nought by my session at awful Artemis' shrine. But I saw my bedfellow dead, and am borne away o'er the deep salt sea, and looking back upon my city, as the ship started on her return and sundered me from the land of Ilium, in my misery I fainted from grief, devoting to curses Helen sister of the Dioscori, and the shepherd of Ida, Paris the dread, since his marriage—no marriage that, but some woe of the avenger—drove me in ruin from my fatherland and exiled me from home. Her may the salt sea ne'er carry back, never may she reach her ancestral home!'

906. τῶν ἀπορθ.—sc. πολέων, partitive gen. Goodwin, § 169. The constr. is imitated by Hor. *Odes* 3. 13, *fies nobilium tu quoque fontium.*

λέξει—Cf. our use of the word 'tell'. This fut. may very possibly be passive; for about 100 Greek verbs, most of them with pure stems, have a passive sense in their fut. middle, e. g. *Alk.* 322, ἀλλ' αὐτίκ' ἐν τοῖς οὐκέτ' οὖσι λέξομαι.

907. νέφος—used of any great number. So Livy 42. 10 *nubes telorum*, and Verg. *Aen.* 12. 254, *facta nube*, cf. Heb. xii. 1 'cloud of witnesses'.

910. ἀποκέκ.—perf. pass. of ἀποκείρω, used here in a middle sense, which accounts for the acc. The phrase ἀποκείρεσθαι κόμας is common enough. See also 114 n. For στεφ. πυργ. cf. Soph. *Ant.* 124, στεφάνωμα πύργων | Ἥφαιστον πευκάενθ' ἑλεῖν.

912. κηλῖδ'.—Pors. makes this dat. and reads οἰκτροτάτῳ, but it is doubtful if final ι of dat. can be so elided. The acc. is a kind of cognate acc.

915. ἦμος—Hom. word. ἐκ δείπνων=*ex cena*, 55 n.

916. κίδναται—or σκίδναται. Same root as *scindo*, quasi σκίνδμι.

918. καταπαύσας—It is easy to supply ἐμέ, though it may be for καταπαυσάμενος, cf. 1108. Various readings so as to introduce an acc. are χοροποιόν and χαροποιόν θυσίαν.

921. ναύταν—adjectival in sense.

926. ἀτερμ. εἰς αὐγὰς—The allusion is to the vista which meets our gaze when we look into a mirror. The Schol. interprets 'round' like ἀπείρονα γαῖαν, making it a transferred epithet. Weil thinks that the mirror looks at one without ceasing.

927. ἐπιδέμνιον—This for ἐπιδέμνιος, which would be very otiose, is due to Pors. [Musgrave conjectured ἐπιδείπνιος.]

931. Ἰλ. σκοπιὰν—i.e. Pergamus. Cf. Homer's Ἴλιος ἠνεμόεσσα.

933. The Dorian girls often wore only a single light garment (χιτώνιον), fastened with clasps down the side. See Mahaffy, *Gk. Antiquities* p. 46.

940. πόδα.—prob. not technically the 'sheet' [*pes* in Catull. 4. 20, *utrumque Iuppiter | simul secundus incidisset in pedem*] but of motion generally. Cf. 1020.

945. αἰνόπαριν—Cf. Hom. *Il.* 3. 39, δύσπαρις, and for the whole sentiment Aesch. *Agam.* 689, ἐλέναυς, ἔλανδρος, ἑλέπτολις (of Helen), and *Androm.* 103, ᾿Ιλίῳ αἰπεινᾷ Πάρις οὐ γάμον ἀλλά τιν᾽ ἄταν | ἠγάγετ᾽.

951. ἄν—sc. Helen.

[952—1022. Enter Polymestor the cruel Thracian king: he hypocritically expresses sorrow for Hecuba's accumulated miseries and excuses his delay in coming. Hecuba puts some searching questions to him about her boy and the treasures sent with him; and on pretence of showing him other treasures hid within the tent she induces him and his children to enter with her.]

953. It seems quite natural that P. overdoing his part should address Priam as well as Hecuba. Nauck and others however condemn the verse.

956. οὐκ οὐδέν—a stronger form of οὐδέν, whereas οὐδέν οὐ would mean 'everything'. Lat. *nihil non*.

957. αὖ—with πράξειν κακῶς.

958. 'And the gods stir them up backwards and forwards, introducing confusion, that through ignorance we may worship them'. αὐτά—i. e. prosperity and adversity. φύρουσι—as if they were the ingredients of a pudding. ἀγνωσίᾳ—causal dative, Goodwin, § 188. The ignorance is of course ignorance of the future.

960. 'But why need one lament over these things, advancing not ahead of his evils?' The metaphor is from the pioneers of an army.

962. 'If thou blame me at all for'. τι—cognate acc. Goodwin, § 159 note 1: the object of μέμφει viz. με is easily understood from the context.

τ. ἑ. ἀπουσίας—causal gen. Goodwin, § 173. 2. μέμφομαι is followed by two constructions: (1) μέμφομαι τινί τι *obicio aliquid alicui*; (2) μ. τινά τινος (as here). Cf. γράφομαι Φίλιππον φόνου.

963. σχἐs—'restrain it' (viz. τὸ μέμφεσθαι): more usually ἐπίσχες: not 'restrain thyself' which would rather be middle, but yet is constantly used for 'stop'.

τυγχάνω—although ἦλθες is aorist. So 1134 δίδωσι and ἦν. 'As it happened I was away in the midland districts of Thrace when thou camest hither, and on my arrival this servant of thine meets me as I am already lifting my foot from the tents'. πόδ' αἴροντι = ἐξιόντι.

967. κλύων—cf. ἄγων 369 note.

968. αἰσχύνομαι προσβλέπειν—'I shrink from looking at'. al. προσβλέπων would mean 'I look upon with shame', cf. 552 note.

971—was suspected by Porson, who proposed either to place it after 972, or to read κἀν for ἐν, οὐκ for κοὐκ. Other editors are more sweeping; Dindorf condemns 970—975, Hartung 973—975.

τυγχάνουσα agrees not with αἰδώς μ' ἔχει but with αἰδοῦμαι for which this is an equivalent: so Ion 927, ὑπεξαντλῶν—αἴρει με (= αἴρομαι). ἵνα—'wherein'.

972. The object of προσβλέπειν is τοῦτον, to be supplied from ὅτῳ. σε which is read generally is omitted in the best MS.

ὀρθαῖς κορ.—'with unaverted eyes', Iph. Aul. χαῖρ' οὐ γὰρ ὀρθοῖς ὄμμασίν σ' ἔτ' εἰσορῶ. Hor. Od. 1. 3, 18, *rectis oculis* (Bentley's conj. for *siccis*).

973. 'But regard it not as enmity to thee'. She really feared to betray her purpose by the hate gleaming from her eyes. αὐτό—i.e. τὸ μή με προσβλέπειν σε. σέθεν—objective gen. after δύσνοιαν. Goodwin, § 167. 3.

μὴ ἡγήσῃ—In prohibitions μὴ λύε, μὴ λύσῃς are good, μὴ λύῃς, μὴ λῦσον bad Greek. Goodwin, § 254. See 871 n.

974. 'And moreover custom also is to some extent the cause that women look not straight at men'. αἴτιον regularly takes acc. and inf.

976. καὶ...γε. 'Ay, and no wonder'. The phrase is common in tragedy.

τίς χρεία σ' ἐμοῦ; 'What need hast thou of me?' sc. ἔχει. Cf. Homer Il. 11. 606, τί δέ σε χρεὼ ἐμεῖο;

977. 'Wherefore didst thou send for me from the house?' τί χρῆμα—Goodwin, § 160. 2, cf. χάριν 892 n. ἐπέμψω = μετε-

πέμψω. The middle often has a causal sense: γράφω, 'I write', γράφομαι, 'I get written'.

978. δή—emphasises ἐμαυτῆς, giving the reason why solitude was desirable.

979. ὀπάονας—his escort, not before mentioned. Euripides has not explained how the same king was on good terms with both Greeks and Trojans. Probably he had in mind the shifting policy of the Thracian kings of his own day.

983. σε χρῆν—so the best MS. The others σὲ χρή.

986. εἰπὲ παῖδα εἰ ζ.—'Tell me if my son yet lives'. Greek emphasises the subject of a dependent clause by making it the object of the principal verb; cf. Eur. *Andr.* 645, τί δῆτ' ἂν εἴποις τοὺς γέροντας ὡς σοφοί.

ἐξ—i.e. having received him from.

988. τὰ ἄ. σε ἐρήσομαι. Greeks could say either ἔρομαι σε or ἔρομαι τι, and here the two constructions are combined: cf. Pind. *Ol.* 6. 81, ἅπαντας ἐν οἴκῳ εἴρετο παῖδα, '(The king) asked all in the house about the child'.

989. μάλιστα—'certainly (he lives)'.

τὸ ἐκείνου μέρος—'with regard to him'. *Rhes.* 405, τὸ σὸν μέρος.

μὲν—virtually='at any rate'. 'Whatever thy other woes, in *him*' &c.

990. Notice here and elsewhere in the play the 'tragic Irony' which consists in the speaker's words meaning much more to the audience than to the person to whom they are addressed.

991. 'What pray in the next place wouldst thou learn of me?' Polym. repeats Hecuba's own word δεύτερον.

992. Verg. *Aen.* 3. 341, *ecqua tamen puero est amissae cura parentis.*

993. 'Yes, and sought to come hither to thee by stealth'. κρύφιος—adj. for adv. Cf. Gray's *Elegy*, 'How *jocund* did they drive their team afield!' ὡς—only in Attic and nearly always 'to' persons.

994. ὃν ἔχων—'in possession of which'. With verbs of coming and the like, the participles ἔχων, φέρων, ἄγων, often mean little more than *cum*, 'together with'.

995. 'Safe, at all events (γε) guarded, &c.'

996. 'Nor lust after what is thy neighbour's'. τὰ πλήσιον=τὰ τῶν πλήσιον is a most rare construction. πλήσιον being an adverb needs the article before it can represent a substantive. ἔρα governs the gen. of the thing aimed at.

997. ἥκιστα—'by no means', *minime;* an instance of softening down.

ὀναίμην—'May I but enjoy my present estate'. *Alk.* 335, τῶνδ' ὄνησιν εὔχομαι | θεοῖς γενέσθαι. Polym. deprecates covetousness; ὀνίναμαι, ἀπολαύω, and other verbs of enjoying, take a gen. which is perhaps partitive.

998, 9. ἅ—τοῦτο—coming together have offended some critics, it would seem without cause. Brunck reads ταῦτα, Porson ὅ.

1000. ἔστ' ὦ φ.—'There is, oh thou that art beloved as thou art now beloved by me'. *P.* What is it that I and my children must know? *H.* Ancient vaults of gold belonging to the house of Priam'. Polymestor in his greedy haste interrupts her, and this accounts for the sing. ἔστι followed by the plural κατώρυχες. This *Schema Pindaricum,* i.e. singular verb with plural noun is rare in Attic, cf. Shakespeare, 'His steeds to water at *those springs* | on chaliced flowers *that lies.*

ὦ. φ. ὦ. σ. ν. ἐ. φ.=ὦ ἔχθιστε. [The usual reading is ἔστω φιλ. 'let it (viz. ὁ λόγος) be beloved as thou art now beloved by me'. But the objections to this are strong.]

1003. ταῦτα—usually refers to what precedes.

1004. 'Certainly, through *thee;* for thou art a pious man', with especial and bitter reference to his impious treatment of her son.

1008. ἵνα—'where are' sc. εἰσίν.

1010. γῆς ὑπερτέλλουσα—'rising above the earth'. Cf. *Or.* 6, κορυφῆς ὑπερτέλλοντα δειμαίνων πέτρον.

1011. ἔτι—'any more', like French *encore,* a virtually comparative particle. τῶν ἐκεῖ—'concerning matters there' =περὶ τῶν ἐκεῖ.

1013. 'Where, pray? or hast thou hidden it within thy robes?' ἦ seems better than ἤ. κρύψασ' ἔχεις—Lat. *occultum habes,* stronger than κέκρυφας.

1014. σκῦλα—spoils, stripped from a fallen enemy (σκύλλω, I strip), but the word is used in a wider signification here.

1015. 'But where? For here are the enclosures where harbours the Achaeans' fleet'. It would of course be hard for Trojan slaves to hide any large amount of gold. Hecuba explains that the tents of the *women* are private.

1016. 'Are things within quite safe, and is there an ab-sence of males?'

1018. ἡμεῖς μόναι. The fem. is no violation of Dawes' canon (cf. 237 n.), for she alludes not to herself alone but to all the Trojan women.

1019. καὶ γάρ—'for in truth'.

1020. λῦσαι πόδα—cf. 940, note.

1021, 2. 'That thou mayest go back with thy children to where thou didst lodge my son'. This is the climax of Hecuba's irony. She means to Hades; Polymestor, not aware that she knew of his treachery, thinks that she means safe away to Thrace.

[1023—1055. Polymestor follows Hecuba into the tents, and the Chorus sing a short ode to prepare the minds of the audience for the cries of Polymestor, who rushes in, his eyes blinded and children slain before his eyes.]

1023. Addressed to Polymestor. ἴσως—'equally', i.e. 'none the less'. Thy punishment is as certain as if already inflicted.

1025 sqq. 'Like a man that has reeled and fallen into some harbourless sea, having forfeited thy being thou shalt lose thy dear life. For where liability to Justice and to the gods coincide, deadly, ay deadly is the calamity' with which the offender expiates his crime. [It is impossible that 'to fall from one's dear life' is good Greek for 'to die', and καρδία is rather the seat of feeling than of life. The verses are in all probability corrupt.] ἄντλος—not 'a hold' but 'bilge-water'; here and in Pindar of the sea; the radical meaning of the word seems to be that of *stagnant water*. λέχριος—otherwise ex-plained 'by a lurch of the vessel' Pflugk. φίλας—an epic epithet, like Homer's φίλον ἦτορ. ἐκπέσῃ, the other reading, is not Attic.

1027. ἀμέρσας—possibly means 'having deprived Poly-mestor of life'; here only is the word used in tragedy. οὗ—the correction of Hemsterhuys for the MS. reading οὐ.

1032. ὁδοῦ—gen. after ψεύσει, involving separation, Goodwin, § 174.

1033. θανάσιμον—' to thy death' proleptic with σέ.

1034. ἀπολέμῳ χειρί—cf. Judg. 9. 54 (Abimelech to his armourbearer), ' Draw thy sword, and slay me, that men say not of me, *A woman slew him* '. The dative is causal, Goodwin, § 188.

1035. Polymestor is heard screaming behind the scenes.

1037. ' Yet again alas for your unhappy butchery '.

1038. 'Dears, terrible evils have been wrought within '. καινά—' fresh ', and so ' strange ', ' terrible '.

1039. 'Be sure ye shall not escape '. οὐ μή with aorist conjunctive is an emphatic *denial*, with future indic. 2nd pers. sing. a strong *prohibition.*

1040. 'For I will strike and burst open the inmost recesses of these tents!' i.e. no seclusion will protect them from his fury.

ἀναρρ.—ἀνα- as in ἀν-οίγω, ἀνα-πετάννυμι. The doubled ρ represents the pronunciation.

1041. 'Look! the blow of his heavy hand is sped forth'. The verse is more appropriate in the mouth of the Chorus.

1042. βούλεσθε—The leader of the Chorus asks the other Trojan dames ἐπεισπέσωμεν—Goodwin, § 256.

1044. μηδέν—adverbial. ἐκβάλλων—'pulling up' from the ground.

1045, 6. οὐ,...οὐ—The asyndeton is for effect.

1046. οὓς ἔκτ. ἑ.—Triumphantly addressed to the audience, and in strong antithesis to ζῶντας.

1047. 'What? didst thou overthrow the Thracian, and hast thou, mistress, the mastery over thy guest-friend?' ἦ γάρ—expressing mixed admiration and surprise,—'Can it be that?'

1050. τυφλῷ π. ποδί—'with blind unsteady step'. A favourite phrase of Euripides, found three times in *Phoen.* 834, 1539, 1616: cf. τυφλὴν χέρα ib. 1699, πόδα τυφλόπουν ib. 1550. Milton, *Samson Agonistes*, 'lend thy guiding hand | to these *dark steps*'.

1054. 'But I will depart and stand out of the way of the most formidable Thracian boiling over with rage'. ἐκποδών— w. dat. cf. 52 note.

1055. ζέοντι—Barnes' correction for the ῥέοντι of the MSS., which does not offer a very good sense. Dem. *de Cor.* p. 272, πολλῷ ῥέοντι καθ' ὑμᾶς, is not strictly parallel. Cf. Soph. *Oed. Col.* 434, ὁπηνίκ' ἔξει θυμός. [Verbs with monosyllabic stem in ε contract only εε and εει, so ζέω, ζεῖς, ζεῖ, ζεῖτον, ζέομεν, ζεῖτε, ζέουσι. Δέω, I bind, is the only exception and is contracted in most forms. Goodwin, § 98 note 1, p. 98.] θυμῷ—dat. of reference.

[1056—1106. Polymestor bursts on to the stage like a wild beast, groping and stumbling, his eyes streaming with blood. He dare not leave his children, yet longs to tear his enemies limb from limb, and calls upon Greeks and Thracians for aid. Whither shall he go? To Orion, or Seirius, or the dark ferry which leads to hell?]

1057. κέλσω—'put in', sc. τὴν ναῦν. Delib. conj. Goodwin, § 256. [The forms κέλλω and ὀκέλλω are collateral: so δύρομαι and ὀδύρομαι. Cf. 740 n.]

1058. 'Setting myself on my hands with the movement of a fourfooted mountain beast'. He is moving on all fours. [Porson would read καὶ κατ' ἴχνος or καὶ ἴχνος in the sense of *vestigium*='foot'. Hermann ἔπι=ἐπιτιθέμενος omitting the comma at κέλσω so as to govern βάσιν.]

1060. ἐξαλλάξω—'shall I take instead' of my present course? So ἐξαμείβω.

1063. τάλαιναι—'cruel'.

1064. ποῖ καὶ—515 n. ποῖ μυχῶν—Adverbs of time and place denoting a point in and of the whole govern a partitive gen. ποῦ γῆς; πηνίκα τῆς ἡμέρας; 'at what time of day?' Lat. *ubi gentium?* Cf. 961 n. Goodwin, § 168. φυγᾷ πτώσσουσι =φεύγουσι and so takes an acc.

1066. Polymestor invokes the sun, as king of light, to give him light and heal his eyes. εἴθε ἀκέσαιο—(from ἀκεσαί-μην) 'O that thou wouldst heal'. τυφλὸν φέγγος=blindness. [Reiske conjectured νέφος for φέγγος. Weil reads ἐπαλλάξας= 'having substituted'.]

1069. 'I perceive the stealthy step of women near'. The Greeks did not accurately distinguish between the various senses, so κτύπον δέδορκα: αἰσθάνομαι is usually 'I perceive with my eyes'. 1200 n.

1070. ἐπᾴξας πόδα—'having rushed'. ἐπᾴσσω is transitive, a force given to it by the preposition. *Aj.* 40, καὶ πρὸς τί δυσλόγιστον ὧδ' ἦξεν χέρα; 'And wherefore darted he thus his senseless hand?'

1071. 'Can I be glutted with their flesh and bones, making myself a banquet on the brutes, winning for myself their destruction as a compensation for my maltreatment?' ἀντίποινα in apposition with λωβάν: cf. *Or.* 8, σφάγιον ἔθετο ματέρα πατρῴων παθέων ἀμοιβάν.

1076. βάκχαις "Αι.—'hell hounds'. Polymestor dare not go far from the tents lest his children's bodies may be mutilated.

διαμοιρᾶσαι—Cf. 1107 φέρειν. *Alk.* 230, πλέον ἦ πελάσσαι.

1077. 'Butchered, food for dogs and outcast on the cruel mountain side'.

1079. κάμψω—'tack'. [Formerly translated 'bend my knee', i.e. rest, but it seems better to make the metaphor of a ship begin from this word.]

1080. 'Gathering up my linen robe like some ship with sea-going rigging, having as my children's guard rushed upon this deadly lair'. ὅπως—of comparison, 398 n. πείσματα— usually the hawsers which bound the ship to the shore, here the rigging. κοίταν—wild beasts' lair, not the *couch* on which the dead children lay.

1085. 'How intolerable the evils which have been wreaked upon thee'. εἴργασται is usually active after the time of Sophokles: but here as 1087 is spurious it must be active: cf. 264 n.

1086. τἀπιτίμια—sc. ἔστιν.

δράσαντι—The Greek theory of retribution was that it was as certain to follow guilt as the night to follow day, δράσαντι παθεῖν as the proverb put it. Cf. Eur. *fragm.* ἡ δίκη...σῖγα καὶ βραδεῖ ποδὶ | στείχουσα μάρψει τοὺς κακοὺς ὅταν τύχῃ. Hor. *Od.* 3. 2. 31, *raro antecedentem scelestum | deseruit pede poena claudo.*

1087. Inserted from 722.

1090. 'O race rejoicing in steeds and inspired by Ares', i.e. warlike.

1094. ἦ and μὴ in iambics form a crasis with οὐ, cf. 1249 n.

1100. 'Shall I fly up to the lofty halls of heaven where Orion or Seirius darts from his eyes flaming rays of fire, or shall I in my misery rush to Hades' black ferry?' Ὠρίων—in Greek the ι is doubtful, in Latin always long. Orion was the Nimrod of Greek mythology, a mighty hunter, and after death became a constellation which rose soon after the summer solstice. ἀμπτάμενος=ἀναπτάμενος from ἀνίπτομαι a collateral form of ἀναπέτομαι. Goodwin, p. 243 s.v. πέτομαι. Cf. ἀμβήσει 1263. Σείριος—properly 'scorching' sc. ἀστήρ. Otherwise known as the dog-star, cf. Verg. *Aen.* 10. 274, *Sirius ardor,* | *ille sitim morbosque ferens mortalibus aegris* | *nascitur, et laevo contristat lumine caelum.* ἀφίησιν belongs in sense both to 'Ωρίων and Σείριος, in grammar only to the latter. Αἴδα πορθμός—the Styx.

1107. ξυγγνώστα—'it is pardonable', pl. for sing.: so ἀδύνατά ἐστιν, 'it is impossible', χαλεπά ἐστιν. Verg. *Aen.* 1. 667, *frater ut Aeneas—iactetur—nota tibi*—'it is known to thee how &c.' [The Chorus advise suicide.]

κρείσσον' ἢ φέρειν—'too heavy to bear' cf. Soph. *O. T.* 1293, τὸ γὰρ νόσημα μεῖζον ἢ φέρειν. ἐξαπαλλάξαι—act. for mid. 918 n. ζόης has been substituted by modern edd. for MS. ζωῆς which does not scan.

[1109—1131. Agamemnon attracted by the uproar joins them, and asks Polymestor who has done the deed. Polymestor longs to clutch Hecuba and tear her limb from limb. Agam. advises less savage measures, saying that he will judge the matter.]

1109. 'For in no quiet tones hath Echo, child of the mountain rock, cried aloud through the host'. This beautiful metaphor illustrates the way in which many a Greek myth arose. Cf. Aesch. *Ag.* 477, κάσις | πηλοῦ ξύνουρος διψία κόνις.

1112. ᾖσμεν—'had we not known'. This reading is derived from the Etymologicon Magnum (about A.D. 1000); the MSS. reading ἴσμεν is clearly wrong. The best Attic forms are ᾔδη, ᾔδησθα, ᾔδει, ᾖστον, ᾔστην, ᾖσμεν, ᾖστε, ᾖσαν.

1113. παρέσχεν—'would have occasioned'. ἄν is not necessary, cf. the Lat. *sustulerat*=sustulisset, Hor. *Od.* 2, 17, 28. [Many editors read παρέσχ' ἄν, but as Elmsley remarks Eur. would have written this παρέσχεν ἄν.]

1114. γάρ—(I appeal to thee) 'for'.

1116. ἔα—out of the verse, as φεῦ 956.

1119. σοί—dat. incommodi. ὅστις ἦν ἄρα—'Whoever he was', 511 n.

1120. 'Nay destroyed me not but worse': i.e. οὐ μόνον ἀπώλεσε. For a similar correction cf. 948, γάμος, οὐ γάμος ἀλλὰ κ.τ.λ. Liv. 39. 28, *nec cum Maronitis, inquit, mihi aut cum Eumene disceptatio est, sed etiam vobiscum Romani.* μειζόνως— Many of these forms are found in Attic writers: Thucydides uses ἐνδεεστέρως, ἀσφαλεστέρως, χαλεπωτέρως, μαλακωτέρως, ὑποδεεστέρως: Sophokles, μειόνως: Euripides, εὐλαβεστέρως.

1122. τί φής;—'What say'st thou?' a formula of surprise. Note the ι subscript.

σὺ...σὺ—Emphatically repeated. A. cannot believe his ears.

εἴργασαι—mid. not pass. cf. 1085 n.

1125. εἰπὲ ποῦ ἐστίν—'tell me where he is', ὅπου is more usual.

1127. οὗτος—'ho there', *heus tu.* The expression could only be used by a superior to his inferior, the barbarian Polymestor being as inferior to Agamemnon as an Indian rajah to the Viceroy of India.

τί πάσχεις;—'what ails thee?'

1128. 'Let me go that I may lay on her my raging hand': Agamemnon had caught hold of him. ἐφεῖναι=ὥστε ἐφεῖναι. μαργάω—desideratives from substantives and adjectives are formed in -άω and -ιάω; so θανατάω, 'I long to die', from θάνατος 'death': φονάω, 'I thirst for blood'.

1129. τὸ βάρβαρον—'thy savagery', viz. 'the non-Hellenic idea that he might take summary vengeance. Euripides throughout draws a contrast between Savagery as represented by Polym. and Hecuba, and Law as typified in the Greeks. He goes so far however as to make Agamemnon almost an Athenian dikast.

[1132—1182. Polymestor shortly excuses his crime: if he had not slain the boy there would have been a nucleus for the Trojans and a second Trojan war with desolation for Thrace would have taken place. He then gives a detailed account of the way in which his children had been butchered and his own eyes put out.]

1132. λέγοιμ' ἄν—'I will gladly speak', modified future.

1134. δίδωσι—historic present. τρέφειν = ἵνα τρέφοιμι. Goodwin, § 265.

1135. ὕποπτος—'suspicious'. Verbals in -τος are usually passive; but we find in an active sense πιστός, 'relying'; μεμπτός, 'blaming'; ἄγευστος, 'not tasting'; ἄψαυστος, 'not touching'; and others.

1137. προμηθίᾳ—see 795 n.

1139. ἀθροίσῃ, ξυνοικίσῃ—are irregular after the historic ἔδεισα, but not so much so as to necessitate the optative being substituted. Cf. 27 n.

1140. 'That one of the house of Priam was alive'. ζῶντα, predicate.

1141. αἶα—for γαῖα to suit the metre, only found in Homer and tragedians.

1142. ἔπειτα—'in the next place'. τάδε—'yon', pointing at them.

1143. Cf. Thuc. 1. 11. (The Greeks at Troy) 'on their arrival conquered the Trojans in battle,—this is clear, for else they would not have been able to build the rampart for their camp,—and evidently not even here did they employ all their forces, but turned their attention to farming the Chersonese and to freebooting'.

1143. γείτονες Τρώων, 'neighbours of the Trojans'. [This is better than translating Τρώων *Troianorum causa.*]

'And that evil might befall us from which we were lately suffering'.

1146. ὡς—with the future participle gives the *avowed* reason, 511 n.; 'pretending to be about to tell me'.

1148. μόνον—not inconsistent with σὺν τέκνοις, but apart from the rest of the camp and therefore where no aid could reach him. *Med.* 513, ξὺν τέκνοις μόνη μόνοις.

1149. εἰδείη—optative after historic present.

1150. κάμψας γόνυ—i.e. resting.

1151. χειρὸς ἐξ ἀριστερᾶς—'on my left hand'. [χεῖρες of all the MSS. is an evident mistake; the correction is due to Milton.]

1152. ὡς δή—'as if forsooth'. δή, δῆτα often, δῆθεν always is sarcastic.

1153. [θάκους ἔχουσαι—This is Hermann's emendation for 'θάκουν and is preferable on two grounds. (1) The augment is not as a rule omitted in Attic Greek, nor can the ε be pródelided after the diphthong of κόραι. (2) The sense is considerably improved.] κερκίδα, cause for effect, lit. the shuttle, here the garment spun. Ἠδωνῆς χερός—'of Edonian make'. The Edonians were a Thracian people, and Edonian means little more than Thracian. ὑπ' αὐγάς—'bringing them under the rays of the light', hence the acc. Goodwin, p. 181.

1155. κάμακα—'spear', part for the whole, properly only the shaft. Θρηκίαν—gives the reason why the women wished to see it.

1156. γυμνόν μ' ἔθηκαν—'they stripped me of'. γυμνός, with other words signifying separation [e.g. κενός, ἔρημος,] govern the gen. Goodwin, § 174.

διπτύχου στολίσματος—'my twofold equipment', i.e. probably, as Weil with one Scholiast suggests, the two spears which heroes carried [not the spear and cloak, for τούσδε πέπλους seems to show that he still had his garments, nor would these be much protection.]

1158. 'Kept dandling them in their hands, that they might be far from their father exchanging them with successions, of hands', i.e. passing them from hand to hand. [χερῶν is doubtful, the two best MSS. having διὰ χερός (which is unmetrical) written over an erasure. χερῶν is very awkward after χεροῖν in 1158.]

1159. γένοιντο has more MS. authority than γένοιτο. Neuters plural usually take a singular verb, but exceptions occur. See 839 n. The verse is deficient in caesura.

1160. κᾇτα=καὶ εἶτα. In a crasis an ι is subscript only when the second word contains an ι: thus κᾆς for καὶ ἐς. ἐκ—'following'. πῶς δοκεῖς;—'Can you believe it?' often inserted thus parenthetically. *Hipp.* 446, τοῦτον λαβοῦσα, πῶς δοκεῖς, καθύβρισεν.

1161. λαβοῦσαι—supply αἱ μὲν to correspond with αἱ δέ, 1162.

1162. 'While others like enemies clutched and held my hands and limbs'. ['Like enemies' is, it must be confessed, very feeble, πολεμίων being a word of wide but not intense meaning, and is much weaker than e.g. ἐχθρός, cf. Xen. *Anab.*

1. 3. 12 ὁ δ' ἀνήρ...χαλεπώτατος δ' ἐχθρὸς ᾧ ἂν πολέμιος ᾖ. A man may be *at war* with another because their countries are at war and yet have no feeling of personal hate against him. The emendation of Mr A. W. Verrall πολυπόδων is worth considering, being much more graphic, and the change is slight. ' Devil fish' grow to great size and strength in the Mediterranean.]

1165. 'Whenever I tried to lift up my face'. ἐξανισταίην —optative of repeated effort. *Iph. Taur.* 325, ἀλλ' εἰ φύγοι τις, ἅτεροι προσκείμενοι | ἔβαλλον αὐτούς.

1166. κόμης—'by the hair', partitive genitive.

1167. πλήθει—'by reason of the crowd', or as our idiom is ' for the crowd', causal dative.

1168. πῆμα πήματος πλέον—'Woe greater than woe', i.e. the intensity of the evil demands some stronger name.

1170. πόρπας—'buckle-pins', the instrument with which Oedipus put out his eyes, *Phoen.* 62, χρυσηλάτοις πόρπαισιν αἱμάξας κόρας, connected with πείρω, pierce.

1172. ἐκπηδήσας—'having bounded forth'. Tmesis is not rare in tragedy, especially in the choruses, and in almost all cases a monosyllabic word stands between the component parts. Very rarely the preposition follows as at 504, Ἀγαμέμνονος πέμψαντος, ὦ γύναι, μέτα.

1173. κύνας—The metaphor is of some great wild beast which turns the tables on the dogs.

1175. τοιάδε πέπονθα—'thus have I suffered'. The cognate accusative is often represented by a neuter adj. or pronoun: the full phrase would be τοιάδε (παθήματα) πέπονθα.

1178. τῶν πρίν—'of the ancients'. εἴρηκεν κακῶς—'has spoken ill of'. εὖ (κακῶς) λέγω (εἴρηκα) takes an acc. like εὖ δρᾶν τινά.

1179. λέγων ἐστίν—an idiomatic form of λέγει, cf. ἦν ἀνέχων, 122. [Porson, after Stobaeus, amends ἢ νῦν λέγει τις ἢ πάλιν, which is neat; but the change does not seem needed.]

1180. συντεμών—'in brief', 'to be concise' = συντόμως εἰπών.

1182. 'He who at any time comes into contact with them knows this well'. ἀεί—with the article and participle, loses its signification 'always' and is usually placed between the two,

but Aesch. *Prom.* 973, θῶπτε τὸν κρατοῦντ' ἀεί.   Cicero (*in Verr.*
5. 12. 29) borrows the idiom, *omnes Siciliae* semper *praetores.*
ἐπίσταται—'knows *well*', Plato opposes ἐπιστήμη, *exact* knowledge, to δόξα.   [Strangely enough no writer has more bitter
sayings against women than Euripides and yet few have drawn
finer characters than Polyxena, Iphigeneia and Alkestis: 'the
poet, who was openly reviled in his own day as the hater of
women and traducer of their sex, has come down to us as their
noblest and most prominent advocate in all Greek literature'.]

1183. τοῖς σ. κακοῖς—'by reason of thy woes', causal
dative.

1184. μέμψῃ—subj. μὴ μέμφῃ the reading of some MSS. is
bad Greek.

1185, 6. Probably spurious. As the verses stand ἐπίφθονοι
must = '*unjustly* hated' which seems impossible. Hermann's
correction ἀντάριθμοι for εἰς ἀριθμόν through a gloss ἰσάριθμοι is
clever: Hartung substitutes πολλῶν for πολλαί: Porson reads
πολλαὶ γὰρ οὐδὲν εἰσ': Reiske τῶν καλῶν. But the verses appear
to be past mending, being the insertion of a copyist who wished
to qualify and expand 1183, 4.

[1187—1237. *Hecuba* (to Agam.) 'Let no specious pleading
make the worse appear the better cause': (turning fiercely to
Polymestor) 'I will expose thy subterfuges, thy *greed* slew my
boy. Why didst thou not, while Troy yet stood, kill him or
send him a prisoner to the Greek camp? Again, thou shouldest
have given the gold to the Greeks when they needed it, but
that thou still holdest. If thou hadst safely guarded my son
thou wouldst have gained fair repute and have found in him a
treasure to supply thy lack of money; now, thou hast lost all!'
(To Agam.) 'Thou wilt be villain if thou shalt help him'.]

1189. ἔδρασε—sc. ὁ ἄνθρωπος understood from ἀνθρώποις.
For the sing. cf. *Androm.* 421, οἰκτρὰ γὰρ τὰ δυστυχῆ | βροτοῖς
ἅπασι κἂν θυραῖος ὢν κυρῇ.

1190. σαθρούς—'unsound'.

1191. τἄδικα —'injustice', subject of δύνασθαι [or 'to
make a good defence of injustice', 1178 n. In either case, the
sophistic and rhetorical plan of making the worse appear the
better reason is alluded to.]

1192. τάδε—i.e. τὸ εὖ λέγειν τἄδικα. ἀκριβόω—'learn accurately', 'reduce to a system', with a disparaging sense of
subtle refinement.

1193. δύναιντ' ἄν—more idiomatic than the variant δύναν-ται: they find out at last that they have not been so clever as they thought.

1194. ἀπώλοντο—'are wont to perish'. See 598 n. Goodwin, § 205. 2.

1195. 'And so stands thy relation to me by way of prelude, now I will turn to *him* and will answer him with my words,—*thou* who sayest that in removing a double toil from the Achaeans thou didst slay my son.' διπλοῦν πόνον—i.e. a second siege of Troy. ἀπαλλάσσων—the present often gives the aim or effort of an action, and so Nauck's ἀπαλλάξων is not needed. ὃς φῇς—for the abrupt change of person cf. Xen. *Anab.* 1. 3. 20, κἂν μὲν ᾖ ἐκεῖ, τὴν δίκην ἔφη χρῄζειν ἐπιθεῖναι αὐτῷ, ἢν δὲ φεύγῃ, ἡμεῖς ἐκεῖ πρὸς ταῦτα βουλευσόμεθα. Ἀχαιῶν—cf. 1141 sq.

1198. ἕκᾱτι—a Doric form; others used in tragedy are Ἀθάνᾱ, δᾱρός, κυνᾱγός, ποδᾱγός, λοχᾱγός, ξενᾱγός, ὀπᾱδός.

1200. ἄν, ἄν—cf. notes on 359, 742.

1201. In bitter allusion to Polymestor's words 1175, τοιάδε σπεύδων κ.τ.λ.

1202. πότερα κηδεύσων—'didst thou mean to make a marriage alliance with one of them?' i.e. with a Greek family.

1203. ἢ τίν' αἰτίαν;—'or what *other* reason?' cf. 1264, ἢ ποίῳ τρόπῳ;

1206. βούλοιο—the optative suggests the improbability that Polymestor will speak the truth.

1207. καὶ κέρδη τὰ σά—'ay, and thy gains', i.e. thy greed.

1208. ἐπεὶ δίδαξον—'or else tell me'; cf. Soph. *Oed. Tyr.* 390, ἐπεὶ φέρ' εἰπέ.

1211. δέ—'I say', resumptive, τί taking up the question of 1208.

1212. θέσθαι χάριν—'to win thyself grace in his eyes'. The middle sense is to be noted.

1214. ἐσμέν—'Now that we are no longer in prosperity'. So the two best MSS., the rest ἦμεν. ἐν φάει—a common metaphor.

1215. 'And the city showed by its smoke that it was in the enemy's hand'. Cf. Aesch. *Ag.* 818, καπνῷ δ' ἁλοῦσα νῦν

E. H.　　　　　　　　　　　　　　　　9

ἔτ' εὔσημος πόλις. [The verse halts somewhat and no satisfactory correction has been made. Canter conjectured καπνός = 'cum hostium manu nihil nisi fumus vestigia urbis significaret'. Weil for ὕπο reads δαμέν 'subdued by the enemy'.]

1216. **κατέκτας**—from stem κτα-, a collateral form of κτείνω: ἔκτᾰν, ἔκτᾰς, ἔκτᾰ, ἔκτᾰμεν. So ἔβην from βαίνω, ἔπτην from πέτομαι, ἔφθην from φθάνω, ἔδρᾱν from διδράσκω, ἔδυν from δύω, and others. Goodwin, § 125.

1217. **φανῇς**—'in order that thou mayest be seen', aorist passive. [φανεῖ, fut. mid. has less authority = 'how thou wilt be seen'.]

1218. **εἴπερ ἦσθα**—the imperfect indicative implies that the excuse was false. Goodwin, § 220. 1. a. (2).

1219. **τοῦδε**—i.e. Polydorus, who has been alluded to 1216.

1223. **τολμᾷς**—'canst not bear', *in animum inducis,* cf. 332.

καρτερεῖς—'persistest'.

1224. **καὶ μὴν**—'and look you', introducing a new phase of her argument, cf. 216 n. **κλέος** [√κλεϝ, 'reputation', whether good or bad, from Indo-Germanic √ΚΡΥ. Cf. Lat. *gloria.*]

1226. Cf. Ennius, quoted by Cicero, *Lael.* 17. 64, *amicus certus in re incerta cernitur.* Shakespeare, *Haml.* III. 2. 217:

'Who not needs shall never lack a friend,
and who in want a hollow friend doth try,
directly seasons him his enemy'.

ἀγαθοὶ=οἱ ἀγαθοί, by crasis, so ἀνήρ=ὁ ἀνήρ.

1227. '*donec eris felix multos numerabis amicos*'. **αὔθ' ἕκαστα**—'in each case of itself', Lat. *ultro.*

1228. **ὁ δὲ**—Polydorus. **εἰ ἐσπάνιζες**—'if thou wast in want'. Goodwin, § 220. 1. a.

1230. **ἐκεῖνον ἄνδρα**—Agamemnon.

1231. **παῖδές τέ σοι**—sc. οἴχονται. [Porson places the comma, not after σοι, but after οἴχεται: when we must supply πράσσουσιν ὧδε.]

1232. **ὧδε**—with a scornful gesture.

1234. **οἷς ἐχρῆν**—sc. πιστὸν εἶναι.

1236. 'We shall say that thou takest pleasure in the wicked and art thyself of like nature'. αὐτὸν gains emphasis from its prominent position.

1237. Hecuba suddenly seems to remember that she is but a captive slave, and in a manner apologises for the vehemence of her words. [It is noteworthy that Hecuba's speech 1187—1237 has exactly the same number of verses as the corresponding one of Polymestor, 1132—1182].

1238. φεῦ φεῦ—'well, well', usually but not always 'particula dolentis'.

[1240—end. Agamemnon decides against Polymestor, who turns upon Hecuba and foretells her change into a cur (the origin of κυνὸς σῆμα), the murder of Kasandra and of Agamemnon himself. Agamemnon orders him away to banishment, Hecuba is to bury her dead, the Chorus of Trojan women to repair to their several masters, time for sailing is at hand. The Chorus end up the play with a short expression of enforced submission.]

1240. ἀχθεινά—the predicate in Greek is often put in the plural where we should have expected the singular; cf. 1107 n.

1242. λαβόντα—not λαβών, because in an accusative and infinitive clause after αἰσχύνην φέρει.

1243. ἐμὴν χάριν—'for my sake', cf. 873 n.

1244. οὔτ' οὖν—'nor indeed', οὖν resumptive. 'Αχαιῶν—sc. χάριν.

1245. ἔχῃς—depending grammatically on δοκεῖς, not on ἀποκτεῖναι, as it strictly should; the mood implies that she charged him with still wishing to keep the gold.

1247. ῥᾴδιον—'a light matter'.

1249. μὴ ἀδικεῖν—to be pronounced μἀδικεῖν. φύγω—deliberative conjunctive, Goodwin, § 256.

1251. τλῆθι—'put up with'.

1252. γυναικὸς ἡσσώμενος—'worsted by a woman'. The genitive may either be due to the comparative notion in the verb, or, as seems more likely, the genitive of the agent (fairly common in poetry, e. g. Soph. *Aj.* 807, φωτὸς ἠπατημένη), a variety of the genitive of the source.

1253. τοῖς κακίοσιν—'to my inferiors'.

1254. Most MSS. give this verse to Agamemnon, but most editors follow Hermann (who says 'regem semel dixisse sententiam sat est') in assigning it to Hecuba.

1256. Cf. *Alk.* 691, χαίρεις ὁρῶν φῶς· πατέρα δ' οὐ χαίρειν δοκεῖς; παιδὸς—'for my child'.

1259. ἀλλ' οὐ τάχα—sc. χαιρήσεις.

1260. ὅρους—'to the boundaries'; this accusative of the place whither, without a preposition, is poetical. Cf. *Bacchae* 5, πάρειμι Δίρκης νάματ' Ἰσμηνοῦ θ' ὕδωρ.

1261. μὲν οὖν—'nay but shall have hidden thee fallen from the mast head'; cf. *immo, immo vero* in the Latin dramatists, used to correct a former statement.

1262. 'At whose hand shall I meet with a forced leap'. τοῦ ; = τίνος ;

1264. ὑποπτέροις νώτοισι—i.e. with wings upon my back.

1265. The accounts of the metamorphosis and death of Hecuba are, as might be expected, very various. Kynossema (κύνος σῆμα) was a promontory in the Thracian Chersonese which was supposed to gain its name from her: Ov. *M.* 13. 568 sq. *rictuque in verba parato | latravit conata loqui. Locus extat et ex re | nomen habet.* Juv. 10. 271, *torva canino | latravit rictu.* Ov. *M.* 13. 565 makes the Thracians stone her to death because of her murder of Polymestor, when she was changed into a dog. Cicero, *Tusc. Disp.* 3. 26, *Hecubam autem putant propter animi acerbitatem quandam et rabiem fingi in canem esse conversam.* Plaut. *Menaechmi,* 701—705.

1267. ὁ Θρῃξὶ μάντις—'the Thracians' seer', the dative differing little in sense from a genitive, cf. *Phoen.* 17, ὦ Θήβαισιν εὐίπποις ἄναξ. [Herodotus 7. 111, 'the Satrae possess the oracle of Dionysus; this oracle is on the highest mountains; the Bessi are those Satrae who give forth the oracles of the shrine, and it is a priestess who delivers them as at Delphi, and (this oracle) is no more intricate'.]

1268. ἔχρησεν—of the god, ἐχρήσατο would mean 'consulted the oracle'.

1269. 'No, for if he had' &c., sc. εἰ ἔχρησεν.

1270. 'Shall I die where I fall or survive and live my life *out* there?' (ἐκ- intensive). [Musgrave says of ἐκπλήσω βίον, 'hoc cum θανοῦσα coniunctum ridiculi aliquid habet; cum ζῶσα tautologici'. So he conjectures πότμον, Brunck μόρον, while Weil would change ἐκπλήσω into ἐκστήσω, i. e. μεταβαλῶ βίον εἰς τάδε.]

1272. ἢ τί comes in parenthetically between the substantive and the article and pronoun qualifying it, and is equivalent to ἢ τί ἄλλο; cf. 1203 n.

1273. κυνὸς σῆμα—cf. 1265 note.

1275. καὶ...δέ—'yes and', the word between being emphatic.

1276. ἀπέπτυσα—cf. 382 n.

1278. μήπω—a modest equivalent of μήποτε. Cf. Soph. *El.* 403, οὐ δῆτα· μήπω νοῦ τοσόνδ' εἴην κακόν. Τυνδαρὶς παῖς—Klytaemnestra: the phrase is pleonastic. Cf. Goodwin, § 129. 9.

1279. τοῦτον—sc. κτενεῖ.

1280. οὗτος—*heus tu*, 1127 n.

1281. The construction involves an ellipse:—'You may kill me if you like, but it will avail you nought, since &c.' The murder thus prophesied is told in the *Agamemnon* of Aeschylus. Strictly speaking, *Mykenae* was the royal city of Agamemnon, but in the time of Euripides the neighbouring town of Argos had put it into the shade.

ἀμμένει—'awaits'=ἀναμένει.

1282. οὐχ ἕλξετε—'drag him forth'. οὐ with the future interrogative is a strong command, Soph. *Phil.* 975, οὐκ εἶ;='begone'.

1284. εἴρηται—'I have said my say', for the force of the tense cf. 236 n. νήσων ἐρήμων depends upon ποι, cf. 455; Goodwin, §§ 168, 182. 2. For the penalty, cf. *Od.* 3. 270 (Aegisthus), δὴ τότε τὸν μὲν ἀοιδὸν ἄγων ἐς νῆσον ἐρήμην | κάλλιπεν οἰωνοῖσιν ἕλωρ καὶ κύρμα γενέσθαι.

1286. καὶ· λίαν=*vel maxime*, καὶ intensive, cf. καὶ μάλα, καὶ πολύ.

1287. διπτύχους—'two'. So Lucr. *duplices oculos.*

1290. πομπίμους—'to convey us', active. ὁρῶ—The Greeks did not accurately distinguish between the various senses, cf. with ὁρῶ πνοάς, Aesch. *Septem*, κτύπον δέδορκα. Cf. 1069 n.

1294. τῶν δεσποσύνων μόχθων—the evils of servitude: cf. Aesch. *Persae* 587, οὐκέτι δεσμοφοροῦσιν δεσποσύνοισιν ἀνάγκαις.

METRICAL NOTES.

59—99. Anapaestic: the difficulties are in the following lines :—

62. λάβετε φέρ | ετε πέμπ | ετ' ἀείρ | ετέ μου. The four short syllables in the first foot are counted as equivalent to an anapaest, $\smile\smile-$, and are justified by the rapid and excited tone which Hecuba assumes. The δέμας of Porson is not necessary.

69. τί ποτ' αἴρομαι ἔννυχος οὕτω. A paroemiac, unless we insert ἆρ' before αἴρομαι, when we have a full but rather ugly anapaestic dim.: Hartung, contrary to all authority, suggests ἐννυχίοις.

76. φοβερὰν | ὄψιν ἔμ | αθον ἐδά | ην. The 3rd foot like the 1st in 62. ἴδον (i.e. εἶδον with augment omitted) has been suggested after ὄψιν.

83. τι νέον, final syllable is lengthened in pause.

90, 91. Dactylic lines, as are 74, 75. The reading ἀνοίκτως removes all difficulty. If ἀνάγκᾳ in 90 and οἰκτρῶς in 91 be retained, then οἰκτρῶς may be repeated and καὶ τόδε μοι δεῖμ' read, the final syllable being elided by *synapheia*.

100—154. Ordinary anapaestic system.

155—177. Anapaestic, spondees predominating: the difficulties are in

164, 5, two paroemiacs together. νῷν is inserted by Musgrave after δαίμων.

168, dactylic.

169. ἀγαστὸς ἐν φάει, dim. iamb. brachycatalectic.

170, 171. Two paroemiacs together as in 164, 165. Herm. puts ποὺς in 170 and reads γηραίᾳ.

178—215. Anapaestic, difficulties being in

186. τί ποτ' ἀναστένεις. A trochaic or dochmiac inter-spersed. ‿ ‿ ‿ — ‿ ‿ ‾

188. τί τόδ' ἀγγέλλεις. To correspond with 186 Herm. read τί δ' ὅ τόδ' ἀγγελεῖς.

191. Πηλείᾳ γέννᾳ, anapaest. monom. hypercat. Herm. reads Πηλείδα, γένν', the ᾰ cut off by *synapheia.*

194. μάνυσον, μᾶτερ, anapaest. monom. hypercat.

201, anapaest. dim. brachycat.

202, anapaest. monom. hypercat. Herm. amends

* * * ἐχθίσταν
ἀρρητάν τ' ὦρσεν δαίμων.

209, 210. Cf. 168, 169.

215. Not a paroemiac, as it should be at the end of a system. Musgrave amends ξυντυχίᾳ κρείσσον' ἔκυρσεν.

444—485. Glyconic, the base of which is a trochee; in Latin glyconic=trochee or spondee followed by two dactyls. Observe that the lines generally begin with a single syllable, long or short, and then break into a dactyl followed by trochees or spondees. Observe also that the concluding lines of στρ. α' and ἀντιστρ. α' have 11 syllables, and that in 474 and 483 a spondee is put for a dactyl.

629—657. Dactylico-trochaic, with rather frequent spondees: 632, 641 must be scanned as *antispasts,* i.e. iambic followed by trochee, any equivalent foot being substituted: thus

Ἀλέξανδρὸς ‖ εἱλᾰτῑ| ναν   κακὸν | τᾷ Σῐ ‖ μούντιδι | γᾷ.

633—642, preponderance of short syllables, which must be contracted: as

ἐ | τᾱμεθ' ᾰ| λῑον ἐπ' | κ.τ.λ.

684 sqq. In the irregular lyric utterances of Hec. we find the general *dochmiac* character (of which according to Herm. there are 48 varieties). The simplest form is ‿——‿—. Iamb. dims. and trims. are interspersed; but we are not to expect a correspondence of str. and antistr.

906—952, dactylico-trochaic.

1025—1034, dochmiac, the long syllables being sometimes resolved. 1030 is pure dochmiac. In 1033 ἰώ is to be counted as one syllable; with the ordinary reading Αἴδαν, the -αν would have to be shortened.

1056—1084. The metre here is very irregular: there is a preponderance of anapaests and dochmiacs. Thus

1056, anap. dim., reading due to Herm.

1057, anap. paroemiac.

1058, dim. dochm.

1059, dim. dochm. with resolved syllables; observe quantity in ποίαν.

1060, 1, anapaest. dim.

1062, dochm. preceded by a resolved cretic (–◡–) Ἰλιάδας.

1063, dochm. dim.

1064, anap. dim.

1065, anap. monometer.

1066, doch. dim.

1067, trim. iamb. brachycatalectic.

1068, doch. monom.

1069 ⎤
1070 ⎥
1071 ⎬ , different anapaests.
1072 ⎥
1073 ⎦

1074, doch. dim.

1075 ⎫
      ⎬ , anapaests.
1076 ⎭

1077, dochmiac.

1078, dochmiac + final cretic: text corrupt.

1079, anapaest. monom. hypercat.

1080, two cretics, unless ἅτε or ὡς be read, when line is dochm.

1081, dochmiac.

1082, anapaest. dim.

1083, iamb. dim. brachycat.

1084, iamb. dim. brachycat.

1088—1105, dochmiac, cretic, iambic and trochaic.

1088, 9, doch. monom.

1090, doch. dim.

1091, troch. dim. *ἰὼ* one syllable. Cf. 1099.

1092, iamb. monom. + cretic.

1093, troch. dim. cat.

1094, iamb. trim. *ἤ* coalesces with *οὐδείς*.

1095, iamb. monom. hyper.

1096, iamb. dim.

1097, troch. dim. cat.

1098, troch. monom. hyper.

1099, troch. dim.

1100, two cretics resolved.

1101, cretic monom. resolved.

1102, troch. dim. cat.

1103, dactylic.

1104, 5, 6, dochmiacs.

1293—1295, ordinary anapaestic system.

INDEX.

prohibition by interrog., 1282
proleptic epithet, 113, 533, 782. 797, 1031
pronoun, understood in adj., 23

P

ρρ = ρs, 8

Σ

σαίρειν, 362
σέθεν, 850
σῖγα and σίγα, 531
σκότος (gender), 1
σπουδῇ, 100
συγκλῄειν, 430
σφε, 260

senses, confusion of in Greek, 1069, 1290
sequence of tenses, 27, 712, 818, 1139, 1149, 1245
subject, change of, 488
substantive (=adj.), 120, 137, 1253
superlative, double, 620
stasimon, 444

T

τἀν (=ἤν), 473, 636
τε, position of, 80, 426
-τι (adv. in), 617
τις (collective), 649
,, (enclitic), 370
τλήμων, 562
τὸ ἐπὶ σε, 514
τοι, 228, 606
τριταῖος, 32
τυγχάνω (w. acc.), 51
τύμβῳ, 41

τύραννος, 366
τῷ (=τίνι), 448

tense, sequence of (see *sequence*)
,, change in (see *change*)
tmesis, 99, 504, 1172

Υ

ὑπό, in comp., 6, 812
,, w. gen., 53
ὕποπτος (active), 1135

Φ

φέγγος, 367
φερτός, 158
φεῦ (of contempt), 863
φεῦ, 1238
φορούμενος, 29
φύλλοις βάλλειν, 574
φύρω, 496

X

χαρακτὴρ, 379
χάριν, 873
χιονώδης, 81
χρεών, 282
χρῆν (=ἐχρῆν), 629
,, (=χρῆναι), 260
χρῶμαι, 311

Ω

ὡς, 622
,, (=ἴσθι ὡς), 346, 400
,, w. participle, 511, 1146
ὡς ἄν, 330
ὥστε (of comparison), 179, 337
ὤφειλον, 394

MACMILLAN'S ELEMENTARY CLASSICS.

18mo., 1s. 6d. each.

"Among the best of the various series of school-books which are just now being published may be mentioned the 'Elementary Classics.' The notes are precisely the sort of notes which are required, which assist a boy without making him lazy."—*Westminster Review.*

The following are ready or in preparation :—

CÆSAR. The Gallic War. Book I. Edited, with Notes and Vocabulary, by A. S. WALPOLE, M.A. [*In the press.*

CÆSAR. The Second and Third Campaigns of the GALLIC WAR. Edited by W. G. RUTHERFORD, M.A., Balliol College, Oxford, and Assistant-Master at St. Paul's School. [*Ready.*

CÆSAR. Scenes from the Fifth and Sixth Books of THE GALLIC WAR. Selected and Edited by C. COLBECK, M.A., Fellow of Trinity College, Cambridge, and Assistant-Master at Harrow. [*Ready.*

CICERO. Select Letters. Edited by Rev. G. E. JEANS, M.A., Fellow of Hertford College, Oxford, and Assistant-Master in Haileybury College. [*In the press.*

EURIPIDES. Hecuba. Edited by Rev. JOHN BOND, M.A., and A. S. WALPOLE, M.A. [*Ready.*

GREEK TESTAMENT. Selections. Edited by Rev. G. F. MACLEAR, M.A., D.D., Warden of St. Augustine's College, Canterbury. [*In preparation.*

HERODOTUS. Selections from Books VII. and VIII. THE EXPEDITION OF XERXES. Edited by A. H. COOKE, B A., Fellow of King's College, Cambridge. [*Ready.*

HOMER'S ILIAD. Book XVIII. The Arms of ACHILLES. Edited by S. R. JAMES, M.A., Scholar of Trinity College, Cambridge, and Assistant-Master at Eton. [*Ready.*

HORACE. The Odes. Books I. II. and III. Edited by T. E PAGE, M.A., late Fellow of St. John's College, Cambridge, and Assistant-Master at the Charterhouse. 1s. 6d. each. [*Ready.*

HORACE. The Fourth Book of the Odes. By the same Editor. [*In preparation.*

HORACE. Select Epodes and Ars Poetica. Edited by Rev. H. A. DALTON, M.A., late Student of Christ Church, Oxford. [*In preparation.*

MACMILLAN AND CO., LONDON.